EVERYMAN, I will go with thee,

and be thy guide,

In thy most need to go by thy side

HENRI BEYLE

Called Stendhal, was born at Grenoble on 23rd
January 1783. Obtained commission in cavalry
regiment 1800, relinquished it in 1802, but in 1806
rejoined service as commissariat officer, and took
part in the Austrian and Russian campaigns on
Napoleon's staff. From 1814 till his death he spent
much of his time in Italy. After Revolution of 1830
became French consul at Civita Vecchia. Died in
Paris, 22nd March 1842.

STENDHAL

Scarlet and Black

A CHRONICLE OF THE NINETEENTH CENTURY

IN TWO VOLUMES · VOLUME ONE

TRANSLATED BY
G. K. SCOTT MONCRIEFF

INTRODUCTION BY
F. C. GREEN, M.C., M.A., DR.PHIL.
*Professor of French Literature
in the University of Edinburgh*

DENT: LONDON
EVERYMAN'S LIBRARY

All rights reserved
Made in Great Britain
at the
Aldine Press · Letchworth · Herts
for
J. M. DENT & SONS LTD
Aldine House · Bedford Street · London
First included in Everyman's Library 1938
Last reprinted 1967

NO. 945

INTRODUCTION

HENRI BEYLE, who probably took his pseudonym, Stendhal, from a little Brunswick town of that name, was born on 23rd January 1783 at Grenoble. Although he liked to imagine that, on the maternal side, he was descended from an Italian whom a trifling murder had driven over the frontier, Henri's parents were respectable, upper middle-class people in easy circumstances. The mother died when the boy was seven. He loved her as passionately as he detested Chérubin Beyle, generally alluded to by his son as *mon bâtard de père*. Henri's childhood was saddened by domestic quarrels, and during the anxious days of the Terror the boy secretly applauded the excesses of the Republicans, especially the execution of Louis XVI. And because the family were not only royalist but piously Catholic, he conceived a hatred of religion. This tendency was fostered by his loathing of the abbé Raillane, Henri's Jesuit tutor, who seemed to him the incarnation of hypocrisy. On the other hand, he adored his grand-aunt, Elizabeth, and his maternal grandfather, Dr Gagnon; the former because of her *espagnolisme* or Cornelian sense of honour; the latter for his eighteenth-century, philosophic outlook.

At the newly founded *École centrale* in Grenoble, young Henri received a grounding in mathematics, drawing, and Latin, and made the acquaintance of Shakespeare whom he revered till the end of his life. But Stendhal, though a promising mathematician, owed little here or in any other subject to his schoolmasters. His knowledge of French literature, for example, was entirely due to his own reading, which was varied and extensive. Rousseau, Helvétius, Tracy, Molière, La Fontaine, Ariosto, were his early favourites.

In 1799 Stendhal was sent to Paris, ostensibly to prepare for the *École polytechnique*. He did not, however, sit the entrance examination. After some weeks of acute loneliness and nostalgia the boy fell ill and was befriended by the Daru family, to which he was distantly related. Pierre Daru, the eldest son, who was later ennobled by Napoleon, then held a high administrative post at the War Office, where a niche was found for Henri. Napoleon was then preparing his Italian campaign, and the young apprentice, to his great delight, crossed the Alps on the heels of Daru and the invading army. His first sight of Italy convinced him that this was the country of his dreams. Thanks once more to Daru, he obtained a commission in the 6th Dragoons, and to his disgust was ordered to leave Milan in the autumn of 1800 to join his regiment at Brescia. This was all the more disagreeable since Henri had fallen in love with a Milanese lady called Gina Pietragrua, the first of many Stendhalian grand passions. She knew nothing then of the havoc she had wrought. Detesting regimental life, Stendhal resigned his commission, and went back to Paris, where, during four years, he read assiduously, dreamed of love and fame, tried unsuccessfully to write plays and, with no better luck, indulged in amorous dalliance. As funds were low Stendhal took a post in a commercial house in Marseilles. This was to annoy the family. To amuse himself he had a liaison with an actress called Mélanie Guilbert. In 1806 Daru very generously interested himself in this ungrateful relative who was given a junior post in the commissariat and, in due course, transferred to the army of occupation in Germany. For some time Stendhal resided at Brunswick, as a sort of area commandant responsible for billeting, levies, and supplies. He went through the terrible Moscow campaign of 1812, and as a reward was appointed *auditeur* in Napoleon's State Council. He also became *Inspecteur du Mobilier de la Couronne*, a lucrative though not exacting office. In 1813 he accompanied the army into Austria, and served as *intendant* at Sagan till the Allies began to close in on France. In 1814 Stendhal was ordered to Grenoble, where he did valuable work organizing the defence of Dauphigny. Bad health and fatigue sent him back to Paris, and when Napoleon went to Elba Stendhal crossed over into Italy. This severed his connection with the imperial régime. Taking up his headquarters in Milan, Stendhal remained in Italy for seven years, frequenting the society of men of letters. Gina Pietragrua now became his mistress, though, in the interval, Stendhal had by no means remained faithful to her memory.

He was now an author, having published in 1814 a book on Haydn and Mozart. Now he explored Italy, ranging far afield to satisfy his curiosity about Italian manners and his passion for the fine arts. His impressions formed the substance of two books, which appeared in 1817. By this time, however, Stendhal had attracted the attention of the Austrian secret police because of his subversive political views so that, in 1821, the Italian sojourn came to an end. He

returned to Paris. In the autumn of that year a brief visit to England put Stendhal in touch with the editor, Colburn, for whose magazines he began to write articles on Parisian life and letters. Stendhal also contributed to various French periodicals. Journalism was his chief source of income until 1830, for his father had died a poor man. This meant the end of his son's dream of a private income, Italian travel, and the leisure to write when he felt inclined. On the other hand, Stendhal was now obliged, for professional reasons, to frequent the literary and political *salons*. This was the period of his most intense literary activity, when he wrote *De l'Amour*, *Racine et Shakespeare*, *La Vie de Rossini*, his first novel *Armance*, *Les Promenades dans Rome*, and, at the close of 1830, *Le Rouge et le Noir*. During these years Stendhal met the great figures in literature, science, and politics—Hugo, Sainte-Beuve, Mérimée, Béranger, Tracy, Cuvier, Thiers, Lafayette, and others.

The 'glorious days' of July brought a change of fortune. Stendhal was appointed consul at Trieste, but was refused his exsequatur by Metternich. He was, therefore, transferred to Civita Vecchia, a seaport which, though close to Rome, was for Stendhal a place of exile. To defeat boredom he threw himself with zeal into his official work, took up archaeology, collected Italian medieval manuscripts, and, whenever possible, escaped from Civita Vecchia. Thanks to the indulgence of his friend, Molé, who had a post in the Cabinet, Stendhal, having been given sick-leave to Paris in 1836, contrived to linger in France till the autumn of 1839. To this we owe *Les Mémoires d'un Touriste*, the journal, published very posthumously, of *Le Voyage dans le Midi*, *La Chartreuse de Parme*, and a few short stories. At Civita Vecchia he wrote the unfinished novel, *Lucien Leuwen*, and fragments of his autobiography. Stendhal on his return to duty had a paralytic stroke but, with great courage, went on with his duties. In October 1841 he was recalled to Paris. In March of the following year a second attack struck him down in the street. He was carried to his house, and died on 22nd March 1842.

Le Rouge et le Noir is the first of Stendhal's works to appear in Everyman's Library. Some may feel that this honour should have been awarded to *La Chartreuse de Parme*. Both are masterpieces, but each reflects, in a different idiom, the peculiar genius of Stendhal. The novel before us offers, I think, the more detailed picture of its author's complex temperament. Probably because *Le Rouge et le Noir* is the earlier of the two works it states the Stendhalian creed of energy in more intransigent terms. Less reticent

here than in *La Chartreuse* Stendhal is more ruthless and sardonic in his review of humanity. Perhaps the satire is less profound, because less universal, than in the later novel. On the other hand, it swings over a wider arc, covering a greater variety of types and professions. One perceives, too, in *La Chartreuse de Parme*, an afterglow of serenity and resignation of which there is no trace in the earlier novel. *Le Rouge et le Noir* has, of course, moments of repose, of Stendhalian reverie. Yet from beginning to end it is a novel of conflict. Its prevailing tone is swiftly tense and dramatic. Julien is not Stendhal, but he possesses many of Stendhal's ideals and principles of conduct. His sensations, also, are those which the author would have had in the situations imagined for the hero. Many of its incidents resemble actual happenings, yet the novel does not offer a mere transcript of Stendhal's experience, of which the artist gives us a critical and sometimes idealized version. What is permanent and purely Stendhalian is Julien's fierce vitality, his profound sense of the duty which he owes, not to the world, but to the ideal he has set himself. It is by this standard that Julien and Stendhal interpret the orthodox Christian maxim: 'For what shall it profit a man if he gain the whole world and lose his own soul?'

The translation here used is by Scott Moncrieff,[1] which means, quite simply, that it is a work of art. Scott Moncrieff was in a class by himself.

The following bibliography comprises the most important of Stendhal's writings. The dates given are those of first publication. The only complete edition of his works is that published by 'Le Divan,' in seventy-nine volumes (1927–38):

La Vie de Haydn, 1814; *Histoire de la peinture en Italie*, 1817; *Rome, Naples et Florence*, 1817; *De l'Amour*, 1822; *Racine et Shakespeare I*, 1823; *Racine et Shakespeare II*, 1825; *Vie de Rossini*, 1824; *Armance*, 1827; *Promenades dans Rome*, 1829; *Le Rouge et le Noir*, 1831; *Mémoires d'un Touriste*, 1838; *La Chartreuse de Parme*, 1839; *L'Abbesse de Castro*, 1839; *Chroniques italiennes*, 1855; *Romans et Nouvelles*, 1854; *Correspondance*, 1855; *Mélanges d'art et de littérature*, 1867; *Vie de Napoléon*, 1876; *Journal*, 1888; *Vie de Henri Brûlard*, 1890; *Souvenirs d'Égotisme*, 1892; *Lucien Leuwen*, 1901. See also M. Josephson, *Stendhal or the Pursuit of Happiness*, 1946.

F. C. G.

[1] By arrangement with Messrs Chatto & Windus.

To O. H. H.

who had every word of both volumes
read to her when she was powerless to resist.

C. K. S. M.

Leghorn—Pisa,
  July–December 1925.

TO THE HAPPY FEW

The drawback of the reign of opinion, which however procures *liberty,* is that it interferes in matters with which it has no concern; such as private life. Hence the gloom of America and England. To avoid touching upon private life, the author has invented a small town, *Verrières,* and when he required a Bishop, a jury, an Assize Court, has placed them all in Besançon, where he has never been.

TRANSLATOR'S NOTE

This translation has been made from the text of *Le Rouge et le Noir, Chronique du XIXe Siècle*, texte établi et annoté avec une préface et une bibliographie par Henri Martineau. . . . Éditions Bossard, Boulevard Saint-Germain, 140, Paris, 1925. This is a reprint of the first edition; the footnotes, giving the corrections and alterations afterwards made in manuscript by Beyle himself, have been incorporated in the text of the translation, the proofs of which have also been collated with the text edited by M. Jules Marsan and published by M. Édouard Champion.

Le Rouge et le Noir was first published by A. Levavasseur, Paris, in 1831, in two volumes octavo, and was reprinted in the same year in six volumes 16mo. It has been many times reprinted by different publishers, among the principal editions being one issued by Alphonse Lemerre in 1886, with a preface by Paul Bourget, and *Le Rouge et le Noir*, texte établi et annoté avec une introduction historique par Jules Marsan, Préface de Paul Bourget, de l'Académie Française, Paris, Librairie ancienne Honoré Champion, Édouard Champion. . . . 5, Quai Malaquais, 1923, 2 vol. in-8. This last forms part of the complete and *definitive* edition in 35 volumes, the first of which appeared in 1912.

C. K. S. M.

CONTENTS

CHAPTER ONE

A SMALL TOWN

Put thousands together
Less bad,
But the cage less gay.
HOBBES.

THE small town of Verrières may be regarded as one of the most attractive in the Franche-Comté. Its white houses with their high pitched roofs of red tiles are spread over the slope of a hill, the slightest contours of which are indicated by clumps of sturdy chestnuts. The Doubs runs some hundreds of feet below its fortifications, built in times past by the Spaniards, and now in ruins.

Verrières is sheltered on the north by a high mountain, a spur of the Jura. The jagged peaks of the Verra put on a mantle of snow in the first cold days of October. A torrent which comes tearing down from the mountain passes through Verrières before emptying its waters into the Doubs, and supplies power to a great number of sawmills; this is an extremely simple industry, and procures a certain degree of comfort for the majority of the inhabitants, who are of the peasant rather than of the burgess class. It is not, however, the sawmills that have made this little town rich. It is to the manufacture of printed calicoes, known as Mulhouse stuffs, that it owes the gen-

eral prosperity which, since the fall of Napoleon, has led
to the refacing of almost all the houses in Verrières.

No sooner has one entered the town than one is startled
by the din of a noisy machine of terrifying aspect. A
score of weighty hammers, falling with a clang which
makes the pavement tremble, are raised aloft by a wheel
which the water of the torrent sets in motion. Each of
these hammers turns out, daily, I cannot say how many
thousands of nails. A bevy of fresh, pretty girls subject
to the blows of these enormous hammers, the little scraps
of iron which are rapidly transformed into nails. This
work, so rough to the outward eye, is one of the industries
that most astonish the traveller who ventures for the first
time among the mountains that divide France from Switzerland. If, on entering Verrières, the traveller inquires to
whom belongs that fine nail factory which deafens everybody who passes up the main street, he will be told in a
drawling accent: "Eh! It belongs to the Mayor."

Provided the traveller halts for a few moments in this
main street of Verrières, which runs from the bank of the
Doubs nearly to the summit of the hill, it is a hundred to
one that he will see a tall man appear, with a busy, important air.

At the sight of him every hat is quickly raised. His
hair is turning grey, and he is dressed in grey. He is
a Companion of several Orders, has a high forehead, an
aquiline nose, and on the whole his face is not wanting in
a certain regularity: indeed, the first impression formed
of it may be that it combines with the dignity of a village
mayor that sort of charm which may still be found in a
man of forty-eight or fifty. But soon the visitor from
Paris is annoyed by a certain air of self-satisfaction and
self-sufficiency mingled with a suggestion of limitations
and want of originality. One feels, finally, that this man's
talent is confined to securing the exact payment of what-

ever is owed to him and to postponing payment till the last possible moment when he is the debtor.

Such is the Mayor of Verrières, M. de Rênal. Crossing the street with a solemn step, he enters the town hall and passes from the visitor's sight. But, a hundred yards higher up, if the visitor continues his stroll, he will notice a house of quite imposing appearance, and, through the gaps in an iron railing belonging to the house, some splendid gardens. Beyond, there is a line of horizon formed by the hills of Burgundy, which seem to have been created on purpose to delight the eye. This view makes the visitor forget the pestilential atmosphere of small financial interests which was beginning to stifle him.

He is told that this house belongs to M. de Rênal. It is to the profits that he has made from his great nail factory that the Mayor of Verrières is indebted for this fine free-stone house which he has just finished building. His family, they say, is Spanish, old, and was or claims to have been established in the country long before Louis XIV conquered it.

Since 1815 he has blushed at his connexion with industry: 1815 made him Mayor of Verrières. The retaining walls that support the various sections of this splendid garden, which, in a succession of terraces, runs down to the Doubs, are also a reward of M. de Rênal's ability as a dealer in iron.

You must not for a moment expect to find in France those picturesque gardens which enclose the manufacturing towns of Germany; Leipsic, Frankfort, Nuremberg, and the rest. In the Franche-Comté, the more walls a man builds, the more he makes his property bristle with stones piled one above another, the greater title he acquires to the respect of his neighbours. M. de Rênal's gardens, honeycombed with walls, are still further admired because he bought, for their weight in gold, certain minute scraps of ground which they cover. For instance that sawmill,

whose curious position on the bank of the Doubs struck
you as you entered Verrières, and on which you noticed
the name *Sorel,* inscribed in huge letters on a board which
overtops the roof, occupied, six years ago, the ground on
which at this moment they are building the wall of the
fourth terrace of M. de Rênal's gardens.

For all his pride, the Mayor was obliged to make many
overtures to old Sorel, a dour and obstinate peasant; he
was obliged to pay him in fine golden louis before he
would consent to remove his mill elsewhere. As for the
public lade which supplied power to the saw, M. de Rênal,
thanks to the influence he wielded in Paris, obtained leave
to divert it. This favour was conferred upon him after
the 182— elections.

He gave Sorel four acres in exchange for one, five hundred yards lower down by the bank of the Doubs. And,
albeit this site was a great deal more advantageous for
his trade in planks of firwood, Père Sorel, as they have
begun to call him now that he is rich, contrived to screw
out of the impatience and *land-owning mania* which
animated his neighbour a sum of 6,000 francs.

It is true that this arrangement was adversely criticised
by the local wiseacres. On one occasion, it was a Sunday,
four years later, M. de Rênal, as he walked home from
church in his mayoral attire, saw at a distance old Sorel,
supported by his three sons, watching him with a smile.
That smile cast a destroying ray of light into the Mayor's
soul; ever since then he has been thinking that he might
have brought about the exchange at less cost to himself.

To win popular esteem at Verrières, the essential thing
is not to adopt (while still building plenty of walls) any
plan of construction brought from Italy by those masons
who in spring pass through the gorges of the Jura on their
way to Paris. Such an innovation would earn the rash
builder an undying reputation for *wrong-headedness,* and

he would be lost forever among the sober and moderate folk who create reputations in the Franche-Comté.

As a matter of fact, these sober folk wield there the most irritating form of *despotism;* it is owing to that vile word that residence in small towns is intolerable to anyone who has lived in that great republic which we call Paris. The tyranny of public opinion (and what an opinion!) is as fatuous in the small towns of France as it is in the United States of America.

CHAPTER TWO

A MAYOR

L'importance! Monsieur, n'est-ce rien? Le respect
des sots, l'ébahissement des enfants, l'envie des riches,
le mépris du sage.

BARNAVE.

FORTUNATELY for M. de Rênal's reputation as
an administrator, a huge retaining wall was
required for the public avenue which skirts the
hillside a hundred feet above the bed of the Doubs. To
this admirable position it is indebted for one of the most
picturesque views in France. But, every spring, torrents
of rainwater made channels across the avenue, carved deep
gullies in it and left it impassable. This nuisance, which
affected everybody alike, placed M. de Rênal under the
fortunate obligation to immortalize his administration by
a wall twenty feet in height and seventy or eighty yards
long.

The parapet of this wall, to secure which M. de Rênal
was obliged to make three journeys to Paris, for the
Minister of the Interior before last had sworn a deadly
enmity to the Verrières avenue; the parapet of this wall
now rises four feet above the ground. And, as though to
defy all Ministers past and present, it is being finished
off at this moment with slabs of dressed stone.

How often, my thoughts straying back to the ball-rooms
of Paris, which I had forsaken overnight, my elbows leaning upon those great blocks of stone of a fine grey with
a shade of blue in it, have I swept with my gaze the vale
of the Doubs! Over there, on the left bank, are five or

[14]

six winding valleys, along the folds of which the eye can make out quite plainly a number of little streams. After leaping from rock to rock, they may be seen falling into the Doubs. The sun is extremely hot in these mountains; when it is directly overhead, the traveller's rest is sheltered on this terrace by a row of magnificent planes. Their rapid growth, and handsome foliage of a bluish tint are due to the artificial soil with which the Mayor has filled in the space behind his immense retaining wall, for, despite the opposition of the town council, he has widened the avenue by more than six feet (although he is a True-Blue and I myself a Liberal, I give him credit for it), that is why, in his opinion and in that of M. Valenod, the fortunate governor of the Verrières poorhouse, this terrace is worthy to be compared with that of Saint-Germain-en-Laye.

For my part, I have only one fault to find with the *Cours de la Fidélité;* one reads this, its official title, in fifteen or twenty places, on marble slabs which have won M. de Rênal yet another Cross; what I should be inclined to condemn in the Cours de la Fidélité is the barbarous manner in which the authorities keep these sturdy plane trees trimmed and pollarded. Instead of suggesting, with their low, rounded, flattened heads, the commonest of kitchen garden vegetables, they would like nothing better than to assume those magnificent forms which one sees them wear in England. But the Mayor's will is despotic, and twice a year every tree belonging to the commune is pitilessly lopped. The Liberals of the place maintain, but they exaggerate, that the hand of the official gardener has grown much more severe since the Reverend Vicar Maslon formed the habit of appropriating the clippings.

This young cleric was sent from Besançon, some years ago, to keep an eye upon the Abbé Chélan and certain parish priests of the district. An old Surgeon-Major of the Army of Italy, in retirement at Verrières, who in his

time had been simultaneously, according to the Mayor, a
Jacobin and a Bonapartist, actually ventured one day to
complain to him of the periodical mutilation of these fine
trees.

"I like shade," replied M. de Rênal with the touch of
arrogance appropriate when one is addressing a surgeon,
a Member of the Legion of Honour; "I like shade, I have
my trees cut so as to give shade, and I do not consider
that a tree is made for any other purpose, unless, like the
useful walnut, it *yields a return.*"

There you have the great phrase that decides everything at Verrières: YIELD A RETURN; it by itself represents
the habitual thought of more than three fourths of the inhabitants.

Yielding a return is the consideration that settles everything in this little town which seemed to you, just now,
so attractive. The stranger arriving there, beguiled by the
beauty of the cool, deep valleys on every side, imagines
at first that the inhabitants are influenced by the idea of
beauty; they are always talking about the beauty of their
scenery: no one can deny that they make a great to-do
about it; but this is because it attracts a certain number of
visitors whose money goes to enrich the innkeepers, and
thus, through the channel of the rate-collector, *yields a
return to the town.*

It was a fine day in autumn and M. de Rênal was strolling along the Cours de la Fidélité, his lady on his arm.
While she listened to her husband, who was speaking with
an air of gravity, Madame de Rênal's eye was anxiously
following the movements of three little boys. The eldest,
who might be about eleven, was continually running to the
parapet as though about to climb on top. A gentle voice
then uttered the name Adolphe, and the child abandoned
his ambitious project. Madame de Rênal looked like a
woman of thirty, but was still extremely pretty.

"He may live to rue the day, that fine gentleman from

Paris," M. de Rênal was saying in a tone of annoyance, his cheek paler even than was its wont. "I myself am not entirely without friends at Court. . . ."

But albeit I mean to speak to you of provincial life for two hundred pages, I shall not be so barbarous as to inflict upon you the tedium and all the *clever turns* of a provincial dialogue.

This fine gentleman from Paris, so odious to the Mayor of Verrières, was none other than M. Appert,[1] who, a couple of days earlier, had contrived to make his way not only into the prison and the poorhouse of Verrières, but also into the hospital, administered gratuitously by the Mayor and the principal landowners of the neighbourhood.

"But," Madame de Rênal put in timidly, "what harm can this gentleman from Paris do you, since you provide for the welfare of the poor with the most scrupulous honesty?"

"He has only come to cast blame, and then he'll go back and have articles put in the Liberal papers."

"You never read them, my dear."

"But people tell us about those Jacobin articles; all that distracts us, and *hinders us from doing good*.[2] As for me, I shall never forgive the curé."

[1] A contemporary philanthropist and prison visitor.
[2] Authentic.

CHAPTER THREE

THE BREAD OF THE POOR

Un curé vertueux et sans intrigue est une Providence
pour le village.

FLEURY.

IT should be explained that the curé of Verrières, an
old man of eighty, but blessed by the keen air of his
mountains with an iron character and strength, had the
right to visit at any hour of the day the prison, the hospital,
and even the poorhouse. It was at six o'clock in the morning precisely that M. Appert, who was armed with an
introduction to the curé from Paris, had had the good sense
to arrive in an inquisitive little town. He had gone at once
to the presbytery.

As he read the letter addressed to him by M. le Marquis
de La Mole, a Peer of France, and the wealthiest land-
owner in the province, the curé Chélan sat lost in thought.

"I am old and liked here," he murmured to himself at
length, "they would never dare!" Turning at once to the
gentleman from Paris, with eyes in which, despite his
great age, there burned that sacred fire which betokens the
pleasure of performing a fine action which is slightly
dangerous:

"Come with me, Sir, and, in the presence of the gaoler
and especially of the superintendents of the poorhouse,
be so good as not to express any opinion of the things we
shall see." M. Appert realized that he had to deal with
a man of feeling; he accompanied the venerable curé,
visited the prison, the hospital, the poorhouse, asked many

questions and, notwithstanding strange answers, did not allow himself to utter the least word of reproach.

This visit lasted for some hours. The curé invited M. Appert to dine with him, but was told that his guest had some letters to write: he did not wish to compromise his kind friend any further. About three o'clock, the gentlemen went back to complete their inspection of the poorhouse, after which they returned to the prison. There they found the gaoler standing in the doorway; a giant six feet tall, with bandy legs; terror had made his mean face hideous.

"Ah, Sir," he said to the curé, on catching sight of him, "is not this gentleman, that I see with you, M. Appert?"

"What if he is?" said the curé.

"Because yesterday I received the most definite instructions, which the Prefect sent down by a gendarme who had to gallop all night long, not to allow M. Appert into the prison."

"I declare to you, M. Noiroud," said the curé, "that this visitor, who is in my company, is M. Appert. Do you admit that I have the right to enter the prison at any hour of the day or night, bringing with me whom I please?"

"Yes, M. le curé," the gaoler murmured in a subdued tone, lowering his head like a bulldog brought reluctantly to obedience by fear of the stick. "Only, M. le curé, I have a wife and children, if I am reported I shall be dismissed; I have only my place here to live on."

"I too should be very sorry to lose mine," replied the worthy curé, in a voice swayed by ever increasing emotion.

"What a difference!" the gaoler answered promptly; "why you, M. le curé, we know that you have an income of 800 livres, a fine place in the sun. . . ."

Such are the events which, commented upon, exaggerated in twenty different ways, had been arousing for the last two days all the evil passions of the little town of Verrières. At that moment they were serving as text

for the little discussion which M. de Rênal was having
with his wife. That morning, accompanied by M. Valenod,
the governor of the poorhouse, he had gone to the curé's
house, to inform him of their extreme displeasure. M.
Chélan was under no one's protection; he felt the full
force of their words.

"Well, gentlemen, I shall be the third parish priest,
eighty years of age, whom the faithful will have seen deprived of his living in this district. I have been here for
six and fifty years; I have christened almost all the inhabitants of the town, which was no more than a village
when I came. Every day I marry young couples whose
grandparents I married long ago. Verrières is my family,
but the fear of leaving it will never make me traffic
with my conscience, or admit any other influence over my
actions; I said to myself, when I saw the stranger: "This
man, who has come from Paris, may indeed be a Liberal,
there are far too many of them; but what harm can he
do to our poor people and our prisoners?'"

The reproaches of M. de Rênal, and above all those of
M. Valenod, the governor of the poorhouse, becoming more
and more bitter:

"Very well, gentlemen, have me deprived," the old curé
had cried, in a quavering voice. "I shall live in the town
all the same. You all know that forty-eight years ago I
inherited a piece of land which brings me 800 livres; I
shall live on that income. I save nothing out of my stipend,
gentlemen, and that may be why I am less alarmed when
people speak of taking it from me."

M. de Rênal lived on excellent terms with his wife; but
not knowing what answer to make to the question, which
she timidly repeated: "What harm can this gentleman
from Paris do to the prisoners?" he was just about to
lose his temper altogether when she uttered a cry. Her
second son had climbed upon the parapet of the wall of
the terrace, and was running along it, though this wall

rose more than twenty feet from the vineyard beneath. The fear of alarming her son and so making him fall restrained Madame de Rênal from calling him. Finally the child, who was laughing at his own prowess, turned to look at his mother, noticed how pale she was, sprang down upon the avenue and ran to join her. He was well scolded.

This little incident changed the course of the conversation.

"I am quite determined to engage young Sorel, the sawyer's son," said M. de Rênal; "he will look after the children, who are beginning to be too much of a handful for us. He is a young priest or thereabouts, a good Latin scholar, and will bring the children on; for he has a strong character, the curé says. I shall give him 300 francs and his board. I had some doubts as to his morals; for he was the Benjamin of that old surgeon, the Member of the Legion of Honour, who on pretence of being their cousin came to live with the Sorels. He might quite well have been nothing better than a secret agent of the Liberals; he said that our mountain air was good for his asthma; but that has never been proved. He had served in all *Buonaparté's* campaigns in Italy, and they even say that he voted against the Empire in his day. This Liberal taught young Sorel Latin, and left him all the pile of books he brought here with him. Not that I should ever have dreamed of having the carpenter's son with my children; but the curé, only the day before the scene which has made a permanent breach between us, told me that this Sorel has been studying theology for the last three years, with the idea of entering the Seminary; so he is not a Liberal, and he is a Latin scholar.

"This arrangement suits me in more ways than one," M. de Rênal went on, looking at his wife with an air of diplomacy; "Valenod is tremendously proud of the two fine Norman horses he has just bought for his calash. But he has not got a tutor for his children."

"He is quite capable of taking this one from us."

"Then you approve of my plan?" said M. de Rênal, thanking his wife, with a smile, for the excellent idea that had just occurred to her. "There, that's settled."

"Oh, good gracious, my dear, how quickly you make up your mind!"

"That is because I have a strong character, as the curé has had occasion to see. Let us make no pretence about it, we are surrounded by Liberals here. All these cloth merchants are jealous of me, I am certain of it; two or three of them are growing rich; very well, I wish them to see M. de Rênal's children go by, out walking in the care of *their tutor*. It will make an impression. My grandfather used often to tell us that in his young days he had had a tutor. It's a hundred crowns he's going to cost me, but that will have to be reckoned as a necessary expense to keep up our position."

This sudden decision plunged Madame de Rênal deep in thought. She was a tall, well made woman, who had been the beauty of the place, as the saying is in this mountain district. She had a certain air of simplicity and bore herself like a girl; in the eyes of a Parisian, that artless grace, full of innocence and vivacity, might even have suggested ideas of a mildly passionate nature. Had she had wind of this kind of success, Madame de Rênal would have been thoroughly ashamed of it. No trace either of coquetry or of affectation had ever appeared in her nature. M. Valenod, the wealthy governor of the poorhouse, was supposed to have paid his court to her, but without success, a failure which had given a marked distinction to her virtue; for this M. Valenod, a tall young man, strongly built, with a vivid complexion and bushy black whiskers, was one of those coarse, brazen, noisy creatures who in the provinces are called fine men.

Madame de Rênal, being extremely shy and liable to be swayed by her moods, was offended chiefly by the restless movements and loud voice of M. Valenod. The distaste that she felt for what at Verrières goes by the name of gaiety had won her the reputation of being extremely proud of her birth. She never gave it a thought, but had been greatly pleased to see the inhabitants of Verrières come less frequently to her house. We shall not attempt to conceal the fact that she was reckoned a fool in the eyes of *their* ladies, because, without any regard for her husband's interests, she let slip the most promising opportunities of procuring fine hats from Paris or Besançon. Provided that she was left alone to stroll in her fine garden, she never made any complaint.

She was a simple soul, who had never risen even to the point of criticising her husband, and admitting that he bored her. She supposed, without telling herself so, that between husband and wife there could be no more tender relations. She was especially fond of M. de Rênal when he spoke to her of his plans for their children, one of whom he intended to place in the army, the second on the bench, and the third in the church. In short, she found M. de Rênal a great deal less boring than any of the other men of her acquaintance.

This wifely opinion was justified. The Mayor of Verrières owed his reputation for wit, and better still for good tone to half a dozen pleasantries which he had inherited from an uncle. This old Captain de Rênal had served before the Revolution in the Duke of Orleans's regiment of infantry, and, when he went to Paris, had had the right of entry into that Prince's drawing-rooms. He had there seen Madame de Montesson, the famous Madame de Genlis, M. Ducrest, the "inventor" of the Palais-Royal. These personages figured all too frequently in M. de Rênal's stories. But by degrees these memories of things that it required so much delicacy to relate had become a burden to him, and for some time now it was only on solemn occasions that he would repeat his anecdotes of the House of Orleans. As he was in other respects most refined, except when the talk ran on money, he was regarded, and rightly, as the most aristocratic personage in Verrières.

CHAPTER FOUR

FATHER AND SON

E sarà mia colpa,
Se così è?

MACHIAVELLI.

"MY wife certainly has a head on her shoulders!"
the Mayor of Verrières remarked to himself the
following morning at six o'clock, as he made
his way down to Père Sorel's sawmill. "Although I said
so to her, to maintain my own superiority, it had never
occurred to me that if I do not take this little priest Sorel,
who, they tell me, knows his Latin like an angel, the governor of the poorhouse, that restless spirit, might very well
have the same idea, and snatch him from me. I can hear
the tone of conceit with which he would speak of his children's tutor! . . . This tutor, once I've secured him, will
he wear a cassock?"

M. de Rênal was absorbed in this question when he saw
in the distance a peasant, a man of nearly six feet in height,
who, by the first dawning light, seemed to be busily
occupied in measuring pieces of timber lying by the side
of the Doubs, upon the towpath. The peasant did not
appear any too well pleased to see the Mayor coming
towards him; for his pieces of wood were blocking the
path, and had been laid there in contravention of the law.

Père Sorel, for it was he, was greatly surprised and
even more pleased by the singular offer which M. de Rênal
made him with regard to his son Julien. He listened to it

nevertheless with that air of grudging melancholy and lack of interest which the shrewd inhabitants of those mountains know so well how to assume. Slaves in the days of Spanish rule, they still retain this facial characteristic of the Egyptian fellahin.

Sorel's reply was at first nothing more than a long-winded recital of all the formal terms of respect which he knew by heart. While he was repeating these vain words, with an awkward smile which enhanced the air of falsehood and almost of rascality natural to his countenance, the old peasant's active mind was seeking to discover what reason could be inducing so important a personage to take his scapegrace of a son into his establishment. He was thoroughly dissatisfied with Julien, and it was for Julien that M. de Rênal was offering him the astounding wage of 300 francs annually, in addition to his food and even his clothing. This last condition, which Père Sorel had had the intelligence to advance on the spur of the moment, had been granted with equal readiness by M. de Rênal.

This demand impressed the Mayor. "Since Sorel is not delighted and overwhelmed by my proposal, as he ought naturally to be, it is clear," he said to himself, "that overtures have been made to him from another quarter; and from whom can they have come, except from Valenod?" It was in vain that M. de Rênal urged Sorel to conclude the bargain there and then: the astute old peasant met him with an obstinate refusal; he wished, he said, to consult his son, as though, in the country, a rich father ever consulted a penniless son, except for form's sake.

A sawmill consists of a shed by the side of a stream. The roof is held up by rafters supported on four stout wooden pillars. Nine or ten feet from the ground, in the middle of the shed, one sees a saw which moves up and down, while an extremely simple mechanism thrusts forward against this saw a piece of wood. This is a wheel set in motion by the mill lade which drives both parts of the machine; that of the saw which moves up and down, and the other which pushes the piece of wood gently towards the saw, which slices it into planks.

As he approached his mill, Père Sorel called Julien in his stentorian voice; there was no answer. He saw only his two elder sons, young giants who, armed with heavy axes, were squaring the trunks of fir which they would afterwards carry to the saw. They were completely engrossed in keeping exactly to the black line traced on the piece of wood, from which each blow of the axe sent huge chips flying. They did not hear their father's voice. He made his way to the shed; as he entered it, he looked in vain for Julien in the place where he ought to have been standing, beside the saw. He caught sight of him five or six feet higher up, sitting astride upon one of the beams of the roof. Instead of paying careful attention to the action of the machinery, Julien was reading a book. Nothing could have been less to old Sorel's liking; he might perhaps have forgiven Julien his slender build, little adapted to hard work, and so different from that of his elder brothers; but this passion for reading he detested: he himself was unable to read.

It was in vain that he called Julien two or three times. The attention the young man was paying to his book, far more than the noise of the saw, prevented him from hearing his father's terrifying voice. Finally, despite his years, the father sprang nimbly upon the trunk that was being cut by the saw, and from there on to the cross beam that held up the roof. A violent blow sent flying into the mill lade the book that Julien was holding; a second blow no less violent, aimed at his head, in the form of a box on the ear, made him lose his balance. He was about to fall from a height of twelve or fifteen feet, among the moving machinery, which would have crushed him, but his father caught him with his left hand as he fell.

"Well, idler! So you keep on reading your cursed books, when you ought to be watching the saw? Read them in the evening, when you go and waste your time with the curé."

Julien, although stunned by the force of the blow, and bleeding profusely, went to take up his proper station beside the saw. There were tears in his eyes, due not so much to his bodily pain as to the loss of his book, which he adored.

"Come down, animal, till I speak to you." The noise of the machine again prevented Julien from hearing this order. His father who had stepped down not wishing to take the trouble to climb up again on to the machine, went to find a long pole used for knocking down walnuts, and struck him on the shoulder with it. No sooner had Julien reached the ground than old Sorel, thrusting him on brutally from behind, drove him towards the house. "Heaven knows what he's going to do to me!" thought the young man. As he passed it, he looked sadly at the mill lade into which his book had fallen; it was the one that he valued most of all, the *Mémorial de Sainte-Hélène*.

His cheeks were flushed, his eyes downcast. He was a slim youth of eighteen or nineteen, weak in appearance, with irregular but delicate features and an aquiline nose. His large dark eyes, which, in moments of calm, suggested a reflective, fiery spirit, were animated at this instant with an expression of the most ferocious hatred. Hair of a dark chestnut, growing very low, gave him a narrow brow, and in moments of anger a wicked air. Among the innumerable varieties of the human countenance, there is perhaps none that is more strikingly characteristic. A slim and shapely figure betokened suppleness rather than strength. In his childhood, his extremely pensive air and marked pallor had given his father the idea that he would not live, or would live only to be a burden upon his family. An object of contempt to the rest of the household. he hated his brothers and father; in the games on Sundays, on the public square, he was invariably beaten.

It was only during the last year that his good looks had begun to win him a few supporters among the girls. Universally despised, as a feeble creature, Julien had adored that old Surgeon-Major who one day ventured to speak to the Mayor on the subject of the plane trees.

This surgeon used now and then to pay old Sorel a day's wage for his son, and taught him Latin and history, that is to say all the history that he knew, that of the 1796 campaign in Italy. On his death, he had bequeathed to him his Cross of the Legion of Honour, the arrears of his pension, and thirty or forty volumes, the most precious of which had just taken a plunge into the *public lade,* diverted by the Mayor's influence.

As soon as he was inside the house, Julien felt his shoulder gripped by his father's strong hand; he trembled, expecting to receive a shower of blows.

"Answer me without lying," the old peasant's harsh voice shouted in his ear, while the hand spun him round as a child's hand spins a lead soldier. Julien's great dark eyes, filled with tears, found themselves staring into the little grey eyes of the old peasant, who looked as though he sought to penetrate to the depths of his son's heart.

CHAPTER FIVE

DRIVING A BARGAIN

Cunctando restituit rem.
ENNIUS.

"ANSWER me, without lying, if you can, you miserable bookworm; how do you come to know Madame de Rênal? When have you spoken to her?"

"I have never spoken to her," replied Julien, "I have never seen the lady except in church."

"But you must have looked at her, you shameless scoundrel?"

"Never! You know that in church I see none but God," Julien added with a hypocritical air, calculated, to his mind, to ward off further blows.

"There is something behind this, all the same," replied the suspicious peasant, and was silent for a moment; "but I shall get nothing out of you, you damned twister. The fact is, I'm going to be rid of you, and my saw will run all the better without you. You have made a friend of the parson or someone, and he's got you a fine post. Go and pack your traps, and I'll take you to M. de Rênal's where you're to be tutor to the children."

"What am I to get for that?"

"Board, clothing and three hundred francs in wages."

"I do not wish to be a servant."

"Animal, who ever spoke of your being a servant? Would I allow my son to be a servant?"

"But, with whom shall I have my meals?"

This question left old Sorel at a loss; he felt that if he spoke he might be guilty of some imprudence; he flew into a rage with Julien, upon whom he showered abuse, accusing him of greed, and left him to go and consult his other sons.

Presently Julien saw them, each leaning upon his axe and deliberating together. After watching them for some time, Julien, seeing that he could make out nothing of their discussion, went and took his place on the far side of the saw, so as not to be taken by surprise. He wanted time to consider this sudden announcement which was altering his destiny, but felt himself to be incapable of prudence; his imagination was wholly taken up with forming pictures of what he would see in M. de Rênal's fine house.

"I must give up all that," he said to himself, "rather than let myself be brought down to feeding with the servants. My father will try to force me; I would sooner die. I have saved fifteen francs and eight sous, I shall run away to-night; in two days, by keeping to side-roads where I need not fear the police, I can be at Besançon; there I enlist as a soldier, and, if necessary, cross the border into Switzerland. But then, good-bye to everything, good-bye to that fine clerical profession which is a stepping-stone to everything."

This horror of feeding with the servants was not natural to Julien; he would, in seeking his fortune, have done other things far more disagreeable. He derived this repugnance from Rousseau's *Confessions*. It was the one book that helped his imagination to form any idea of the world. The collection of reports of the Grand Army and the *Mémorial de Sainte-Hélène* completed his Koran. He would have gone to the stake for those three books. Never did he believe in any other. Remembering a saying of

the old Surgeon-Major, he regarded all the other books
in the world as liars, written by rogues in order to obtain advancement.

With his fiery nature Julien had one of those astonishing memories so often found in foolish people. To win
over the old priest Chélan, upon whom he saw quite clearly
that his own future depended, he had learned by heart the
entire New Testament in Latin; he knew also M. de
Maistre's book *Du Pape,* and had as little belief in one
as in the other.

As though by a mutual agreement, Sorel and his son
avoided speaking to one another for the rest of the day.
At dusk, Julien went to the curé for his divinity lesson,
but did not think it prudent to say anything to him of
the strange proposal that had been made to his father.
"It may be a trap," he told himself; "I must pretend to
have forgotten about it."

Early on the following day, M. de Rênal sent for old
Sorel, who, after keeping him waiting for an hour or two,
finally appeared, beginning as he entered the door a hundred excuses interspersed with as many reverences. By
dint of giving voice to every sort of objection, Sorel succeeded in gathering that his son was to take his meals
with the master and mistress of the house, and on days
when they had company in a room by himself with the
children. Finding an increasing desire to raise difficulties
the more he discerned a genuine anxiety on the Mayor's
part, and being moreover filled with distrust and bewilderment, Sorel asked to see the room in which his son was
to sleep. It was a large chamber very decently furnished,
but the servants were already engaged in carrying into
it the beds of the three children.

At this the old peasant began to see daylight; he at
once asked with assurance to see the coat which would
be given to his son. M. de Rênal opened his desk and
took out a hundred francs.

"With this money, your son can go to M. Durand, the clothier, and get himself a suit of black."

"And supposing I take him away from you," said the peasant, who had completely forgotten the reverential forms of address. "Will he take this black coat with him?"

"Certainly."

"Oh, very well!" said Sorel in a drawling tone, "then there's only one thing for us still to settle: the money you're to give him."

"What!" M. de Rênal indignantly exclaimed, "we agreed upon that yesterday: I give three hundred francs; I consider that plenty, if not too much."

"That was your offer, I do not deny it," said old Sorel, speaking even more slowly; then, by a stroke of genius which will astonish only those who do not know the Franc-Comtois peasant, he added, looking M. de Rênal steadily in the face: *"We can do better elsewhere."*

At these words the Mayor was thrown into confusion. He recovered himself, however, and, after an adroit conversation lasting fully two hours, in which not a word was said without a purpose, the peasant's shrewdness prevailed over that of the rich man, who was not dependent on his for his living. All the innumerable conditions which were to determine Julien's new existence were finally settled; not only was his salary fixed at four hundred francs, but it was to be paid in advance, on the first day of each month.

"Very well! I shall let him have thirty-five francs," said M. de Rênal.

"To make a round sum, a rich and generous gentleman like our Mayor," the peasant insinuated in a coaxing voice, "will surely go as far as thirty-six."

"All right," said M. de Rênal, "but let us have no more of this."

For once, anger gave him a tone of resolution. The peasant saw that he could advance no farther. Thereupon M. de Rênal began in turn to make headway. He utterly refused to hand over the thirty-six francs for the first month to old Sorel, who was most eager to receive the money on his son's behalf. It occurred to M. de Rênal that he would be obliged to describe to his wife the part he had played throughout this transaction.

"Let me have back the hundred francs I gave you," he said angrily. "M. Durand owes me money. I shall go with your son to choose the black cloth."

After this bold stroke, Sorel prudently retired upon his expressions of respect; they occupied a good quarter of an hour. In the end, seeing that there was certainly nothing more to be gained, he withdrew. His final reverence ended with the words:

"I shall send my son up to the *château*."

It was thus that the Mayor's subordinates spoke of his house when they wished to please him.

Returning to his mill, Sorel looked in vain for his son. Doubtful as to what might be in store for him, Julien had left home in the dead of night. He had been anxious to find a safe hiding-place for his books and his Cross of the Legion of Honour. He had removed the whole of his treasures to the house of a young timber-merchant, a friend of his, by the name of Fouqué, who lived on the side of the high mountain overlooking Verrières.

When he reappeared: "Heaven knows, you damned idler," his father said to him, "whether you will ever have enough honour to pay me for the cost of your keep, which I have been advancing to you all these years! Pack up your rubbish, and off with you to the Mayor's."

Julien, astonished not to receive a thrashing, made haste to set off. But no sooner was he out of sight of his terrible father than he slackened his pace. He decided that it would serve the ends of his hypocrisy to pay a visit to the church.

The idea surprises you? Before arriving at this horrible idea, the soul of the young peasant had had a long way to go.

When he was still a child, the sight of certain dragoons of the 6th, in their long, white cloaks, and helmets adorned with long crests of black horsehair, who were returning from Italy, and whom Julien saw tying their horses to the barred window of his father's house, drove him mad with longing for a military career. Later on he listened with ecstasy to the accounts of the battles of the Bridge of Lodi, Arcole and Rivoli given him by the old Surgeon-Major. He noticed the burning gaze which the old man directed at his Cross.

But when Julien was fourteen, they began to build a church at Verrières, one that might be called magnificent for so small a town. There were, in particular, four marble pillars the sight of which impressed Julien; they became famous throughout the countryside, owing to the deadly enmity which they aroused between the Justice of the Peace and the young Vicar, sent down from Besançon, who was understood to be the spy of the *Congregation*. The Justice of the Peace came within an ace of losing his post, such at least was the common report. Had he not dared to have a difference of opinion with a priest who, almost every fortnight, went to Besançon, where he saw, people said, the Right Reverend Lord Bishop?

In the midst of all this, the Justice of the Peace, the father of a large family, passed a number of sentences which appeared unjust; all of these were directed against such of the inhabitants as read the *Constitutionnel*. The right party was triumphant. The sums involved amounted, it was true, to no more than four or five francs; but one of these small fines was levied upon a nailsmith, Julien's godfather. In his anger, this man exclaimed: "What a change! And to think that, for twenty years and more, the Justice was reckoned such an honest man!" The Surgeon-Major, Julien's friend, was dead.

All at once Julien ceased to speak of Napoleon; he announced his intention of becoming a priest, and was constantly to be seen, in his father's sawmill, engaged in learning by heart a Latin Bible which the curé had lent him. The good old man, amazed at his progress, devoted whole evenings to instructing him in divinity. Julien gave utterance in his company to none but pious sentiments. Who could have supposed that that girlish face, so pale and gentle, hid the unshakable determination to expose himself to the risk of a thousand deaths rather than fail to make his fortune?

To Julien, making a fortune meant in the first place leaving Verrières; he loathed his native place. Everything that he saw there froze his imagination.

From his earliest boyhood, he had had moments of exaltation. At such times he dreamed with rapture that one day he would be introduced to the beautiful ladies of Paris; he would manage to attract their attention by some brilliant action. Why should he not be loved by one of them, as Bonaparte, when still penniless, had been loved by the brilliant Madame de Beauharnais? For many years now, perhaps not an hour of Julien's life had passed without his reminding himself that Bonaparte, an obscure subaltern with no fortune, had made himself master of the world with his sword. This thought consoled him for his misfortunes which he deemed to be great, and enhanced his joy when joy came his way.

The building of the church and the sentences passed oy the Justice brought him sudden enlightenment; an idea which occurred to him drove him almost out of his senses for some weeks, and finally took possession of him with the absolute power of the first idea which a passionate nature believes itself to have discovered.

"When Bonaparte made a name for himself, France was in fear of being invaded; military distinction was necessary and fashionable. To-day we see priests at forty drawing stipends of a hundred thousand francs, that is to say three times as much as the famous divisional commanders under Napoleon. They must have people to support them. Look at the Justice here, so wise a man, always so honest until now, sacrificing his honour, at his age, from fear of offending a young vicar of thirty. I must become a priest."

On one occasion, in the midst of his new-found piety, after Julien had been studying divinity for two years, he was betrayed by a sudden blaze of the fire that devoured his spirit. This was at M. Chélan's; at a dinner party of priests, to whom the good curé had introduced him as an educational prodigy, he found himself uttering frenzied praise of Napoleon. He bound his right arm across his chest, pretending that he had put the arm out of joint when shifting a fir trunk, and kept it for two months in this awkward position. After this drastic penance, he forgave himself. Such is the young man of eighteen, but weak in appearance, whom you would have said to be, at the most, seventeen, who, carrying a small parcel under his arm, was entering the magnificent church of Verrières.

He found it dark and deserted. In view of some festival, all the windows in the building had been covered with crimson cloth; the effect of this, when the sun shone, was a dazzling blaze of light, of the most imposing and most religious character. Julien shuddered. Being alone in the church, he took his seat on the bench that had the most handsome appearance. It bore the arms of M. de Rênal.

On the desk in front, Julien observed a scrap of printed paper, spread out there as though to be read. He looked at it closely and saw:

"Details of the execution and of the last moments of Louis Jenrel, executed at Besançon, on the . . ."

The paper was torn. On the other side he read the opening words of a line, which were: "The first step."

"Who can have put this paper here?" said Julien. "Poor wretch!" he added with a sigh, "his name has the same ending as mine." And he crumpled up the paper.

On his way out, Julien thought he saw blood by the holy water stoup; it was some of the water that had been spilt: the light from the red curtains which draped the windows made it appear like blood.

Finally, Julien felt ashamed of his secret terror.

"Should I prove coward?" he said to himself. *"To arms!"*

This phrase, so often repeated in the old Surgeon's accounts of battles, had a heroic sound in Julien's ears. He rose and walked rapidly to M. de Rênal's house.

Despite these brave resolutions, as soon as he caught sight of the house twenty yards away he was overcome by an unconquerable shyness. The iron gate stood open; it seemed to him magnificent. He would have now to go in through it.

Julien was not the only person whose heart was troubled by his arrival in this household. Madame de Rênal's extreme timidity was disconcerted by the idea of this stranger who, in the performance of his duty, would be constantly coming between her and her children. She was accustomed to having her sons sleep in her own room. That morning, many tears had flowed when she saw their little beds being carried into the apartment intended for the tutor. In vain did she beg her husband to let the bed of Stanislas Xavier, the youngest boy, be taken back to her room.

Womanly delicacy was carried to excess in Madame de Rênal. She formed a mental picture of a coarse, unkempt creature, employed to scold her children, simply because he knew Latin, a barbarous tongue for the sake of which her sons would be whipped.

CHAPTER SIX

DULNESS

Non so più cosa son,
Cosa facio.

MOZART (*Figaro*).

WITH the vivacity and grace which came naturally
to her when she was beyond the reach of male
vision, Madame de Rênal was coming out
through the glass door which opened from the drawing-
room into the garden, when she saw, standing by the front
door, a young peasant, almost a boy still, extremely pale
and shewing traces of recent tears. He was wearing a
clean white shirt and carried under his arm a neat jacket
of violet ratteen.

This young peasant's skin was so white, his eyes were
so appealing, that the somewhat romantic mind of Madame
de Rênal conceived the idea at first that he might be a
girl in disguise, come to ask some favour of the Mayor.
She felt sorry for the poor creature, who had come to
a standstill by the front door, and evidently could not
summon up courage to ring the bell. Madame de Rênal
advanced, oblivious for the moment of the bitter grief that
she felt at the tutor's coming. Julien, who was facing
the door, did not see her approach. He trembled when a
pleasant voice sounded close to his ear:

"What have you come for, my boy?"

Julien turned sharply round, and, struck by the charm
of Madame de Rênal's expression, forgot part of his shy-

ness. A moment later, astounded by her beauty, he forgot everything, even his purpose in coming. Madame de
Rênal had repeated her question.

"I have come to be tutor, Madame," he at length informed her, put to shame by his tears which he dried
as best he might.

Madame de Rênal remained speechless; they were standing close together, looking at one another. Julien had
never seen a person so well dressed as this, let alone
a woman with so exquisite a complexion, to speak to him in
a gentle tone. Madame de Rênal looked at the large tears
which lingered on the cheeks (so pallid at first and now
so rosy) of this young peasant. Presently she burst out
laughing, with all the wild hilarity of a girl; she was
laughing at herself, and trying in vain to realise the full
extent of her happiness. So this was the tutor whom
she had imagined an unwashed and ill-dressed priest, who
was coming to scold and whip her children.

"Why, Sir!" she said to him at length, "do you know
Latin?"

The word "Sir" came as such a surprise to Julien that
he thought for a moment before answering.

"Yes, ma'am," he said shyly.

Madame de Rênal felt so happy that she ventured to say
to Julien:

"You won't scold those poor children too severely?"

"Scold them? I?" asked Julien in amazement. "Why
should I?"

"You will, Sir," she went on after a brief silence and
in a voice that grew more emotional every moment, "you
will be kind to them, you promise me?"

To hear himself addressed again as "Sir," in all seri-
ousness, and by a lady so fashionably attired, was more
than Julien had ever dreamed of; in all the cloud castles
of his boyhood, he had told himself that no fashionable
lady would deign to speak to him until he had a smart

uniform. Madame de Rênal, for her part, was completely taken in by the beauty of Julien's complexion, his great dark eyes and his becoming hair which was curling more than usual because, to cool himself, he had just dipped his head in the basin of the public fountain. To her great delight, she discovered an air of girlish shyness in this fatal tutor, whose severity and savage tone she had so greatly dreaded for her children's sake. To Madame de Rênal's peace-loving nature the contrast between her fears and what she now saw before her was a great event. Finally she recovered from her surprise. She was astonished to find herself standing like this at the door of her house with this young man almost in his shirtsleeves and so close to her.

"Let us go indoors, Sir," she said to him with an air of distinct embarrassment.

Never in her life had a purely agreeable sensation so profoundly stirred Madame de Rênal; never had so charming an apparition come in the wake of more disturbing fears. And so those sweet children, whom she had tended with such care, were not to fall into the hands of a dirty, growling priest. As soon as they were in the hall, she turned to Julien who was following her shyly. His air of surprise at the sight of so fine a house was an additional charm in the eyes of Madame de Rênal. She could not believe her eyes; what she felt most of all was that the tutor ought to be wearing a black coat.

"But is it true, Sir," she said to him, again coming to a halt, and mortally afraid lest she might be mistaken, so happy was the belief making her, "do you really know Latin?"

These words hurt Julien's pride and destroyed the enchantment in which he had been living for the last quarter of an hour.

"Yes, Ma'am," he informed her, trying to adopt a chilly

air; "I know Latin as well as M. le curé; indeed, he is sometimes so kind as to say that I know it better."

Madame de Rênal felt that Julien had a very wicked air; he had stopped within arm's length of her. She went nearer to him, and murmured:

"For the first few days, you won't take the whip to my children, even if they don't know their lessons?"

This gentle, almost beseeching tone coming from so fine a lady at once made Julien forget what he owed to his reputation as a Latin scholar. Madame de Rênal's face was close to his own, he could smell the perfume of a woman's summer attire, so astounding a thing to a poor peasant. Julien blushed deeply, and said with a sigh and in a faint voice:

"Fear nothing, Ma'am, I shall obey you in every respect."

It was at this moment only, when her anxiety for her children was completely banished, that Madame de Rênal was struck by Julien's extreme good looks. The almost feminine cast of his features and his air of embarrassment did not seem in the least absurd to a woman who was extremely timid herself. The manly air which is generally considered essential to masculine beauty would have frightened her.

"How old are you, Sir?" she asked Julien.

"I shall soon be nineteen."

"My eldest son is eleven," went on Madame de Rênal, completely reassured; "he will be almost a companion for you, you can talk to him seriously. His father tried to beat him once, the child was ill for a whole week, and yet it was quite a gentle blow."

"How different from me," thought Julien. "Only yesterday my father was thrashing me. How fortunate these rich people are!"

Madame de Rênal had by this time arrived at the stage

of remarking the most trivial changes in the state of the
tutor's mind; she mistook this envious impulse for shyness, and tried to give him fresh courage.

"What is your name, Sir?" she asked him with an accent and a grace the charm of which Julien could feel
without knowing from whence it sprang.

"They call me Julien Sorel, Ma'am; I am trembling
as I enter a strange house for the first time in my life;
I have need of your protection, and shall require you to
forgive me many things at first. I have never been to
College, I was too poor; I have never talked to any other
men, except my cousin the Surgeon-Major, a Member of
the Legion of Honour, and the Reverend Father Chélan.
He will give you a good account of me. My brothers
have always beaten me, do not listen to them if they speak
evil of me to you; pardon my faults, Ma'am, I shall never
have any evil intention."

Julien plucked up his courage again during this long
speech; he was studying Madame de Rênal. Such is the
effect of perfect grace when it is natural to the character,
particularly when she whom it adorns has no thought of
being graceful. Julien, who knew all that was to be
known about feminine beauty, would have sworn at that
moment that she was no more than twenty. The bold idea
at once occurred to him of kissing her hand. Next, this
idea frightened him; a moment later, he said to himself:
"It would be cowardly on my part not to carry out an
action which may be of use to me, and diminish the scorn
which this fine lady probably feels for a poor workman,
only just taken from the sawbench." Perhaps Julien was
somewhat encouraged by the words "good looking boy"
which for the last six months he had been used to hearing
on Sundays on the lips of various girls. While he debated
thus with himself, Madame de Rênal offered him a few
suggestions as to how he should begin to handle her chil-

dren. The violence of Julien's effort to control himself made him turn quite pale again; he said, with an air of constraint:

"Never, Ma'am, will I beat your children; I swear it before God."

And so saying he ventured to take Madame de Rênal's hand and carry it to his lips. She was astonished at this action, and, on thinking it over, shocked. As the weather was very warm, her arm was completely bare under her shawl, and Julien's action in raising her hand to his lips had uncovered it to the shoulder. A minute later she scolded herself; she felt that she had not been quickly enough offended.

M. de Rênal, who had heard the sound of voices, came out of his study; with the same majestic and fatherly air that he assumed when he was conducting marriages in the Town Hall, he said to Julien:

"It is essential that I speak to you before the children see you."

He ushered Julien into one of the rooms and detained his wife, who was going to leave them together. Having shut the door, M. de Rênal seated himself with gravity.

"The curé has told me that you were an honest fellow, everyone in this house will treat you with respect, and if I am satisfied I shall help you to set up for yourself later on. I wish you to cease to see anything of either your family or your friends, their tone would not be suited to my children. Here are thirty-six francs for the first month; but I must have your word that you will not give a penny of this money to your father."

M. de Rênal was annoyed with the old man, who, in this business, had proved more subtle than he himself.

"And now, *Sir,* for by my orders everyone in this house is to address you as Sir, and you will be conscious of the advantage of entering a well ordered household; now, Sir, it is not proper that the children should see you in a jacket.

Have the servants seen him?" M. de Rênal asked his wife.

"No, dear," she replied with an air of deep thought.

"Good. Put on this," he said to the astonished young man, handing him one of his own frock coats. "And now let us go to M. Durand, the clothier."

More than an hour later, when M. de Rênal returned with the new tutor dressed all in black, he found his wife still seated in the same place. She felt soothed by Julien's presence; as she studied his appearance she forgot to feel afraid. Julien was not giving her a thought; for all his mistrust of destiny and of mankind, his heart at that moment was just like a child's; he seemed to have lived whole years since the moment when, three hours earlier, he stood trembling in the church. He noticed Madame de Rênal's frigid manner, and gathered that she was angry because he had ventured to kiss her hand. But the sense of pride that he derived from the contact of garments so different from those which he was accustomed to wear caused him so much excitement, and he was so anxious to conceal his joy that all his gestures were more or less abrupt and foolish. Madame de Rênal gazed at him with eyes of astonishment.

"A little gravity, Sir," M. de Rênal told him, "if you wish to be respected by my children and my servants."

"Sir," replied Julien, "I am uncomfortable in these new clothes; I, a humble peasant, have never worn any but short jackets; with your permission, I shall retire to my bedroom."

"What think you of this new acquisition?" M. de Rênal asked his wife.

With an almost instinctive impulse, of which she herself certainly was not aware, Madame de Rênal concealed the truth from her husband.

"I am by no means as enchanted as you are with this little peasant; your kindness will turn him into an imperti-

nent rascal whom you will be obliged to send packing within
a month."

"Very well! We shall send him packing; he will have
cost me a hundred francs or so, and Verrières will have
grown used to seeing a tutor with M. de Rênal's children.
That point I should not have gained if I had let Julien
remain in the clothes of a working man. When I dismiss
him, I shall of course keep the black suit which I have
just ordered from the clothier. He shall have nothing but
the coat I found ready made at the tailor's, which he is
now wearing."

The hour which Julien spent in his room seemed like
a second to Madame de Rênal. The children, who had
been told of their new tutor's arrival, overwhelmed their
mother with questions. Finally Julien appeared. He was
another man. It would have been straining the word
to say that he was grave; he was gravity incarnate. He
was introduced to the children, and spoke to them with an
air that surprised M. de Rênal himself.

"I am here, young gentlemen," he told them at the end
of his address, "to teach you Latin. You know what is
meant by repeating a lesson. Here is the Holy Bible,"
he said, and shewed them a tiny volume in 32mo, bound
in black. "It is in particular the story of Our Lord Jesus
Christ, that is the part which is called the New Testament.
I shall often make you repeat lessons; now you must make
me repeat mine."

Adolphe, the eldest boy, had taken the book.

"Open it where you please," Julien went on, "and tell
me the first three words of a paragraph. I shall repeat by
heart the sacred text, the rule of conduct for us all, until
you stop me."

Adolphe opened the book, read a couple of words, and
Julien repeated the whole page as easily as though he
were speaking French. M. de Rênal looked at his wife
with an air of triumph. The children, seeing their par-

ents' amazement, opened their eyes wide. A servant came to the door of the drawing-room, Julien went on speaking in Latin. The servant at first stood motionless and then vanished. Presently the lady's maid and the cook appeared in the doorway; by this time Adolphe had opened the book at eight different places, and Julien continued to repeat the words with the same ease.

"Eh, what a bonny little priest," the cook, a good and truly devout girl, said aloud.

M. de Rênal's self-esteem was troubled; so far from having any thought of examining the tutor, he was engaged in ransacking his memory for a few words of Latin; at last, he managed to quote a line of Horace. Julien knew no Latin apart from the Bible. He replied with a frown:

"The sacred ministry to which I intend to devote myself has forbidden me to read so profane a poet."

M. de Rênal repeated a fair number of alleged lines of Horace. He explained to his children what Horace was; but the children, overcome with admiration, paid little attention to what he was saying. They were watching Julien.

The servants being still at the door, Julien felt it incumbent upon him to prolong the test.

"And now," he said to the youngest boy, "Master Stanislas Xavier too must set me a passage from the Holy Book."

Little Stanislas, swelling with pride, read out to the best of his ability the opening words of a paragraph, and Julien repeated the whole page. That nothing might be wanting to complete M. de Rênal's triumph, while Julien was reciting, there entered M. Valenod, the possessor of fine Norman horses, and M. Charcot de Maugiron, Sub-Prefect of the district. This scene earned for Julien the title "Sir"; the servants themselves dared not withhold it from him.

That evening, the whole of Verrières flocked to M. de

Rênal's to behold the marvel. Julien answered them all with an air of gloom which kept them at a distance. His fame spread so rapidly through the town that, shortly afterwards, M. de Rênal, afraid of losing him, suggested his signing a contract for two years.

"No, Sir," Julien replied coldly, "if you chose to dismiss me I should be obliged to go. A contract which binds me without putting you under any obligation is unfair, I must decline."

Julien managed so skilfully that, less than a month after his coming to the house, M. de Rênal himself respected him. The curé having quarrelled with MM. de Rênal and Valenod, there was no one who could betray Julien's former passion for Napoleon, of whom he was careful to speak with horror.

CHAPTER SEVEN

ELECTIVE AFFINITIES

Ils ne savent toucher le cœur qu'en le froissant.

A MODERN.

THE children adored him, he did not care for them;
his thoughts were elsewhere. Nothing that these
urchins could do ever tried his patience. Cold,
just, impassive, and at the same time loved, because his
coming had in a measure banished dulness from the house,
he was a good tutor. For his part, he felt only hatred
and horror for the high society in which he was allowed
to occupy the very foot of the table, a position which may
perhaps explain his hatred and horror. There were certain formal dinners at which he could barely contain his
loathing of everything round about him. On Saint Louis's
day in particular, M. Valenod was laying down the law
at M. de Rênal's; Julien almost gave himself away; he
escaped into the garden, saying that he must look after
the children. "What panegyrics of honesty!" he exclaimed;
"anyone would say that was the one and only virtue; and
yet what consideration, what a cringing respect for a man
who obviously has doubled and tripled his fortune since
he has been in charge of the relief of the poor! I would
wager that he makes something even out of the fund
set apart for the foundlings, those wretches whose need
is even more sacred than that of the other paupers. Ah,
monsters! Monsters! And I too, I am a sort of found-
ling, hated by my father, my brothers, my whole family."
Some days earlier, Julien walking by himself and say-

ing his office in a little wood, known as the Belvedere, which overlooks the Cours de la Fidélité, had tried in vain to avoid his two brothers, whom he saw approaching him by a solitary path. The jealousy of these rough labourers had been so quickened by the sight of their brother's handsome black coat, and air of extreme gentility, as well as by the sincere contempt which he felt for them, that they had proceeded to thrash him, leaving him there unconscious and bleeding freely. Madame de Rênal, who was out walking with M. Valenod and the Sub-Prefect, happened to turn into the little wood; she saw Julien lying on the ground and thought him dead. She was so overcome as to make M. Valenod jealous.

His alarm was premature. Julien admired Madame de Rênal's looks, but hated her for her beauty; it was the first reef on which his fortune had nearly foundered. He spoke to her as seldom as possible, in the hope of making her forget the impulse which, at their first encounter, had led him to kiss her hand.

Elisa, Madame de Rênal's maid, had not failed to fall in love with the young tutor; she often spoke of him to her mistress. Miss Elisa's love had brought upon Julien the hatred of one of the footmen. One day he heard this man say to Elisa: "You won't speak to me any more, since that greasy tutor has been in the house." Julien did not deserve the epithet; but, with the instinct of a good looking youth, became doubly attentive to his person. M. Valenod's hatred was multiplied accordingly. He said in public that such effeminate ways were not becoming in a young cleric. Barring the cassock, Julien now wore clerical attire.

Madame de Rênal observed that he was speaking more often than before to Miss Elisa; she learned that these conversations were due to the limitations of Julien's extremely small wardrobe. He had so scanty a supply of linen that he was obliged to send it out constantly to be washed, and it was in performing these little services that Elisa made herself useful to him.

This extreme poverty, of which she had had no suspicion, touched Madame de Rênal; she longed to make him presents, but did not dare; this inward resistance was the first feeling of regret that Julien caused her. Until then the name of Julien and the sense of a pure and wholly intellectual joy had been synonymous to her. Tormented by the idea of Julien's poverty, Madame de Rênal spoke to her husband about making him a present of linen:

"What idiocy!" he replied. "What! Make presents to a man with whom we are perfectly satisfied, and who is serving us well? It is when he neglects his duty that we should stimulate his zeal."

Madame de Rênal felt ashamed of this way of looking at things; before Julien came she would not have noticed it. She never saw the young cleric's spotless, though very simple, toilet without asking herself: "Poor boy, how ever does he manage?"

As time went on she began to feel sorry for Julien's deficiencies, instead of being shocked by them.

Madame de Rênal was one of those women to be found in the provinces whom one may easily take to be fools until one has known them for a fortnight. She had no experience of life, and made no effort at conversation. Endowed with a delicate and haughty nature, that instinct for happiness natural to all human beings made her, generally speaking, pay no attention to the actions of the coarse creatures into whose midst chance had flung her.

She would have been remarkable for her naturalness and quickness of mind, had she received the most scanty education; but in her capacity as an heiress she had been brought up by nuns who practised a passionate devotion to the Sacred Heart of Jesus, and were animated by a violent hatred of the French as being enemies of the

Jesuits. Madame de Rênal had sufficient sense to forget at once, as absurdities, everything she had learned in the convent; but she put nothing else in its place, and ended by knowing nothing. The flatteries of which she had been the precocious object, as the heiress to a large fortune, and a marked tendency towards passionate devotion, had bred in her an attitude towards life that was wholly inward. With an outward show of the most perfect submission, and a self-suppression which the husbands of Verrières used to quote as an example to their wives, and which was a source of pride to M. de Rênal, her inner life was, as a matter of fact, dictated by the most lofty disdain. Any princess who is quoted as an illustration of pride pays infinitely more attention to what her gentlemen are doing round about her than this meekest of women, so modest in appearance, gave to anything that her husband said or did. Until Julien arrived, she had really paid no attention to anyone but her children. Their little illnesses, their sorrows, their little pleasures absorbed the whole sensibility of this human soul, which had never, in the whole of her life, adored anyone save God, while she was at the Sacred Heart in Besançon.

Although she did not condescend to say so to anyone, a feverish attack coming to one of her sons threw her almost into the same state as if the child had died. A burst of coarse laughter, a shrug of the shoulders, accompanied by some trivial maxim as to the foolishness of women, had regularly greeted the confessions of grief of this sort which the need of an outlet had led her to make to her husband during the first years of their married life. Witticisms of this sort, especially when they bore upon the illnesses of the children, turned the dagger in Madame de Rênal's heart. This was all the substitute she found for the obsequious, honeyed flatteries of the Jesuitical convent in which she had passed her girlhood. She was educated in the school of suffering. Too proud to speak of griefs of this sort, even to her friend Madame Derville, she imagined that all men resembled her husband, M. Valenod, and the Sub-Prefect Charcot de Maugiron. Coarse wit and the most brutal insensibility to everything that did not promise money, promotion or a Cross; a blind hatred of every argument that went against them seemed to her to be things natural to the male sex, like the wearing of boots and felt hats.

After many long years, Madame de Rênal had not yet grown accustomed to these money-grubbing creatures among whom she had to live.

Hence the success of the little peasant Julien. She found much pleasant enjoyment, radiant with the charm of novelty, in the sympathy of this proud and noble spirit. Madame de Rênal had soon forgiven him his extreme ignorance, which was an additional charm, and the roughness of his manners, which she succeeded in improving. She found that it was worth her while to listen to him, even when they spoke of the most ordinary things, even when it was a question of a poor dog that had been run over, as it was crossing the street, by a peasant's cart going by at a trot. The sight of such a tragedy made her husband utter his coarse laugh, whereas she saw Julien's fine, beautifully arched black eyebrows wince. Generosity, nobility of soul, humanity, seemed to her, after a time, to exist only in this young cleric. She felt for him alone all the sympathy and even admiration which those virtues arouse in well-bred natures.

In Paris, Julien's position with regard to Madame de Rênal would very soon have been simplified; but in Paris love is the child of the novels. The young tutor and his timid mistress would have found in three or four novels, and even in the lyrics of the Gymnase a clear statement of their situation. The novels would have outlined for them the part to be played, shewn them the model to copy; and this model, sooner or later, albeit without the slightest pleasure, and perhaps with reluctance, vanity would have compelled Julien to follow.

In a small town of the Aveyron or the Pyrenees, the slightest incident would have been made decisive by the ardour of the climate. Beneath our more sombre skies, a penniless young man, who is ambitious only because the refinement of his nature puts him in need of some of those pleasures which money provides, is in daily contact with a woman of thirty who is sincerely virtuous, occupied with her children, and never looks to novels for examples of conduct. Everything goes slowly, everything happens by degrees in the provinces: life is more natural.

Often, when she thought of the young tutor's poverty, Madame de Rênal was moved to tears. Julien came upon her, one day, actually crying.

"Ah, Ma'am, you have had some bad news!"

"No, my friend," was her answer: "Call the children, let us go for a walk."

She took his arm and leaned on it in a manner which Julien thought strange. It was the first time that she had called him "my friend."

Towards the end of their walk, Julien observed that she was blushing deeply. She slackened her pace.

"You will have heard," she said without looking at him, "that I am the sole heiress of a very rich aunt who lives at Besançon. She loads me with presents. My sons are making . . . such astonishing progress . . . that I should like to ask you to accept a little present, as a token of my gratitude. It is only a matter of a few louis to supply you with linen. But——" she added, blushing even more deeply, and was silent.

"What, Ma'am?" said Julien.

"It would be unnecessary," she went on, lowering her head, "to speak of this to my husband."

"I may be humble, Ma'am, but I am not base," replied Julien coming to a standstill, his eyes ablaze with anger, and drawing himself up to his full height. "That is a point which you have not sufficiently considered. I should be less than a footman if I put myself in the position of hiding from M. de Rênal anything that had to do with *my money.*"

Madame de Rênal was overwhelmed.

"The Mayor," Julien went on, "has given me thirty-six francs five times since I came to live in his house; I am prepared to shew my account-book to M. de Rênal or to anyone else, including M. Valenod who hates me."

This outburst left Madame de Rênal pale and trembling, and the walk came to an end before either of them could find an excuse for renewing the conversation. Love for Madame de Rênal became more and more impossible in the proud heart of Julien: as for her, she respected, she admired him; she had been scolded by him. On the pretext of making amends for the humiliation which she had unintentionally caused him, she allowed herself to pay him the most delicate attentions. The novelty of this procedure kept her happy for a week. Its effect was to some extent to appease Julien's anger; he was far from seeing anything in it that could be mistaken for personal affection.

"That," he said to himself, "is what rich people are like: they humiliate one, and then think they can put things right by a few monkey-tricks."

Madame de Rênal's heart was too full, and as yet too innocent for her, notwithstanding the resolutions she had made, not to tell her husband of the offer she had made to Julien and the manner in which she had been repulsed.

"What," M. de Rênal retorted, with keen annoyance, "could you tolerate a refusal from a *servant?*"

And as Madame de Rênal protested at this word:

"I speak, Ma'am, as the late Prince de Condé spoke, when presenting his Chamberlains to his bride: 'All these people,' he told her, 'are our servants.' I read you the passage from Besenval's *Memoirs,* it is essential in questions of precedence. Everyone who is not a gentleman, who lives in your house and receives a salary, is your servant. I shall say a few words to this Master Julien, and give him a hundred francs."

"Ah, my dear," said Madame de Rênal trembling, "please do not say anything in front of the servants."

"Yes, they might be jealous, and rightly," said her husband as he left the room, thinking of the magnitude of the sum.

Madame de Rênal sank down on a chair, almost fainting with grief. "He is going to humiliate Julien, and it is my fault!" She felt a horror of her husband, and hid her face in her hands. She promised herself that she would never confide anything in him again.

When she next saw Julien, she was trembling all over, her bosom was so contracted that she could not manage to utter a single word. In her embarrassment she took his hands and wrung them.

"Well, my friend," she said to him after a little, "are you pleased with my husband?"

"How should I not be?" Julien answered with a bitter smile; "he has given me a hundred francs."

Madame de Rênal looked at him as though uncertain what to do.

"Give me your arm," she said at length with an accent of courage which Julien had never yet observed in her.

She ventured to enter the shop of the Verrières bookseller, in spite of his terrible reputation as a Liberal. There she chose books to the value of ten louis which she gave to her sons. But these books were the ones which she knew that Julien wanted. She insisted that there, in the bookseller's shop, each of the children should write his own name in the books that fell to his share. While Madame de Rênal was rejoicing at the partial reparation which she had had the courage to make to Julien, he was lost in amazement at the quantity of books which he saw on the bookseller's shelves. Never had he dared to set foot in so profane a place; his heart beat violently. So far from his having any thought of trying to guess what was occurring in the heart of Madame de Rênal, he was plunged in meditation as to how it would be possible for a young student of divinity to procure some of these books. At length the idea came to him that it might be possible, by a skilful approach, to persuade M. de Rênal that he ought to set his sons, as the subject for an essay, the lives of the celebrated gentlemen who were natives of the province. After a month of careful preliminaries, he saw his idea prove successful, so much so that, shortly afterwards, he ventured, in speaking to M. de Rênal, to mention an action considerably more offensive to the noble Mayor; it was a matter of contributing to the prosperity of a Liberal, by taking out a subscription at the library. M. de Rênal entirely agreed that it was wise to let his eldest son have a *visual impression* of various works which he would hear mentioned in conversation when he went to the Military School; but Julien found the Mayor obdurate in refusing to go any farther. He suspected a secret reason, which he was unable to guess.

"I was thinking, Sir," he said to him one day, "that it would be highly improper for the name of a respectable gentleman like a Rênal to appear on the dirty ledger of the librarian."

M. de Rênal's face brightened.

"It would also be a very bad mark," Julien went on, in a humbler tone, "against a poor divinity student, if it should one day be discovered that his name had been on the ledger of a bookseller who keeps a library. The Liberals might accuse me of having asked for the most scandalous books; for all one knows they might even go so far as to write in after my name the titles of those perverse works."

But Julien was going off the track. He saw the Mayor's features resume their expression of embarrassment and ill humour. Julien was silent. "I have my man hooked," he said to himself.

A few days later, on the eldest boy's questioning Julien as to a book advertised in the *Quotidienne,* in M. de Rênal's presence:

"To remove all occasion for triumph from the Jacobin Party," said the young tutor, "and at the same time to enable me to answer Master Adolphe, one might open a subscription at the library in the name of the lowest of your servants."

"That is not at all a bad idea," said M. de Rênal, obviously delighted.

"Only it would have to be specified," said Julien with that grave and almost sorrowful air which becomes certain people so well, when they see the success of the projects which have been longest in their minds, "it would have to be specified that the servant shall not take out any novels. Once they were in the house, those dangerous works might corrupt Madame's maids, not to speak of the servant himself."

"You forget the political pamphlets," added M. de Rênal, in a haughty tone. He wished to conceal the admiration that he felt for the clever middle course discovered by his children's tutor.

Julien's life was thus composed of a series of petty negotiations; and their success was of far more importance to him than the evidence of a marked preference for himself which was only waiting for him to read it in the heart of Madame de Rênal.

The moral environment in which he had been placed all his life was repeated in the household of the worshipful Mayor of Verrières. There, as in his father's sawmill, he profoundly despised the people with whom he lived, and was hated by them. He saw every day, from the remarks made by the Sub-Prefect, by M. Valenod and by the other friends of the family, with reference to the things that had just happened under their eyes, how remote their ideas were from any semblance of reality. Did an action strike him as admirable, it was precisely what called forth blame from the people round about him. His unspoken retort was always: "What monsters!" or "What fools!" The amusing thing was that, with all his pride, frequently he understood nothing at all of what was being discussed.

In his whole life, he had never spoken with sincerity except to the old Surgeon-Major; the few ideas that he had bore reference to Napoleon's campaigns in Italy, or to surgery. His youthful courage took delight in detailed accounts of the most painful operations; he said to himself: "I should not have flinched."

The first time that Madame de Rênal attempted a conversation with him on a subject other than that of the children's education, he began to talk of surgical operations; she turned pale, and begged him to stop.

Julien knew nothing apart from these matters. And so, as he spent his time with Madame de Rênal, the strangest silence grew up between them as soon as they were alone together. In her own drawing-room, humble as his bearing was, she found in his eyes an air of intellectual superiority over everyone that came to the house. Were she left alone for a moment with him, she saw him grow visibly embarrassed. This troubled her, for her womanly instinct made her realize that his embarrassment was not in the least degree amorous.

In consequence of some idea derived from a description of good society, as the old Surgeon-Major had beheld it, as soon as conversation ceased in a place where he found himself in the company of a woman, Julien felt abashed, as though he himself were specially to blame for this silence. This sensation was a hundred times more painful when they were alone. His imagination, full of the most extravagant, the most Spanish notions as to what a man ought to say, when he is alone with a woman, offered him in his agitation none but inadmissible ideas. His soul was in the clouds, and yet he was incapable of breaking the most humiliating silence. Thus his air of severity, during his long walks with Madame de Rênal and the children, was intensified by the most cruel sufferings. He despised himself hideously. If by mischance he forced himself to speak, he found himself saying the most ridiculous things. To increase his misery, he saw and exaggerated his own absurdity; but what he did not see was the expression in his eyes, they were so fine and revealed so burning a soul that, like good actors, they imparted at times a charming meaning to what was meaningless. Madame de Rênal remarked that, when alone with her, he never expressed himself well except when he was distracted by some unforeseen occurrence, he never thought of turning a compliment. As the friends of the family did not spoil her by offering her new and brilliant ideas, she took a delight in the flashes of Julien's intellect.

Since the fall of Napoleon, all semblance of gallantry in speech has been sternly banished from the code of provincial behaviour. People are afraid of losing their posts. The unscrupulous seek support from the *Congregation;* and hypocrisy has made the most brilliant advances even among the Liberal classes. Dulness increases. No pleasure is left, save in reading and agriculture.

Madame de Rênal, the wealthy heiress of a religious aunt, married at sixteen to a worthy gentleman, had never in her life felt or seen anything that bore the faintest resemblance to love. Her confessor, the good curé Chélan, was the only person almost who had ever spoken to her of love, with reference to the advances of M. Valenod, and he had drawn so revolting a picture of it that the word conveyed nothing to her but the idea of the most abject immorality. She regarded as an exception, or rather as something quite apart from nature, love such as she had found it in the very small number of novels that chance had brought to her notice. Thanks to this ignorance, Madame de Rênal, entirely happy, occupied incessantly with the thought of Julien, was far from reproaching herself in the slightest degree.

CHAPTER EIGHT

MINOR EVENTS

Then there were sighs, the deeper for suppression,
    And stolen glances, sweeter for the theft,
And burning blushes, though for no transgression.
                                    Don Juan, I. 74.

THE angelic sweetness which Madame de Rênal derived from her own character as well as from her present happiness was interrupted only when she happened to think of her maid Elisa. This young woman received a legacy, went to make her confession to the curé Chélan, and revealed to him her intention to marry Julien. The curé was genuinely delighted at his friend's good fortune; but his surprise was great when Julien informed him with a resolute air that Miss Elisa's offer could not be accepted.

"Pay good heed, my son, to what is taking place in your heart," said the curé, frowning; "I congratulate you on your vocation, if it is to it alone that must be ascribed your scorn of a more than adequate provision. For fifty-six years and more have I been curé at Verrières, and yet, so far as one can see, I am going to be deprived. This distresses me, albeit I have an income of eight hundred livres. I tell you of this detail in order that you may not be under any illusion as to what is in store for you in the priestly calling. If you think of paying court to the men in power, your eternal ruin is assured. You may make your fortune, but you will have to injure the poor and needy, flatter the Sub-Prefect, the Mayor, the important person, and minister to his passions: such conduct, which in the world is called the art of life, may, in a layman, be not wholly incompatible with salvation; but in our calling, we have to choose; we must make our fortune either in this world or in the next, there is no middle way. Go, my dear friend, reflect, and come back in three days' time with a definite answer. I am sorry to see underlying your character, a smouldering ardour which does not suggest to my mind the moderation and complete renunciation of earthly advantages necessary in a priest; I augur well from your intelligence; but, allow me to tell you," the good curé went on, with tears in his eyes, "in the calling of a priest, I shall tremble for your salvation."

Julien was ashamed of his emotion; for the first time in his life, he saw himself loved; he wept for joy, and went to hide his tears in the great woods above Verrières.

"Why am I in this state?" he asked himself at length; "I feel that I would give my life a hundred times over for that good Father Chélan, and yet he has just proved to me that I am no better than a fool. It is he above all that I have to deceive, and he sees through me. That secret ardour of which he speaks is my plan for making my fortune. He thinks me unfit to be a priest, at the very moment when I imagined that the sacrifice of an income of fifty louis was going to give him the most exalted idea of my piety and my vocation.

"For the future," Julien continued, "I shall rely only upon those elements of my character which I have tested. Who would ever have said that I should find pleasure in shedding tears? That I should love the man who proves to me that I am nothing more than a fool?"

Three days later, Julien had found the pretext with which he should have armed himself from the first; this pretext was a calumny, but what of that? He admitted to the curé, after much hesitation, that a reason which

he could not explain to him, because to reveal it would
injure a third party, had dissuaded him from the first
from the projected marriage. This was tantamount to an
indictment of Elisa's conduct. M. Chélan detected in
his manner a fire that was wholly mundane, and very
different from that which should have inspired a young
Levite.

"My friend," he appealed to him again, "be an honest
yeoman, educated and respected, rather than a priest
without a vocation."

Julien replied to these fresh remonstrances extremely
well, so far as words went; he hit upon the expressions
which a fervent young seminarist would have employed;
but the tone in which he uttered them, the ill-concealed
fire that smouldered in his eyes alarmed M. Chélan.

We need not augur ill for Julien's future; he hit upon
the correct form of words of a cunning and prudent hypocrisy. That is not bad at his age. As for his tone and
gestures, he lived among country folk; he had been de-
barred from seeing the great models. In the sequel, no
sooner had he been permitted to mix with these gentlemen than he became admirable as well in gesture as in
speech.

Madame de Rênal was surprised that her maid's newly
acquired fortune had not made the girl more happy; she
saw her going incessantly to the curé's, and returning
with tears in her eyes; finally Elisa spoke to her mistress of her marriage.

Madame de Rênal believed herself to have fallen ill;
a sort of fever prevented her enjoying any sleep; she
was alive only when she had her maid or Julien before
her eyes. She could think of nothing but them and the
happiness they would find in their married life. The
poverty of the small house in which people would be
obliged to live, with an income of fifty louis, portrayed
itself to her in enchanting colours. Julien might very well

become a lawyer at Bray, the Sub-Prefecture two leagues from Verrières; in that event she would see something of him.

Madame de Rênal sincerely believed that she was going mad; she said so to her husband, and finally did fall ill. That evening, as her maid was waiting upon her, she noticed that the girl was crying. She loathed Elisa at that moment, and had spoken sharply to her; she begged the girl's pardon. Elisa's tears increased; she said that if her mistress would allow it, she would tell her the whole tale of her distress.

"Speak," replied Madame de Rênal.

"Well, the fact is, Ma'am, he won't have me; wicked people must have spoken evil of me to him, and he believes them."

"Who won't have you?" said Madame de Rênal, scarcely able to breathe.

"And who could it be, Ma'am, but M. Julien?" the maid replied through her sobs. "His Reverence has failed to overcome his resistance; for His Reverence considers that he ought not to refuse a decent girl, just because she has been a lady's maid. After all, M. Julien's own father is no better than a carpenter; and he himself, how was he earning his living before he came to Madame's?"

Madame de Rênal had ceased to listen; surfeit of happiness had almost deprived her of the use of her reason. She made the girl repeat to her several times the assurance that Julien had refused in a positive manner, which would not permit of his coming to a more reasonable decision later on.

"I wish to make a final effort," she said to her maid. "I shall speak to M. Julien."

Next day after luncheon, Madame de Rênal gave herself the exquisite sensation of pleading her rival's cause, and of seeing Elisa's hand and fortune persistently refused for an hour on end.

Little by little Julien abandoned his attitude of studied reserve, and ended by making spirited answers to the sound arguments advanced by Madame de Rênal. She could not hold out against the torrent of happiness which now poured into her heart after all those days of despair. She found herself really ill. When she had come to herself, and was comfortably settled in her own room, she asked to be left alone. She was in a state of profound astonishment.

"Can I be in love with Julien?" she asked herself at length.

This discovery, which at any other time would have filled her with remorse and with a profound agitation, was no more to her than a singular spectacle, but one that left her indifferent. Her heart, exhausted by all that she had just undergone, had no sensibility left to place at the service of her passions.

Madame de Rênal tried to work, and fell into a deep sleep; when she awoke, she was less alarmed than she should have been. She was too happy to be able to take anything amiss. Artless and innocent as she was, this honest provincial had never tormented her soul in an attempt to wring from it some little sensibility to some novel shade of sentiment or distress. Entirely absorbed, before Julien came, in that mass of work which, outside Paris, is the lot of a good wife and mother, Madame de Rênal thought about the passions, as we think about the lottery: a certain disappointment and a happiness sought by fools alone.

The dinner bell rang; Madame de Rênal blushed deeply when she heard Julien's voice as he brought in the children. Having acquired some adroitness since she had fallen in love, she accounted for her colour by complaining of a splitting headache.

"There you have women," put in M. de Rênal, with a

coarse laugh. "There's always something out of order in their machinery."

Accustomed as she was to this form of wit, the tone of his voice hurt Madame de Rênal. She sought relief in studying Julien's features; had he been the ugliest man in the world, he would have charmed her at that moment.

Always zealous in imitating the habits of the Court, with the first fine days of spring M. de Rênal removed his household to Vergy; it is the village rendered famous by the tragic adventure of Gabrielle.[1] A few hundred yards from the picturesque ruins of the old gothic church, M. de Rênal owned an old castle with its four towers, and a garden laid out like that of the Tuileries, with a number of box borders, and chestnut alleys trimmed twice in the year. An adjoining field, planted with apple trees, allowed the family to take the air. Nine or ten splendid walnuts grew at the end of the orchard; their massive foliage rose to a height of some eighty feet.

"Each of those damned walnuts," M. de Rênal would say when his wife admired them, "costs me half an acre of crop; the corn will not grow in their shade."

The rustic scene appeared to come as a novelty to Madame de Rênal; her admiration knew no bounds. The feeling that animated her gave her a new spirit and determination. On the second day after their removal to Vergy, M. de Rênal having returned to town upon some official business, his wife engaged labourers at her own expense. Julien had given her the idea of a little gravelled path, which should run round the orchard and beneath the big walnuts, and would allow the children to walk there in the early morning without wetting their shoes in the dew. This plan was put into execution within twenty-four hours of its conception. Madame de Rênal spent a long and happy day with Julien supervising the labourers.

[1] Gabrielle de Vergy, the heroine of a mediæval romance.
C. K. S. M.

When the Mayor of Verrières returned from the town, he was greatly surprised to find the path finished. His coming surprised Madame de Rênal also; she had forgotten that he existed. For the next two months, he continued to speak with annoyance of their presumption in having carried out, without consulting him, so important a repair, but Madame de Rênal had done it at her own expense, and this to some extent consoled him.

She spent her days running about the orchard with her children, and chasing butterflies. They had made a number of large nets of light-coloured gauze, with which they caught the unfortunate *lepidoptera*. This was the outlandish name which Julien taught Madame de Rênal. For she had sent to Besançon for the handsome work on the subject by M. Godart; and Julien read to her the strange habits of these insects.

They fastened them, without compunction, with pins upon a large sheet of pasteboard, also prepared by Julien.

At last Madame de Rênal and Julien had a subject for conversation; he was no longer exposed to the frightful torture inflicted on him by intervals of silence.

They conversed incessantly, and with extreme interest, although always of the most innocent things. This life, active, occupied and cheerful, suited everyone, except Miss Elisa, who found herself worked to death. "Even at carnival-time," she said, "when there is a ball at Verrières, Madame has never taken so much trouble over her dress; she changes her clothes two or three times a day."

As it is our intention to flatter no one, we shall not conceal the fact that Madame de Rênal, who had a superb skin, had dresses made for her which exposed her arms and bosom freely. She was very well made, and this way of dressing suited her to perfection.

"You have never *been so young,* Ma'am," her friends from Verrières used to tell her when they came to dine at Vergy. (It is a local form of speech.)

A curious point, which our readers will scarcely believe, was that Madame de Rênal had no deliberate intention in taking such pains with her appearance. She enjoyed doing so; and, without giving the matter any particular thought, whenever she was not chasing butterflies with the children and Julien, she was engaged with Elisa making dresses. Her one expedition to Verrières was due to a desire to purchase new summer clothes which had just arrived there from Mulhouse.

She brought back with her to Vergy a young woman, one of her cousins. Since her marriage, Madame de Rênal had gradually formed an intimate friendship with Madame Derville, who in their younger days had been her schoolfellow at the Sacré-Cœur.

Madame Derville laughed heartily at what she called her cousin's absurd ideas. "If I were alone, they would never occur to me," she used to say. These sudden ideas, which in Paris would have been called sallies, made Madame de Rênal feel ashamed, as of something foolish, when she was with her husband; but Madame Derville's presence gave her courage. She began by telling her what she was thinking in a timid voice; when the ladies were by themselves for any length of time, Madame de Rênal would become animated, and a long, undisturbed morning passed in a flash and left the friends quite merry. On this visit, the sensible Madame Derville found her cousin much less merry and much happier.

Julien, meanwhile, had been living the life of a child since he had come to the country, as happy to be running after butterflies as were his pupils. After so much constraint and skilful diplomacy, alone, unobserved by his fellow-men, and, instinctively, feeling not in the least afraid of Madame de Rênal, he gave himself up to the pleasure of being alive, so keen at his age, and in the midst of the fairest mountains in the world.

As soon as Madame Derville arrived, Julien felt that

*C 945

she was his friend; he hastened to shew her the view that was to be seen from the end of the new path; as a matter of fact it was equal, if not superior to the most admirable scenery which Switzerland and the Italian lakes have to offer. By climbing the steep slope which began a few yards farther on, one came presently to high precipices fringed with oakwoods, which projected almost over the bed of the river. It was to the summits of these sheer rocks that Julien, happy, free, and indeed something more, lord of the house, led the two friends, and relished their admiration of those sublime prospects.

"To me it is like Mozart's music," said Madame Derville.

His brothers' jealousy, the presence of a despotic and ill tempered father had spoiled the country round Verrières in Julien's eyes. At Vergy, he found no trace of these unpleasant memories; for the first time in his life, he could see no one that was his enemy. When M. de Rênal was in town, as frequently happened, he ventured to read; soon, instead of reading at night, and then taking care, moreover, to shade his lamp with an inverted flowerpot, he could take his full measure of sleep; during the day, in the interval between the children's lessons, he climbed up among these rocks with the book that was his sole rule of conduct, and the sole object of his transports. He found in it at once happiness, ecstasy and consolation in moments of depression.

Certain things which Napoleon says of women, various discussions of the merits of the novels in vogue during his reign, furnished him now, for the first time, with several ideas which would long since have been familiar to any other young man of his age.

The hot weather came. They formed the habit of spending the evening under a huge lime a few yards from the house. There the darkness was intense. One evening, Julien was talking with emphasis, he was revelling in the pleasure of talking well and to young married women; as he gesticulated, he touched the hand of Madame de Rênal, who was leaning on the back of one of those chairs of painted wood that are placed in gardens.

The hand was hurriedly withdrawn; but Julien decided that it was his *duty* to secure that the hand should not be withdrawn when he touched it. The idea of a duty to be performed, and of making himself ridiculous, or rather being left with a sense of inferiority if he did not succeed in performing it, at once took all the pleasure from his heart.

CHAPTER NINE

AN EVENING IN THE COUNTRY

La Didon de M. Guérin, esquisse charmant!
STROMBECK.

WHEN he saw Madame de Rênal again, the next morning, there was a strange look in his eyes; he watched her like an enemy with whom he would presently be engaged. This expression, so different from his expression overnight, made Madame de Rênal lose her head; she had been kind to him, and he appeared vexed. She could not take her eyes from his.

Madame Derville's presence excused Julien from his share of the conversation, and enabled him to concentrate his attention upon what he had in mind. His sole occupation, throughout the day, was that of fortifying himself by reading the inspired text which refreshed his soul.

He greatly curtailed the children's lessons, and when, later on, the presence of Madame de Rênal recalled him to the service of his own vanity, decided that it was absolutely essential that this evening she should allow her hand to remain in his.

The sun as it set and so brought nearer the decisive moment made Julien's heart beat with a strange excitement. Night fell. He observed, with a joy that lifted a huge weight from his breast, that it was very dark. A sky packed with big clouds, kept in motion by a hot breeze, seemed to forebode a tempest. The two women continued strolling until a late hour. Everything that they did this evening seemed strange to Julien. They were enjoying this weather, which, in certain delicate natures, seems to enhance the pleasure of love.

At last they sat down, Madame de Rênal next to Julien, and Madame Derville on the other side of her friend. Preoccupied with the attempt he must shortly make, Julien could think of nothing to say. The conversation languished.

"Shall I tremble like this and feel as uncomfortable the first time I have to fight a duel?" Julien wondered; for he had too little confidence either in himself or in others not to observe the state he was in.

In this agonising uncertainty, any danger would have seemed to him preferable. How often did he long to see Madame de Rênal called by some duty which would oblige her to return to the house and so leave the garden! The violence of the effort which Julien had to make to control himself was such that his voice was entirely altered; presently Madame de Rênal's voice became tremulous also, but Julien never noticed this. The ruthless warfare which his sense of duty was waging with his natural timidity was too exhausting for him to be in a condition to observe anything outside himself. The quarter before ten had sounded from the tower clock, without his having yet ventured on anything. Julien, ashamed of his cowardice, told himself: "At the precise moment when ten o'clock strikes, I shall carry out the intention which, all day long, I have been promising myself that I would fulfil this evening, or I shall go up to my room and blow my brains out."

After a final interval of tension and anxiety, during which the excess of his emotion carried Julien almost out of his senses, the strokes of ten sounded from the clock overhead. Each stroke of that fatal bell stirred an echo in his bosom, causing him almost a physical revulsion.

Finally, while the air was still throbbing with the last stroke of ten, he put out his hand and took that of Madame de Rênal, who at once withdrew it. Julien, without exactly knowing what he was doing, grasped her hand again. Although greatly moved himself, he was struck by the icy coldness of the hand he was clasping; he pressed it with convulsive force; a last attempt was made to remove it from him, but finally the hand was left in his grasp.

His heart was flooded with joy, not because he loved Madame de Rênal, but because a fearful torment was now at an end. So that Madame Derville should not notice anything, he felt himself obliged to speak; his voice, now, was loud and ringing. Madame de Rênal's, on the other hand, betrayed such emotion that her friend thought she must be ill and suggested to her that they should go indoors. Julien saw the danger: "If Madame de Rênal returns to the drawing-room, I am going to fall back into the horrible position I have been in all day. I have not held this hand long enough to be able to reckon it as a definite conquest."

When Madame Derville repeated her suggestion that they should go into the drawing-room, Julien pressed the hand that lay in his.

Madame de Rênal, who was preparing to rise, resumed her seat, saying in a faint tone:

"I do, as a matter of fact, feel a little unwell, but the fresh air is doing me good."

These words confirmed Julien's happiness, which, at this moment, was extreme: he talked, forgot to dissimulate, appeared the most charming of men to his two hearers. And yet there was still a slight want of courage in this eloquence which had suddenly come to him. He was in a deadly fear lest Madame Derville, exhausted by the wind which was beginning to rise, and heralded the storm, might decide to go in by herself to the drawing-room. Then he would be left alone with Madame de Rênal. He had found almost by accident the blind courage which was sufficient for action; but he felt that it lay beyond his power to utter the simplest of words to Madame de Rênal. However mild her reproaches might be, he was going to be defeated, and the advantage which he had just gained wiped out.

Fortunately for him, this evening, his touching and emphatic speeches found favour with Madame Derville, who as a rule found him as awkward as a schoolboy, and by no means amusing. As for Madame de Rênal, her hand lying clasped in Julien's, she had no thought of anything; she was allowing herself to live. The hours they spent beneath this huge lime, which, local tradition maintained, had been planted by Charles the Bold, were for her a time of happiness. She listened with rapture to the moaning of the wind in the thick foliage of the lime, and the sound of the first few drops that were beginning to fall upon its lowest leaves. Julien did not notice a detail which would have greatly reassured him; Madame de Rênal, who had been obliged to remove her hand from his, on rising to help her cousin to pick up a pot of flowers which the wind had overturned at their feet, had no sooner sat down again than she gave him back her hand almost without difficulty, and as though it had been an understood thing between them.

Midnight had long since struck; at length it was time to leave the garden: the party broke up. Madame de Rênal, transported by the joy of being in love, was so ignorant that she hardly reproached herself at all. Happiness robbed her of sleep. A sleep like lead carried off Julien, utterly worn out by the battle that had been raging all day in his heart between timidity and pride.

Next morning he was called at five o'clock; and (what would have been a cruel blow to Madame de Rênal had she known of it) he barely gave her a thought. He had done *his duty, and a heroic duty.* Filled with joy by this sentiment, he turned the key in the door of his bedroom and gave himself up with an entirely new pleasure to reading about the exploits of his hero.

When the luncheon bell sounded, he had forgotten, in reading the reports of the Grand Army, all the advantages he had won overnight. He said to himself, in a careless tone, as he went down to the drawing-room: "I must tell this woman that I love her."

Instead of that gaze charged with passion which he expected to meet, he found the stern face of M. de Rênal, who, having arrived a couple of hours earlier from Verrières, did not conceal his displeasure on finding that Julien was wasting the whole morning without attending to the children. No sight could have been so unprepossessing as that of this self-important man, conscious of a grievance and confident of his right to let it be seen.

Each of her husband's harsh words pierced Madame de Rênal to the heart. As for Julien, he was so plunged in ecstasy, still so absorbed in the great events which for the last few hours had been happening before his eyes, that at first he could barely lower the pitch of his attention to listen to the stern voice of M. de Rênal. At length he answered him, sharply enough:

"I was unwell."

The tone of this reply would have stung a man far less susceptible than the Mayor of Verrières; it occurred to him to reply to Julien with an immediate dismissal. He was restrained only by the maxim which he had laid down for himself, never to be too hasty in business matters.

"This young fool," he soon reminded himself, "has made himself a sort of reputation in my house; Valenod may take him on, or else he will marry Elisa, and, in either case, he can afford to laugh at me in his heart."

Despite the wisdom of these reflexions, M. de Rênal's displeasure found an outlet nevertheless in a succession of coarse utterances which succeeded in irritating Julien. Madame de Rênal was on the point of subsiding in tears. As soon as the meal was ended, she asked Julien to give her his arm for their walk; she leaned upon it in a friendly way. To all that Madame de Rênal said to him, Julien could only murmur in reply:

"This is what rich people are like!"

M. de Rênal kept close beside them; his presence increased Julien's anger. He noticed suddenly that Madame de Rênal was leaning upon his arm in a marked manner; this action horrified him, he repulsed her violently, freeing his arm from hers.

Fortunately M. de Rênal saw nothing of this fresh impertinence; it was noticed only by Madame Derville; her friend burst into tears. At this moment M. de Rênal began flinging stones at a little peasant girl who was trespassing by taking a short cut across a corner of the orchard.

"Monsieur Julien, kindly control yourself, remember that we are all of us liable to moments of ill temper," Madame Derville said hastily.

Julien looked at her coldly with eyes in which the loftiest contempt was portrayed.

This look astonished Madame Derville, and would have surprised her far more could she have guessed its full meaning; she would have read in it a vague hope of the most terrible revenge. It is doubtless to such moments of humiliation that we owe men like Robespierre.

"Your Julien is very violent, he frightens me," Madame Derville murmured to her friend.

"He has every reason to be angry," the other replied. "After the astonishing progress the children have made with him, what does it matter if he spends a morning without speaking to them? You must admit that gentlemen are very hard."

For the first time in her life, Madame de Rênal felt a sort of desire to be avenged on her husband. The intense hatred that animated Julien against rich people was about to break forth. Fortunately M. de Rênal called for his gardener, with whom for the rest of the time he busied himself in stopping up with faggots of thorn the short cut that had been made across the orchard. Julien did not utter a single word in reply to the attentions that were shewn him throughout the remainder of the walk. As soon as M. de Rênal had left them, the two ladies, on the plea that they were tired, had asked him each for an arm.

As he walked between these women whose cheeks were flushed with the embarrassment of an intense discomfort, Julien's sombre and decided air formed a striking contrast. He despised these women, and all tender feelings.

"What!" he said to himself, "not even an allowance of five hundred francs to complete my studies! Ah! How I should send her packing!"

Absorbed in these drastic thoughts, the little that he deigned to take in of the polite speeches of the two ladies displeased him as being devoid of meaning, silly, feeble, in a word *feminine*.

By dint of talking for talking's sake, and of trying to keep the conversation alive, Madame de Rênal found herself saying that her husband had come from Verrières because he had made a bargain, for the purchase of maize straw, with one of his farmers. (In this district maize straw is used to stuff the palliasses of the beds.)

"My husband will not be joining us again," Madame de Rênal went on: "he will be busy with the gardener and his valet changing the straw in all the palliasses in the house. This morning he put fresh straw on all the beds on the first floor, now he is at work on the second."

Julien changed colour; he looked at Madame de Rênal in an odd manner, and presently drew her apart, so to speak, by increasing his pace. Madame Derville allowed them to move away from her.

"Save my life," said Julien to Madame de Rênal, "you alone can do it; for you know that the valet hates me like poison. I must confess to you, Ma'am, that I have a portrait; I have hidden it in the palliasse on my bed."

At these words, Madame de Rênal in turn grew pale.

"You alone, Ma'am, can go into my room at this moment; feel, without letting yourself be observed, in the corner of the palliasse nearest to the window; you will find there a small box of shiny black pasteboard."

"It contains a portrait?" said Madame de Rênal, barely able to stand.

Her air of disappointment was noticed by Julien, who at once took advantage of it.

"I have a second favour to ask of you, Ma'am; I beg you not to look at the portrait, it is my secret."

"It is a secret!" repeated Madame de Rênal, in faint accents.

But, albeit she had been reared among people proud of their wealth, and sensible of pecuniary interests alone, love had already instilled some generosity into her heart. Though cruelly wounded, it was with an air of the simplest devotion that Madame de Rênal put to Julien the questions necessary to enable her to execute his commission properly.

"And so," she said, as she left him, "it is a little round box, of black pasteboard, and very shiny."

"Yes, Ma'am," replied Julien in that hard tone which danger gives a man.

She mounted to the second floor of the house, as pale as though she were going to her death. To complete her misery she felt that she was on the point of fainting, but the necessity of doing Julien a service restored her strength.

"I must have that box," she said to herself as she quickened her pace.

She could hear her husband talking to the valet, actually in Julien's room. Fortunately they moved into the room in which the children slept. She lifted the mattress and plunged her hand into the straw with such force as to scratch her fingers. But, although extremely sensitive to slight injuries of this sort, she was now quite unconscious

of the pain, for almost immediately she felt the polished
surface of the pasteboard box. She seized it and fled.

No sooner was she rid of the fear of being surprised by
her husband, than the horror inspired in her by this box
made her feel that in another minute she must unquestion-
ably faint.

"So Julien is in love, and I have here the portrait of
the woman he loves."

Seated on a chair in the sitting-room of this apartment,
Madame de Rênal fell a prey to all the horrors of jealousy.
Her extreme ignorance was of service to her again at this
moment; astonishment tempered her grief. Julien appeared, snatched the box, without thanking her, without
saying a word, and ran into his bedroom, where he struck
a light and immediately destroyed it. He was pale,
speechless; he exaggerated to himself the risk he had been
running.

"The portrait of Napoleon," he said to himself with a
toss of the head, "found hidden in the room of a man who
professes such hatred for the usurper! Found by M. de
Rênal, so *ultra* and so angry! and, to complete the imprudence, on the white card at the back of the portrait,
lines in my writing! And lines that can leave no doubt
as to the warmth of my admiration! And each of those
transports of love is dated! There was one only two days
ago!

"All my reputation brought down, destroyed in a moment!" Julien said to himself as he watched the box burn,
"and my reputation is all I have, I live by it alone . . . and
what a life at that, great God!"

An hour later, his exhaustion and the pity he felt for
himself disposed him to feel affection. He met Madame
de Rênal and took her hand which he kissed with more
sincerity than he had ever yet shewn. She coloured with
delight, and almost simultaneously repulsed Julien with
the anger of a jealous woman. Julien's pride, so recently

wounded, made a fool of him at that moment. He saw in Madame de Rênal only a rich woman. he let fall her hand with contempt, and strode away. He went out and walked pensively in the garden; presently a bitter smile appeared on his lips.

"Here I am walking about as calm as a man who is his own master! I am not looking after the children! I am exposing myself to the humiliating remarks of M. de Rênal, and he will be justified." He hastened to the children's room.

The caresses of the youngest boy, to whom he was greatly attached, did something to soothe his agonizing pain.

"This one does not despise me yet," thought Julien. But presently he blamed himself for this relief from pain, as for a fresh weakness. "These children fondle me as they might fondle the puppy that was bought yesterday."

CHAPTER TEN

A LARGE HEART AND A SMALL FORTUNE

> But passion most dissembles, yet betrays,
>   Even by its darkness; as the blackest sky
> Foretells the heaviest tempest.
>
> *Don Juan,* I. 73.

M. DE RÊNAL, who was visiting every room in the house, reappeared in the children's room with the servants who brought back the palliasses refilled. The sudden entry of this man was the last straw to Julien.

Paler, more sombre than usual, he advanced towards him. M. de Rênal stood still and looked at his servants.

"Sir," Julien began, "do you suppose that with any other tutor your children would have made the same progress that they have made with me? If your answer is no," he went on without giving M. de Rênal time to speak, "how dare you presume to reproach me with neglecting them?"

M. de Rênal, who had barely recovered from his alarm, concluded from the strange tone which he saw this young peasant adopt that he had in his pocket some more attractive offer and was going to leave him. Julien's anger increasing as he spoke:

"I can live without you, Sir," he concluded.

"I am extremely sorry to see you so agitated," replied M. de Rênal, stammering a little. The servants were a few feet away, and were occupied in making the beds.

"That is not enough for me, Sir," Julien went on, beside himself with rage; "think of the abominable things you said to me, and in the presence of ladies, too!"

M. de Rênal was only too well aware of what Julien was asking, and conflicting passions did battle in his heart. It so happened that Julien, now really mad with rage, exclaimed:

"I know where to go, Sir, when I leave your house."

On hearing these words, M. de Rênal had a vision of Julien established in M. Valenod's household.

"Very well, Sir," he said at length with a sigh, and the air of a man calling in a surgeon to perform the most painful operation, "I agree to your request. From the day after to-morrow, which is the first of the month, I shall give you fifty francs monthly."

Julien wanted to laugh and remained speechless: his anger had completely vanished.

"I did not despise the animal enough," he said to himself. "This, no doubt, is the most ample apology so base a nature is capable of making."

The children, who had listened to this scene openmouthed, ran to the garden to tell their mother that M. Julien was in a great rage, but that he was to have fifty francs a month.

Julien went after them from force of habit, without so much as a glance at M. de Rênal, whom he left in a state of intense annoyance.

"That's a hundred and sixty-eight francs," the Mayor said to himself, "that M. Valenod has cost me. I must really say a few firm words to him about his contract to supply the foundlings."

A moment later, Julien again stood before him.

"I have a matter of conscience to discuss with M. Chélan. I have the honour to inform you that I shall be absent for some hours."

"Ah, my dear Julien," said M. de Rênal, laughing in

the most insincere manner, "the whole day, if you wish,
the whole of to-morrow, my worthy friend. Take the
gardener's horse to go to Verrières.

"There," M. de Rênal said to himself, "he's going with
an answer to Valenod; he's given me no promise, but we
must let the young hothead cool down."

Julien made a speedy escape and climbed up among the
big woods through which one can go from Vergy to
Verrières. He was in no hurry to reach M. Chélan's.
So far from desiring to involve himself in a fresh display
of hypocrisy, he needed time to see clearly into his own
heart, and to give audience to the swarm of conflicting feelings that disturbed it.

"I have won a battle," he said to himself as soon as he
found himself in the shelter of the woods and out of sight
of anyone, "I have really won a battle!"

The last word painted his whole position for him in
glowing colours, and restored some degree of tranquillity
to his heart.

"Here I am with a salary of fifty francs a month; M. de
Rênal must be in a fine fright. But of what?"

His meditation as to what could have frightened the
prosperous and powerful man against whom, an hour
earlier, he had been seething with rage completely restored
Julien's serenity. He was almost conscious, for a moment,
of the exquisite beauty of the woods through which he was
walking. Enormous fragments of bare rock had in times
past fallen into the heart of the forest from the side of the
mountain. Tall beeches rose almost as high as these rocks
whose shadow provided a delicious coolness within a few
yards of places where the heat of the sun's rays would
have made it impossible to stop.

Julien paused for a breathing-space in the shadow of
these great rocks, then went on climbing. Presently, by
following a narrow path, barely visible and used only by
goatherds, he found himself standing upon an immense

rock, where he could be certain of his complete isolation from his fellow-men. This natural position made him smile, it suggested to him the position to which he was burning to attain in the moral sphere. The pure air of these lofty mountains breathed serenity and even joy into his soul. The Mayor of Verrières might still, in his eyes, be typical of all the rich and insolent denizens of the earth, but Julien felt that the hatred which had convulsed him that afternoon contained, notwithstanding its violence, no element of personal ill-feeling. Should he cease to see M. de Rênal, within a week he would have forgotten him, the man himself, his house, his dogs, his children and all that was his. "I have forced him, I do not know how, to make the greatest of sacrifices. What, more than fifty crowns a year? A moment earlier I had just escaped from the greatest danger. That makes two victories in one day; the second contains no merit, I must try to discover the reason. But we can leave such arduous research for to-morrow."

Julien, erect upon his mighty rock, gazed at the sky, kindled to flame by an August sun. The grasshoppers were chirping in the patch of meadow beneath the rock; when they ceased everything around him was silence. Twenty leagues of country lay at his feet. From time to time a hawk, risen from the bare cliffs above his head, caught his eye as it wheeled silently in its vast circles. Julien's eye followed mechanically the bird of prey. Its calm, powerful motion impressed him, he envied such strength, he envied such isolation.

It was the destiny of Napoleon, was it one day to be his own?

CHAPTER ELEVEN

NIGHT THOUGHTS

Yet Julia's very coldness still was kind,
    And tremulously gentle her small hand
Withdrew itself from his, but left behind
    A little pressure, thrilling, and so bland
And slight, so very slight, that to the mind
    'Twas but a doubt.

                                    Don Juan, I. 71.

HE must, however, let himself be seen at Verrières. As he left the Presbytery the first person he met was, by a happy chance, M. Valenod, whom he hastened to inform of the increase in his salary.

On his return to Vergy, Julien did not go down to the garden until night had set in. His heart was worn out by the multitude of powerful emotions that had assailed it in the course of the day. "What shall I say to them?" he asked himself anxiously, thinking of the ladies. It never occurred to him that his spirits were precisely at the level of the trivial happenings that as a rule occupy the whole interest of women. Often Julien was unintelligible to Madame Derville, and even to her friend, while he in turn only half understood all that they were saying to him. Such was the effect of the force, and, if I may use the word, of the magnitude of the waves of passion on which the heart of this ambitious youth was being tossed. In this strange creature almost every day was one of storm.

When he went into the garden that evening, Julien was ready to listen with interest to the thoughts of the fair cousins. They awaited his coming with impatience. He took his accustomed seat, by Madame de Rênal's side. The darkness soon became intense. He attempted to clasp a white hand which for some time he had seen close beside him, resting on the back of a chair. There was some hesitation shewn, but finally the hand was withdrawn from him in a manner which betokened displeasure. Julien was prepared to regard this as final, and to continue the conversation in a light tone, when he heard M. de Rênal approach.

The rude words of the morning still rang in Julien's ears. "Would it not," he said to himself, "be a good way of scoring off this creature, so lavishly endowed with every material advantage, to take possession of his wife's hand under his very eyes? Yes, I will do it, I, for whom he has shewn such contempt."

From that moment peace of mind, so ill assorted to Julien's character, speedily vanished; he desired most anxiously, and without being able to fix his mind on anything else, that Madame de Rênal might consent to let him hold her hand.

M. de Rênal talked politics in an angry tone: two or three manufacturers at Verrières were becoming decidedly richer than himself, and wished to oppose him at the elections. Madame Derville listened to him. Julien, irritated by this talk, moved his chair nearer to Madame de Rênal's. The darkness hid every movement. He ventured to place his hand close to the pretty arm which her gown left bare. Troubled, no longer conscious of what he was doing, he moved his cheek in the direction of this pretty arm, and made bold to press his lips to it.

Madame de Rênal shuddered. Her husband was a few feet away, she hastened to give Julien her hand, at the same time thrusting him slightly from her. While M. de Rênal continued his abuse of the good-for-nothings and Jacobins who were making fortunes, Julien covered the hand which had been left in his with passionate kisses, or so at least they seemed to Madame de Rênal. And yet the poor woman had been furnished with proof, on this fatal day, that the heart of the man whom she adored without confessing it was pledged elsewhere! Throughout the hours of Julien's absence, she had been a prey to the most abject misery, which had made her think.

"What," she said to herself, "am I to love, to have love offered to me? Am I, a married woman, to fall in love? But," she reminded herself, "I have never felt that dark passion for my husband, and so I cannot tear my mind from Julien. At heart he is only a boy filled with respect for me! This folly will pass. How can it concern my husband what feelings I may entertain for this young man? M. de Rênal would be bored by the talks I have with Julien, about things of the imagination. He himself thinks only about his business. I am taking nothing from him to give to Julien."

No trace of hypocrisy came to sully the purity of this simple soul, carried away by a passion such as she had never felt. She was deceived, but quite unawares, and at the same time a virtuous instinct had taken alarm. Such were the conflicts that were agitating her when Julien appeared in the garden. She heard his voice, almost at the same moment she saw him sit down by her side. Her heart was so to speak carried away by this charming happiness which for the last fortnight had astonished even more than it had bewitched her. Everything was unexpected to her. And yet after a few moments: "So Julien's presence is enough," she said to herself, "to wipe out all memory of his misconduct?" She took fright; then it was that she withdrew her hand from his.

His kisses, filled with passion and such as she had never yet received, made her at once forget the possibility of his loving another woman. Soon he was no longer guilty in her eyes. The cessation of her poignant grief, born of suspicion, the presence of a happiness of which she had never even dreamed, plunged her in transports of affection and wild gaiety. That evening was delightful for them all, except for the Mayor of Verrières, who could not forget the growing wealth of his competitors. Julien no longer thought of his dark ambition, nor of his plans that would be so difficult of execution. For the first time in his life, he was carried away by the power of beauty. Lost in a vague and pleasant dream, so foreign to his nature, gently pressing that hand which pleased him as an example of perfect beauty, he gave a divided attention to the rustle of the leaves of the lime, stirred by the gentle night breeze, and to the dogs at the mill by the Doubs, barking in the distance.

But this emotion was a pleasure and not a passion. On returning to his room he thought of one happiness only, that of going on with his favourite book; at twenty, the thought of the world and of the impression one is going to make on it, prevails over everything else.

Presently, however, he put down the book. By dint of dreaming of Napoleon's victories, he had discerned a new element in his own. "Yes, I have won a battle," he told himself, "but I must follow it up, I must crush the arrogance of this proud gentleman while he is still retreating. That is Napoleon out and out. He reproaches me with neglecting his children. I must ask him for three days' holiday, to go and see my friend Fouqué. If he refuses, I again offer to break the agreement; but he will give way."

Madame de Rênal could not close an eye. She felt that she had never lived until that moment. She could not tear her mind from the happiness of feeling Julien cover her hand with burning kisses.

Suddenly the horrid word *adultery* occurred to her. All the most disgusting implications that the vilest debauchery can impart to the idea of sensual love came crowding into her imagination. These ideas sought to tarnish the tender

and godlike image that she had made for herself of Julien
and of the pleasure of loving him. The future portrayed
itself in terrible colours. She saw herself an object of
scorn.

It was a frightful moment; her soul journeyed into
strange lands. That evening she had tasted an unknown
happiness; now she suddenly found herself plunged in
appalling misery. She had no conception of such sufferings; they began to affect her reason. The thought occurred
to her for a moment of confessing to her husband that she
was afraid of falling in love with Julien. It would have
allowed her to speak of him. Fortunately she recalled a
piece of advice given her long ago by her aunt, on the
eve of her marriage. It warned her of the danger of con-
fiding in a husband, who is after all a master. In the
intensity of her grief she wrung her hands.

She was carried away indiscriminately by conflicting and
painful imaginings. At one moment she was afraid of
not being loved in return, at another the fearful thought
of the crime tortured her as though on the morrow she
would have to be exposed in the pillory, on the public
square of Verrières, with a placard proclaiming her
adultery to the populace.

Madame de Rênal was without any experience of life;
even when wide awake and in the full exercise of her
reason, she would have seen no distinction between being
guilty in the sight of God and finding herself publicly
greeted with all the most flagrant marks of general
opprobrium.

When the frightful idea of adultery and of all the
ignominy which (she supposed) that crime brings in its
train gave her at length a respite, and she began to dream
of the delight of living with Julien innocently, as in the
past, she found herself swept away by the horrible thought
that Julien was in love with another woman. She saw
once again his pallor when he was afraid of losing her

CHAPTER TWELVE

A JOURNEY

On trouve à Paris des gens élégants, il peut y avoir
en province des gens à caractère.

SIEYÈS.

NEXT morning, at five o'clock, before Madame de
Rênal was visible, Julien had obtained from her
husband three days' leave of absence. Contrary
to his expectation, Julien found himself longing to see
her again, and could think of nothing but that shapely
hand. He went down to the garden, Madame de Rênal
was long in coming. But if Julien had been in love with
her he would have seen her, behind her half-closed shutters
on the first floor, her face pressed to the glass. She was
watching him. At length, in spite of her resolutions, she
decided to shew herself in the garden. Her customary
pallor had given place to the most glowing colour. This
simple-minded woman was evidently agitated: a feeling of
constraint and even of resentment marred that expression
of profound serenity, as though raised above all the common interests of life, which gave such charm to that
heavenly face.

Julien lost no time in joining her; he admired those fine
arms which a shawl flung in haste across her shoulders
left visible. The coolness of the morning air seemed to
increase the brilliance of a complexion which the agitation
of the past night made all the more sensible to every
impression. This beauty, modest and touching, and yet
full of thoughts which are nowhere to be found among the

portrait, or of compromising her by letting it be seen. For the first time, she had surprised signs of fear on that calm and noble countenance. Never had he shewn himself in such a state for her or for her children. This additional grief carried her to the utmost intensity of anguish which the human soul is able to endure. Unconsciously, Madame de Rênal uttered cries which roused her maid. Suddenly she saw appear by her bedside the light of a lamp, and recognised Elisa.

"Is it you that he loves?" she cried in her frenzy.

The maid, amazed at the fearful distress in which she found her mistress, paid no attention fortunately to this singular utterance. Madame de Rênal realized her own imprudence: "I am feverish," she told her, "and I think, a little light-headed; stay beside me."

Thoroughly awakened by the necessity of controlling herself, she felt less wretched; reason resumed the sway of which her state of drowsiness had deprived it. To escape from the fixed stare of her maid, she ordered her to read the newspaper aloud, and it was to the monotonous sound of the girl's voice, reading a long article from the *Quotidienne,* that Madame de Rênal formed the virtuous resolution to treat Julien with absolute coldness when next she saw him.

lower orders, seemed to reveal to Julien an aspect of her nature of which he had never yet been aware. Wholly absorbed in admiration of the charms which his greedy eye surprised, Julien was not thinking of the friendly greeting which he might expect to receive. He was all the more astonished by the icy coldness that was shewn him, beneath which he even thought he could make out a deliberate intention to put him in his place.

The smile of pleasure faded from his lips; he remembered the rank that he occupied in society, especially in the eyes of a noble and wealthy heiress. In a moment, his features shewed nothing but pride and anger with himself. He felt a violent disgust at having been so foolish as to postpone his departure by more than an hour, only to receive so humiliating a greeting.

"Only a fool," he told himself, "loses his temper with other people: a stone falls because it is heavy. Am I always to remain a boy? When am I going to form the good habit of giving these people their exact money's worth and no more of my heart and soul? If I wish to be esteemed by them and by myself, I must shew them that it is my poverty that deals with their wealth, but that my heart is a thousand leagues away from their insolence, and is placed in too exalted a sphere to be reached by their petty marks of contempt or favour."

While these sentiments came crowding into the young tutor's mind, his features assumed an expression of injured pride and ferocity. Madame de Rênal was greatly distressed by this. The virtuous coldness which she had meant to impart to her greeting gave way to an expression of interest, and of an interest animated by the surprise of the sudden change which she had just beheld in him. The flow of idle words that people exchange in the morning with regard to one another's health, to the beauty of the day, and so forth, dried up at once in them both. Julien, whose judgment was not disturbed by any passion, soon found a way of letting Madame de Rênal see how little he regarded himself as being on terms of friendship with her; he said nothing to her of the little expedition on which he was starting, bowed to her, and set off.

As she watched him go, overwhelmed by the sombre pride which she read in that glance, so friendly the evening before, her eldest son, who came running up from the other end of the garden, said to her as he embraced her:

"We have a holiday, M. Julien is going on a journey."

At these words Madame de Rênal felt herself frozen by a deadly chill; she was unhappy in her virtue, and more unhappy still in her weakness.

This latest development now occupied the whole of her imagination; she was carried far beyond the wise resolutions which were the fruit of the terrible night she had passed. It was a question no longer of resisting this charming lover, but of losing him for ever.

She was obliged to take her place at table. To add to her misery, M. de Rênal and Madame Derville spoke of nothing but Julien's departure. The Mayor of Verrières had remarked something unusual in the firm tone with which he had demanded a holiday.

"The young peasant has doubtless an offer from some one in his pocket. But that some one, even if it should be M. Valenod, must be a little discouraged by the sum of 600 francs, which he must now be prepared to spend annually. Yesterday, at Verrières, he will have asked for three days in which to think things over; and this morning, so as not to be obliged to give me an answer, the young gentleman goes off to the mountains. To have to reckon with a wretched workman who puts on airs, that's what we've come to!"

"Since my husband, who does not know how deeply he has wounded Julien, thinks he is going to leave us, what am I to suppose?" Madame de Rênal asked herself. "Ah! It is all settled!"

So as to be able at least to weep in freedom, and without having to answer Madame Derville's questions, she pleaded a splitting headache, and retired to bed.

"There you have a woman all over," M. de Rênal repeated; "there's always something wrong with those complicated machines." And he went on his way jeering.

While Madame de Rênal was at the mercy of the most cruel inflictions of the terrible passion into which accident had led her, Julien was making his way light-heartedly amid the loveliest views that mountain scenery has to offer. He was obliged to pass over the high range to the north of Vergy. The path which he followed, rising gradually amid great beechwoods, forms an endless series of zigzags on the side of the high mountain which bounds the valley of the Doubs on the north. Presently the traveller's gaze, passing over the lower ridges which confine the course of the Doubs on the south, was able to sweep the fertile plains of Burgundy and Beaujolais. Irresponsive as the heart of this ambitious youth might be to this kind of beauty, he could not refrain from stopping now and again to gaze at so vast and so imposing a prospect.

At length he came to the summit of the high mountain, beneath which he must pass in order to arrive, by this diagonal route, at the lonely valley in which his friend Fouqué, the young timber merchant, lived. Julien was in no hurry to see him, or any other human being for that matter. Concealed like a bird of prey, amid the bare rocks which crowned the high mountain, he could see a long way off anyone that might be coming his way. He discovered a small cave in the almost perpendicular face of one of the rocks. He set his course for it, and presently was ensconced in this retreat. "Here," he said, his eyes sparkling with joy, "men can do me no harm." It occurred to him to indulge in the pleasure of writing down his thoughts, so dangerous to him in any other place. A smooth block of stone served as his table. His pen flew:

he saw nothing of the scene round about him. At length he noticed that the sun was setting behind the distant mountains of Beaujolais.

"Why should I not spend the night here?" he asked himself; "I have bread, and *I am free!*" At the sound of that great word his heart leaped, his hypocrisy meant that he was not free even with Fouqué. His head supported on both his hands, Julien stayed in this cave happier than he had ever been in his life, engrossed in his dreams and in the joy of freedom. Without heeding it he saw fade and die, one after another, the last rays of evening light. In the midst of that vast darkness, his soul wandered in contemplation of what he imagined that he would one day find in Paris. This was first and foremost a woman far more beautiful and of a far higher intelligence than any it had been his lot to see in the country. He loved with passion, he was loved in return. If he tore himself from her for a few moments, it was to cover himself with glory and earn the right to be loved more warmly still.

Even if we allow him Julien's imagination, a young man brought up among the melancholy truths of Paris would have been aroused at this stage in his romance by the cold touch of irony; the mighty deeds would have vanished with the hope of performing them, to give place to the well-known maxim: "When a man leaves his mistress, he runs the risk of being betrayed two or three times daily." The young peasant saw no obstacle between himself and the most heroic actions, save want of opportunity.

But black night had succeeded the day, and he had still two leagues to cover before coming down to the hamlet in which Fouqué lived. Before leaving the little cave, Julien struck a light and carefully destroyed all that he had written.

He greatly astonished his friend by knocking at his door at one o'clock in the morning. He found Fouqué engaged in making up his accounts. He was a young man of tall stature, none too well made, with large, hard features, a huge nose, and plenty of good nature concealed beneath this repellent aspect.

"You've quarrelled with your M. de Rênal, then, that you come here of a sudden like this?"

Julien related to him, with suitable omissions, the events of the previous evening.

"Stay with me," Fouqué said to him; "I see that you know M. de Rênal, M. Valenod, the Sub-Prefect Maugiron, the curé Chélan; you have grasped all the subtle points of their natures; you're ripe now to put yourself up for auction. You know arithmetic better than I do, you shall keep my books; I am making a big profit from my business. The impossibility of doing everything by myself and the fear of hitting upon a rogue in the man I might take as my partner prevent me every day from doing the most profitable deals. Not a month ago I put six thousand francs in the pocket of Michaud of Saint-Amand, whom I had not seen for six years, and met quite by chance at the Pontarlier sale. Why should not you have made those six thousand francs yourself, or three thousand at least? For if I had had you with me that day, I should have gone on bidding for that lot of timber, and the other would soon have left me with it. Be my partner."

This offer annoyed Julien; it unsettled his erratic mind; throughout supper, which the friends cooked for themselves, like Homeric heroes, for Fouqué lived by himself, he shewed Julien his books, and proved to him what advantages his trade in timber offered. Fouqué had the highest opinion of Julien's intelligence and character.

When at length the latter found himself alone in his little room walled with planks of firwood, "It is true," he said to himself, "I can make a few thousand francs here, then return with advantage to the calling of soldier or priest, according to the fashion prevailing in France at the time. The little hoard that I shall have amassed will remove all difficulties of detail. Alone on this mountain-side, I can do something to dispel my present appalling ignorance of so many of the things that occupy the minds of all these fashionable gentlemen. But Fouqué is giving up the thought of marriage, he has told me again and again that solitude is making him melancholy. It is obvious that if he is taking a partner who has no money to put into his business, it is in the hope of providing himself with a companion who will never leave him.

"Shall I prove false to my friend?" exclaimed Julien angrily. This creature, for whom hypocrisy and the absence of all fellow feeling were the ordinary line of conduct, could not on this occasion bear the thought of the slightest want of delicacy towards a man who loved him.

But all at once Julien became happy, he had a reason for refusing. "What, I should be idly wasting seven or eight years! I should thus arrive at eight and twenty; but, at that age, Napoleon had already done his greatest deeds! After I have obscurely scraped together a little money by going round all these timber sales, and winning the favour of various minor rascals, who can say whether I shall still preserve the sacred fire with which one makes oneself a name?"

The following morning, Julien replied with great coolness to the worthy Fouqué, who looked upon the matter of their partnership as settled, that his vocation to the sacred ministry of the altar did not allow him to accept. Fouqué could not believe his ears.

"But do you realize," he kept on saying, "that I make you my partner, or, if you prefer, give you four thousand francs a year? And you want to go back to your M. de Rênal, who despises you like the mud on his shoes! When you have two hundred louis in hand, what is to prevent you from entering the Seminary? I will say more, I under-take to procure for you the best parish in the district. For," Fouqué went on, lowering his voice, "I supply firewood to the ——, and the ——, and M. ——. I give them the best quality of oak, for which they pay me the price of white wood, but never was money better invested."

Nothing could prevail against Julien's vocation. In the end Fouqué decided that he must be slightly mad. On the third day, at dawn, Julien left his friend to pass the day among the rocks of the big mountain. He found his little cave again, but he no longer enjoyed peace of mind, his friend's offers had destroyed it. Like Hercules he found himself called upon to choose not between vice and virtue, but between mediocrity ending in an assured comfort and all the heroic dreams of his youth. "So I have no real firmness of character," he told himself; and this was the doubt that pained him most. "I am not of the stuff of which great men are made, since I am afraid that eight years spent in providing myself with bread may rob me of that sublime energy which makes men do extraordinary things."

CHAPTER THIRTEEN

OPEN-WORK STOCKINGS

Un roman: c'est un miroir qu'on promène le long d'un chemin.

SAINT-RÉAL.

WHEN Julien caught sight of the picturesque ruins of the old church of Vergy, it occurred to him that for two whole days he had not once thought of Madame de Rênal. "The other day, as I was leaving, that woman reminded me of the vast gulf that separates us, she treated me like a workman's son. No doubt she wished to shew me that she repented of having let me hold her hand the night before. . . . It is a lovely hand, all the same! What charm, what nobility dwells in that woman's glance!"

The possibility of making a fortune with Fouqué gave a certain facility to the course of Julien's reasoning; it was less often interrupted by irritation, and the keen sense of his own poverty and humble position in the eyes of the world. As though perched on a lofty promontory, he was able to judge, and, so to speak, overlooked extreme poverty on the one hand and that life of comfort which he still called riches on the other. He was far from considering his position like a philosopher, but he had sufficient perception to feel that he was *different* after this little expedition among the mountains.

He was struck by the extreme uneasiness with which Madame de Rênal listened to the short account of his journey, for which she had asked him.

Fouqué had had thoughts of marriage, unhappy love affairs; the conversation between the friends had been filled with long confidences of this nature. After finding happiness too soon, Fouqué had discovered that he was not the sole possessor of his mistress's heart. These disclosures had astonished Julien; he had learned much that was new to him. His solitary life, compounded of imagination and suspicion, had kept him aloof from everything that could have enlightened him.

During his absence, life had been for Madame de Rênal nothing more than a succession of torments, each different but all alike intolerable; she was really ill.

"You must not, on any account," Madame Derville told her when she saw Julien return, "feeling as you do, sit in the garden this evening, the damp air would make you worse."

Madame Derville was surprised to see that her friend, who was always being scolded by M. de Rênal for the undue simplicity of her attire, had put on open-work stockings and a pair of charming little shoes that had arrived from Paris. For the last three days Madame de Rênal's sole distraction had been to cut out and make Elisa put together in all haste a summer gown, of a charming little fabric greatly in fashion. It was just possible to finish this gown a few minutes after Julien's arrival; Madame de Rênal at once put it on. Her friend had no longer any doubt. "She is in love, poor woman!" Madame Derville said to herself. She understood all the strange symptoms of her illness.

She saw her speak to Julien. Pallor took the place of the most vivid blushes. Anxiety stood revealed in her eyes, fastened on those of the young tutor. Madame de Rênal expected every moment that he was going to offer an explanation, and announce that he was leaving the house, or would remain. It never occurred to Julien to say anything about this subject, which had not entered his thoughts. After a terrible struggle, Madame de Rênal at last ventured to say to him, in a tremulous voice, in which the whole extent of her passion lay revealed:

"Are you going to leave your pupils to take a post elsewhere?"

Julien was struck by her quavering voice and by the look in her eyes. "This woman loves me," he said to himself; "but after this passing weakness for which her pride is reproaching her, and as soon as she is no longer afraid of my going, she will return to her arrogance." This glimpse of their respective positions came to Julien like a flash of lightning; he replied, hesitatingly:

"I should greatly regret leaving such attractive and *well born* children, but perhaps it will be inevitable. A man has duties towards himself also."

As he uttered the words *well born* (this was one of the aristocratic expressions which Julien had recently acquired), he burned with a strong feeling of antipathy.

"To this woman," he said to himself, "I am not well born."

Madame de Rênal, as she listened to him, was admiring his intelligence, his beauty, her heart was pierced by the possibility of departure which he dangled before her. All her friends from Verrières who, during Julien's absence, had come out to dine at Vergy, had almost vied in complimenting her upon the astonishing young man that her husband had had the good fortune to unearth. This was not to say that they understood anything of the progress that the children had made. The fact of his knowing the Bible by heart, and in Latin, too, had provoked in the inhabitants of Verrières an admiration that will endure for, it may be, a century.

Julien, who spoke to no one, knew nothing of all this. If Madame de Rênal had had the slightest self-control, she would have congratulated him on the reputation he had won, and Julien, his pride set at rest, would have been pleasant and affable to her, all the more as her new gown seemed to him charming. Madame de Rênal, also pleased with her pretty gown, and with what Julien said to her about it, had proposed a turn in the garden; soon she had confessed that she was not well enough to walk. She had taken the returned traveller's arm, and, far from restoring her strength, the contact of that arm deprived her of what little strength remained to her.

It was dark; no sooner were they seated than Julien, relying on the privilege he had already won, ventured to press his lips to the arm of his pretty neighbour, and to take her hand. He was thinking of the boldness which Fouqué had used with his mistresses, and not of Madame de Rênal; the phrase *well born* still weighed upon his heart. His own hand was pressed, but this afforded him no pleasure. Far from his being proud, or even grateful for the affection which Madame de Rênal betrayed this evening by unmistakable signs, beauty, elegance, freshness found him almost unconscious of their appeal. Purity of heart, freedom from any feeling of hatred, serve doubtless to prolong the duration of youth. It is the face that ages first in the majority of beautiful women.

Julien was sullen all the evening; hitherto he had been angry only with fortune and with society; now that Fouqué had offered him an ignoble way of arriving at comfort, he was angry with himself. Absorbed in his own thoughts, although now and then he addressed a few words to the ladies, Julien ended by unconsciously letting go Madame de Rênal's hand. This action completely nonplussed the poor woman; she saw in it an indication of her fate.

Had she been certain of Julien's affection, her virtue might perhaps have found strength to resist him. Trembling at the thought of losing him for ever, her passion carried her to the point of seizing Julien's hand, which, in his distraction, he had allowed to rest upon the back of a chair. This action stirred the ambitious youth; he would have liked it to be witnessed by all those proud nobles who, at table, when he was at the lower end with the children, used to look at him with so patronizing a smile. "This woman cannot despise me any longer: in that case," he said to himself, "I ought to be stirred by her beauty; I owe it to myself to be her lover." Such an idea would never have occurred to him before he received the artless confidences of his friend.

\ The sudden resolution he had just made formed a pleasing distraction. He said to himself: "I must have one of these two women"; he realized that he would greatly have preferred to pay his court to Madame Derville; it was not that she was more attractive, but she had seen him always as a tutor honoured for his learning, and not as a working carpenter, with a ratteen jacket folded under his arm, as he had first appeared to Madame de Rênal.

It was precisely as a young workman, blushing to the whites of his eyes, hesitating outside the door of the house and not venturing to ring the bell, that Madame de Rênal delighted most to picture him. This woman, whom the townsfolk called so haughty, rarely thought of rank, and the slightest achievement went a long way farther, in her mind, than the promise of character held out by the rank of a man. A carter who had shewn valour would have been more gallant to her mind than a terrible captain of hussars adorned with moustaches and pipe. She believed Julien's heart to be nobler than that of any of her cousins, all of whom were gentlemen of family, and many of them bearing titles.

As he followed up this survey of his position, Julien saw that he must not think of attempting the conquest of Madame Derville, who had probably noticed the weakness that Madame de Rênal shewed for him. Forced to return to the latter: "What do I know of this woman's character?" Julien asked himself. "Only this: before I went away,

I took her hand, she withdrew it; to-day I withdraw my hand, she seizes it and presses it. A good opportunity to repay her all the contempt she has shewn for me. God knows how many lovers she has had! Perhaps she is deciding in my favour only because of the facilities for our meeting."

Such is, alas, the drawback of an excessive civilization. At the age of twenty, the heart of a young man, if he has any education, is a thousand leagues from that devil-may-care attitude without which love is often only the most tedious duty.

"I owe it to myself all the more," went on Julien's petty vanity, "to succeed with this woman, so that if I ever make my fortune, and some one reproaches me with having filled the humble post of tutor, I may let it be understood that it was love that brought me into that position."

Julien once more withdrew his hand from that of Madame de Rênal, then took her hand again and pressed it. As they returned to the drawing-room, towards midnight, Madame de Rênal murmured in his ear:

"Are you leaving us, are you going away?"

Julien answered with a sigh:

"I must indeed go away, for I love you passionately; it is a sin . . . and what a sin for a young priest!"

Madame de Rênal leaned upon his arm, bending towards him until her cheek felt the warmth of his.

The night passed for these two people very differently. Madame de Rênal was exalted by transports of the most lofty moral pleasure. A coquettish girl who falls in love early grows accustomed to the distress of love; when she comes to the age of true passion, the charm of novelty is lacking. As Madame de Rênal had never read any novels, all the refinements of her happiness were new to her. No melancholy truth came to freeze her heart, not even the spectre of the future. She saw herself as happy

in ten years' time as she was at that moment. Even the
thought of virtue and of the fidelity she had vowed to M.
de Rênal, which had distressed her some days before,
presented itself in vain, she dismissed it like an importunate
stranger. "Never will I allow Julien to take any liberty,"
Madame de Rênal told herself, "we shall live in future as
we have been living for the last month. He shall be a
friend."

CHAPTER FOURTEEN

THE ENGLISH SCISSORS

A girl of sixteen had a rosy complexion, and put on rouge.

POLIDORI.

AS for Julien, Fouqué's offer had indeed destroyed all his happiness; he could not decide upon any course.

"Alas! Perhaps I am wanting in character, I should have made Napoleon a bad soldier. Anyhow," he went on, "my little intrigue with the lady of the house is going to distract me for the moment."

Fortunately for him, even in this minor incident, his inward feelings bore no relation to his cavalier language. He was afraid of Madame de Rênal because of her pretty gown. This gown was in his eyes the advance guard of Paris. His pride was determined to leave nothing to chance and to the inspiration of the moment. Drawing upon Fouqué's confessions and the little he had read about love in the Bible, he prepared a plan of campaign in great detail. Since, though he did not admit it to himself, he was extremely anxious, he committed this plan to writing.

The following morning, in the drawing-room, Madame de Rênal was alone with him for a moment.

"Have you no other name besides Julien?" she asked him.

Our hero did not know what answer to give to so flattering a question. No provision had been made in his plan for such an event. But for the stupid mistake of making a plan, Julien's quick mind would soon have come to his rescue, his surprise would only have added to the keenness of his perceptions.

He was awkward and exaggerated his own awkwardness. Madame de Rênal soon forgave him that. She saw in it the effect of a charming candour. And the one thing lacking, to her mind, in this man, who was considered so brilliant, was an air of candour.

"I don't at all trust your little tutor," Madame Derville said to her on several occasions. "He seems to me to be always thinking and to act only from motives of policy. He's crafty."

Julien remained deeply humiliated by the disaster of not having known what answer to make to Madame de Rênal.

"A man of my sort owes it to himself to make up for this check"; and, seizing the moment at which she passed from one room to another, he did what he considered his duty by giving Madame de Rênal a kiss.

Nothing could have been less appropriate, less agreeable either to himself or to her, nor could anything have been more imprudent. They barely escaped being caught. Madame de Rênal thought him mad. She was frightened and even more shocked. This stupidity reminded her of M. Valenod.

"What would happen to me," she asked herself, "if I were left alone with him?" All her virtue returned, for her love was in eclipse.

She arranged matters so that there should always be one of her children with her.

The day passed slowly for Julien, he spent the whole of it in clumsily carrying out his plan of seduction. He never once looked at Madame de Rênal without embodying a question in his look; he was not, however, such a fool as not to see that he was failing completely to be agreeable, let alone seductive.

Madame de Rênal could not get over her astonishment at finding him so awkward and at the same time so bold. "It is the timidity of love in a man of parts!" she said to herself at length, with an inexpressible joy. "Can it be possible that he has never been loved by my rival!"

After luncheon, Madame de Rênal returned to the drawing-room to entertain M. Charcot de Maugiron, the Sub-Prefect of Bray. She was working at a little tapestry frame on a tall stand. Madame Derville was by her side. It was in this position, and in the full light of day, that our hero thought fit to thrust forward his boot and press the pretty foot of Madame de Rênal, whose open-work stocking and smart Parisian shoe were evidently attracting the gaze of the gallant Sub-Prefect.

Madame de Rênal was extremely alarmed; she let fall her scissors, her ball of wool, her needles, and Julien's movement could thus pass for a clumsy attempt to prevent the fall of the scissors, which he had seen slipping down. Fortunately these little scissors of English steel broke, and Madame de Rênal could not sufficiently express her regret that Julien had not been nearer at hand.

"You saw them falling before I did, you might have caught them; your zeal has only succeeded in giving me a violent kick."

All this play-acting took in the Sub-Prefect, but not Madame Derville. "This pretty youth has very bad manners!" she thought; the worldly-wisdom of a provincial capital can never pardon mistakes of this sort. Madame de Rênal found an opportunity of saying to Julien:

"Be careful, I order you."

Julien realized his own clumsiness, and was annoyed. For a long time he debated within himself whether he ought to take offence at the words: "I order you." He was foolish enough to think: "She might say to me 'I order you' if it was something to do with the children's education: but in responding to my love, she assumes equality. One cannot love without *equality*"; and he lost himself in composing commonplaces on the subject of equality. He repeated angrily to himself the verse of Corneille which Madame Derville had taught him a few days earlier:

Love creates equalities, it does not seek them.

Julien, insisting upon playing the part of a Don Juan, he who had never had a mistress in his life, was deadly dull for the rest of the day. He had only one sensible idea; bored with himself and with Madame de Rênal, he saw with alarm the evening approach when he would be seated in the garden, by her side and in the dark. He told M. de Rênal that he was going to Verrières to see the curé; he set off after dinner, and did not return until late at night.

At Verrières, Julien found M. Chélan engaged in packing up; he had at last been deprived of his benefice; the vicar Maslon was to succeed him. Julien helped the good curé, and it occurred to him to write to Fouqué that the irresistible vocation which he felt for the sacred ministry had prevented him at first from accepting his friend's obliging offer, but that he had just witnessed such an example of injustice, that perhaps it would be more advantageous to his welfare were he not to take holy orders.

Julien applauded his own deftness in making use of the deprivation of the curé of Verrières to leave a door open for himself and so return to commerce, should the sad voice of prudence prevail, in his mind, over heroism.

CHAPTER FIFTEEN

COCK-CROW

Amour en latin faict amor;
Or donc provient d'amour la mort,
Et, par avant, soulcy qui mord,
Deuil, plours, pieges, forfaitz, remord. . . .

Blason d'amour.

IF Julien had had a little of that discernment which he
so gratuitously supposed himself to possess, he might
have congratulated himself next day on the effect produced by his visit to Verrières. His absence had made his
clumsiness be forgotten. All that day too, he was inclined
to sulk; towards nightfall a preposterous idea occurred to
him, and he imparted it to Madame de Rênal with a rare
intrepidity.

No sooner had they sat down in the garden than, without
waiting for a sufficient cloak of darkness, Julien put his
lips to Madame de Rênal's ear, and, at the risk of compromising her horribly, said to her:

"To-night, Ma'am, at two o'clock, I am coming to your
room, I have something to say to you."

Julien was trembling lest his request should be granted;
the part of a seducer was so horrible a burden that if he
had been free to follow his own inclination, he would have
retired to his room for some days, and not set eyes on
the ladies again. He realized that, by his clever tactics
of yesterday, he had squandered all the promise of the
day before, and really he did not know where to turn.

Madame de Rênal replied with a genuine and by no
means exaggerated indignation to the impertinent an-

nouncement which Julien had had the audacity to make. He thought he could read scorn in her brief answer. It was certain that in this answer, uttered in the lowest of tones, the word "Fie!" had figured. Making the excuse that he had something to say to the children, Julien went up to their room, and on his return placed himself by the side of Madame Derville and at a distance from Madame de Rênal. He thus removed from himself all possibility of taking her hand. The conversation took a serious turn, and Julien held his own admirably, apart from a few intervals of silence during which he cudgelled his brains. "Why cannot I think of some fine plan," he asked himself, "to force Madame de Rênal to shew me those unmistakable marks of affection which made me imagine, three days ago, that she was mine!"

Julien was extremely disconcerted by the almost desperate situation into which he had been led. And yet nothing could have embarrassed him so much as success.

When the party broke up at midnight, his pessimism led him to believe that Madame Derville looked upon him with contempt, and that probably he stood no higher in the favour of Madame de Rênal.

Being in an extremely bad temper and deeply humiliated, Julien could not sleep. He was a thousand leagues from any thought of abandoning all pretence, all his plans, and of living from day to day with Madame de Rênal, contenting himself like a child with the happiness that each day would bring.

He wearied his brain in devising clever stratagems; a moment later, he felt them to be absurd; he was in short extremely wretched, when two struck from the clock tower.

This sound aroused him as the crow of the cock aroused Saint Peter. He saw himself arrived at the moment of the most distressing event. He had not thought once again of his impertinent suggestion, from the moment in which he had made it. It had met with so hostile a reception!

"I told her that I should come to her at two o'clock," he said to himself as he rose; "I may be inexperienced and coarse, as is natural in the son of a peasant, Madame Derville has let me see that plainly enough; but at any rate I will not be weak."

Julien had every right to praise his own courage, never had he set himself a more painful task. As he opened the door of his room, he trembled so much that his knees gave way beneath him, and he was obliged to lean against the wall.

He was in his stocking feet. He went to listen at M. de Rênal's door, through which he could hear him snoring. This dismayed him. He had no longer any excuse for not going to her. But, great God! What should he do when he got there? He had no plan, and even if he had had one, he was in such distress of mind that he would not have been in a fit state to put it into practice.

Finally, with an anguish a thousand times keener than if he had been going to the scaffold, he entered the little corridor that led to Madame de Rênal's room. He opened the door with a trembling hand, making a fearful noise as he did so.

There was a light in the room, a night light was burning in the fireplace; he had not expected this fresh calamity. Seeing him enter, Madame de Rênal sprang quickly out of bed. "Wretch!" she cried. There was some confusion. Julien forgot his futile plans and returned to his own natural character. Not to please so charming a woman seemed to him the greatest disaster possible. His only answer to her reproaches was to fling himself at her feet, clasping her round the knees. As she spoke to him with extreme harshness, he burst into tears.

Some hours later, when Julien emerged from Madame de Rênal's room, one might have said, in the language of

romance, that there was nothing more left for him to
wish. And indeed, he was indebted to the love he had inspired and to the uncontrollable impression made on him
by her seductive charms for a victory to which not all his
misplaced ingenuity would ever have led him.

But, in the most delicious moments, the victim of a
freakish pride, he still attempted to play the part of a
man in the habit of captivating women: he made incredible
efforts to destroy his natural amiability. Instead of his
paying attention to the transports which he excited, and
to the remorse that increased their vivacity, the idea of
duty was continually before his eyes. He feared a terrible remorse, and undying ridicule, should he depart
from the ideal plan that he had set himself to follow.
In a word, what made Julien a superior being was precisely what prevented him from enjoying the happiness
that sprang up at his feet. He was like a girl of sixteen
who has a charming complexion and, before going to a
ball, is foolish enough to put on rouge.

In mortal terror at the apparition of Julien, Madame
de Rênal was soon a prey to the cruellest alarms. Julien's
tears and despair distressed her greatly.

Indeed, when she had no longer anything to refuse
him, she thrust him from her, with genuine indignation,
and then flung herself into his arms. No purpose was
apparent in all this behaviour. She thought herself damned
without remission, and sought to shut out the vision of
hell by showering the most passionate caresses on Julien.
In a word, nothing would have been wanting to complete
our hero's happiness, not even a burning sensibility in the
woman he had just vanquished, had he been capable of
enjoying it. Julien's departure brought no cessation of the
transports which were shaking her in spite of herself, nor
of her struggle with the remorse that was tearing her.

"Heavens! Is to be happy, to be loved, no more than
that?" Such was Julien's first thought on his return to

his own room. He was in that state of astonishment and uneasy misgivings into which a heart falls when it has just obtained what it has long desired. It has grown used to desiring, finds nothing left to desire, and has not yet acquired any memories. Like a soldier returning from a parade, Julien was busily engaged in reviewing all the details of his conduct. "Have I failed in one of the duties I owe to myself? Have I really played my part?"

And what a part! The part of a man accustomed to shine before women.

CHAPTER SIXTEEN

THE DAY AFTER

He turn'd his lips to hers, and with his hand
Call'd back the tangles of her wandering hair.
Don Juan, I. 170.

FORTUNATELY for Julien's pride, Madame de
Rênal had been too greatly agitated and surprised
to notice the fatuity of the man who in a moment
had become everything in the world to her.

As she was imploring him to withdraw, seeing the day
begin to break:

"Oh, Heavens!" she said, "if my husband has heard
any sound, I am lost."

Julien, who had leisure for composing phrases, remembered one to the point:

"Should you regret your life?"

"Ah! Very much at this moment, but I should not
regret having known you."

Julien found that his dignity required him to return
to his room in broad daylight and with deliberate want
of precaution.

The continuous attention with which he watched his
own slightest actions, in the insane idea of being taken
for a man of experience, had this one advantage; when
he saw Madame de Rênal again, at luncheon, his behaviour
was a miracle of prudence.

As for her, she could not look at him without blushing
to the whites of her eyes, and could not live for an instant without looking at him; she noticed her own confusion, and her efforts to conceal it increased. Julien

raised his eyes to hers once only. At first, Madame de Rênal admired his prudence. Presently, seeing that this solitary glance was not repeated, she took alarm: "Can it be that he does not love me any more," she asked herself; "alas, I am far too old for him; I am ten years his senior."

On the way from the dining-room to the garden, she pressed Julien's hand. In the surprise that he felt at so extraordinary a token of affection, he gazed at her with passion; for she had struck him as looking very pretty at luncheon, and, without raising his eyes, he had spent his time making a detailed catalogue of her charms. This look consoled Madame de Rênal; it did not remove all her uneasiness; but her uneasiness removed, almost entirely, the remorse she felt when she thought of her husband.

At luncheon, the said husband had noticed nothing; not so with Madame Derville; she feared Madame de Rênal to be on the point of succumbing. All through the day, her bold, incisive friendship did not spare the other those hinted suggestions intended to portray in hideous colours the danger that she was running.

Madame de Rênal was burning to be left alone with Julien; she wanted to ask him whether he still loved her. Despite the unalterable gentleness of her nature, she was more than once on the point of letting her friend know what a nuisance she was making of herself.

That evening, in the garden, Madame Derville arranged things so skilfully that she found herself placed between Madame de Rênal and Julien. Madame de Rênal, who had formed a delicious image of the pleasure of pressing Julien's hand and carrying it to her lips, could not so much as address a word to him.

This catastrophe increased her agitation. Remorse for one thing was gnawing her. She had so scolded Julien

for the imprudence he had shewn in coming to her room
the night before, that she trembled lest he might not
come that night. She left the garden early, and went
up to wait in her room. But, beside herself with impatience, she rose and went to glue her ear to Julien's
door. Despite the uncertainty and passion that were devouring her, she did not dare enter. This action seemed
to her the last word in lowness, for it serves as text to a
country maxim.

The servants were not all in bed. Prudence obliged her
finally to return to her own room. Two hours of waiting
were two centuries of torment.

But Julien was too loyal to what he called his duty,
to fail in the execution, detail by detail, of what he had
laid down for himself.

As one o'clock struck, he slipped quietly from his room,
made sure that the master of the house was sound asleep,
and appeared before Madame de Rênal. On this occasion he found greater happiness with his mistress, for
he was less continually thinking of the part he had to
play. He had eyes to see and ears to hear. What Madame
de Rênal said to him about his age contributed to give
him some degree of self-assurance.

"Alas! I am ten years older than you! How can you
love me?" she repeated without any object, simply because the idea oppressed her.

Julien could not conceive such a thing, but he saw that
her distress was genuine, and almost entirely forgot his
fear of being ridiculous.

The foolish idea of his being regarded as a servile lover,
at his mistress's beck and call, on account of his humble
birth, vanished likewise. In proportion as Julien's transports reassured his coy mistress, she recovered some
degree of happiness and the faculty of criticising her lover.
Fortunately, he shewed almost nothing, on this occasion,
of that borrowed air which had made their meeting the

night before a victory, but not a pleasure. Had she noticed his intentness upon playing a part, the painful discovery would have robbed her of all happiness for ever. She could have seen in it nothing else than a painful consequence of their disparity of age.

Albeit Madame de Rênal had never thought about theories of love, difference of age is, next to difference of fortune, one of the great commonplaces of provincial humour, whenever there is any talk of love.

In a few days, Julien, all the ardour of his youth restored, was madly in love.

"One must admit," he said to himself, "that her kindness of heart is angelic, and that no one could be prettier."

He had almost entirely lost the idea of a part to be played. In a moment of unrestrained impulse, he even confessed to her all his anxieties. This confidence raised to its climax the passion that he inspired. "So I have not had any fortunate rival," Madame de Rênal said to herself with ecstasy. She ventured to question him as to the portrait in which he took such an interest; Julien swore to her that it was that of a man.

When Madame de Rênal was calm enough to reflect, she could not get over her astonishment that such happiness could exist and that she had never had the slightest idea of it.

"Ah!" she said to herself, "if I had known Julien ten years ago, when I might still be considered pretty!"

Julien's thoughts were worlds apart from these. His love was still founded in ambition: it was the joy of possessing —he, a poor creature so unfortunate and so despised —so noble and beautiful a woman. His acts of adoration, his transports at the sight of his mistress's charms, ended by reassuring her somewhat as to the difference in age. Had she possessed a little of that worldly wisdom a woman of thirty has long enjoyed in more civilized lands, she would have shuddered for the continuance of a love which seemed to exist only upon surprise and the titillation of self-esteem.

In the moments when he forgot his ambition, Julien went into transports over everything that Madame de Rênal possessed, including her hats and gowns. He could not tire of the pleasure of inhaling their perfume. He opened her wardrobe and stood for hours on end marvelling at the beauty and neat arrangement of everything inside. His mistress, leaning upon his shoulder, gazed at him; he himself gazed at those ornaments and fripperies which on a wedding day are displayed among the presents.

"I might have married a man like this!" Madame de Rênal sometimes thought; "What a fiery spirit! What a rapturous life with him!"

As for Julien, never had he found himself so close to those terrible weapons of feminine artillery. "It is impossible," he told himself, "that in Paris there can be anything finer!" After which he could find no objection to his happiness. Often his mistress's sincere admiration, and her transports of passion made him forget the fatuous theory that had kept him so restrained and almost ridiculous in the first moments of their intimacy. There were moments when, despite his hypocritical habits, he found an intense pleasure in confessing to this great lady who admired him his ignorance of any number of little usages. His mistress's rank seemed to raise him above himself. Madame de Rênal, for her part, found the most exquisite moral satisfaction in thus instructing in a heap of little things this young man endowed with genius whom everyone regarded as bound one day to go so far. Even the Sub-Prefect and M. Valenod could not help admiring him: she thought the better of them accordingly. As for Madame Derville, these were by no means her sentiments. In despair at what she thought she could discern, and seeing that her wise counsel was becoming hateful to a woman who had positively lost her head, she left Vergy without offering an explanation for which she was not asked. Madame de Rênal shed a few tears at her departure, and soon it seemed to her that her happiness was doubled. By the withdrawal of her guest she found herself left alone with her lover almost all day long.

Julien gave himself all the more readily to the pleasant society of his mistress inasmuch as, whenever he was left too long by himself, Fouqué's fatal offer recurred to his mind to worry him. In the first days of this new life, there were moments when he, who had never loved, who had never been loved by anyone, found so exquisite a pleasure in being sincere, that he was on the point of confessing to Madame de Rênal the ambition which until then had been the very essence of his existence. He would have liked to be able to consult her as to the strange temptation which he felt in Fouqué's offer, but a trifling occurrence put a stop to all frankness.

CHAPTER SEVENTEEN

THE PRINCIPAL DEPUTY

O! how this spring of love resembleth
The uncertain glory of an April day,
Which now shews all the beauty of the sun,
And by and by a cloud takes all away!
The Two Gentlemen of Verona.

ONE evening as the sun set, sitting by his mistress, at the end of the orchard, safe from disturbance, he was deep in thought. "Will such delicious moments," he was wondering, "last for ever?" His thoughts were absorbed in the difficulty and necessity of adopting a profession, he was deploring this great and distressing problem which puts an end to boyhood and spoils the opening years of manhood when one has no money.

"Ah!" he cried, "Napoleon was indeed the man sent by God to help the youth of France! Who is to take his place? What will the poor wretches do without him, even those who are richer than I, who have just the few crowns needed to procure them a good education, and then not enough money to purchase a man at twenty and launch themselves in a career! Whatever happens," he added with deep sigh, "that fatal memory will for ever prevent us from being happy!"

He saw Madame de Rênal frown suddenly; she assumed a cold, disdainful air; this line of thought seemed to her worthy of a servant. Brought up in the idea that she was extremely rich, it seemed to her a thing to be taken for granted that Julien was also. She loved him a thousand times more than life itself, she would have loved him even had he been ungrateful and faithless, and money to her meant nothing.

Julien was far from guessing what was in her mind. This frown brought him back to earth. He had presence of mind enough to arrange his sentence and to make it plain to the noble lady, seated so close beside him on the bank of verdure, that the words he had just uttered were some that he had heard during his expedition to his friend the timber merchant. This was the reasoning of the impious.

"Very well! Don't mix any more with such people," said Madame de Rênal, still preserving a trace of that glacial air which had suddenly taken the place of an expression of the tenderest and most intimate affection.

This frown, or rather his remorse for his imprudence, was the first check administered to the illusion that was bearing Julien away. He said to himself: "She is good and kind, her feeling for me is strong, but she has been brought up in the enemy's camp. They are bound to be specially afraid of that class of men of spirit who, after a good education, have not enough money to enter upon a career. What would become of these nobles, if it were granted us to fight them with equal weapons? Myself, for instance, as Mayor of Verrières, well intentioned, honest as M. de Rênal is at heart, how I should deal with the vicar, M. Valenod and all their rascalities! How justice should triumph in Verrières. It is not their talents that would prove an obstacle. They are endlessly feeling their way."

Julien's happiness was, that day, on the point of becoming permanent. What our hero lacked was the courage to be sincere. He needed the courage to give battle, but *on the spot;* Madame de Rênal had been surprised by his speech, because the men whom she was in the habit of meeting were always saying that the return of Robespierre was made possible especially by these young men of the lower orders, who had been too well educated. Madame de Rênal's cold manner persisted for some time, and seemed to Julien to be marked. This was because the fear of having said to him indirectly something unpleasant followed her repugnance at his unfortunate speech. This distress was clearly shewn on her pure countenance; so simple when she was happy and away from bores.

Julien no longer dared give himself up freely to his dreams. More calm and less amorous, he decided that it was imprudent in him to go to Madame de Rênal in her room. It would be better if she came to him; if a servant saw her moving about the house, there would be a score of possible reasons to account for her action.

But this arrangement also had its drawbacks. Julien had received from Fouqué certain books for which he, as a student of divinity, could never have asked a bookseller. He ventured to open them only at night. Often he would have been just as well pleased not to be interrupted by an assignation, the tension of waiting for which, even before the little scene in the orchard, would have left him incapable of reading.

He was indebted to Madame de Rênal for an entirely new understanding of the books he read. He had ventured to ply her with questions as to all sorts of little things ignorance of which seriously handicaps the intelligence of a young man born outside the ranks of society, whatever natural genius one may choose to attribute to him.

This education in love, given by an extremely ignorant woman, was a blessing. Julien was at once enabled to see society as it is to-day. His mind was not perplexed by accounts of what it was in the past, two thousand years ago, or sixty years ago merely, in the days of Voltaire and Louis XV. To his unspeakable joy a cloud passed from before his eyes; he understood at last the things that were happening at Verrières.

In the foreground appeared the highly complicated intrigues woven, for the last two years, round the Prefect at Besançon. They were supported by letters that came from Paris, and bore all the most illustrious signatures. It was a question of making M. de Moirod, the most bigoted man in the place, the Principal instead of the Second Deputy to the Mayor of Verrières.

His rival was an extremely rich manufacturer, whom it was absolutely essential to confine to the post of Second Deputy.

Julien at last understood the hints that he had overheard, when the cream of local society came to dine with M. de Rênal. This privileged class was greatly taken up with this selection of a Principal Deputy, of which the rest of the town and especially the Liberals did not even suspect the possibility. What gave it its importance was that, as everybody knew, the eastern side of the main street of Verrières must be carried back more than nine feet, for this street was now a royal highway.

Well, if M. de Moirod, who owned three houses that would have to be carried back, succeeded in becoming Principal Deputy, and so Mayor in the event of M. de Rênal's being returned to Parliament, he would shut his eyes, and it would be possible to make little, imperceptible repairs to the houses that encroached on the public thoroughfare, as a result of which they would be good for a hundred years. Despite the great piety and admitted probity of M. de Moirod, it was certain that he *could be managed,* for he had a large family. Among the houses that would have to be carried back, nine belonged to the very best people in Verrières.

In Julien's eyes, this intrigue was far more important than the history of the battle of Fontenoy, a name which he saw for the first time in one of the books that Fouqué had sent him. Many things had astonished Julien during the five years since he had begun to spend his evenings with the curé. But discretion and a humble spirit being the chief qualities required in a divinity student, it had always been impossible for him to ask any questions.

One day, Madame de Rênal had given an order to her husband's valet, Julien's enemy.

"But, Ma'am, to-day is the last Friday of the month," the man answered her with a curious expression.

"Go," said Madame de Rênal.

"Well," said Julien, "he is going to that hay store, which used to be a church, and was recently restored to the faith; but why? That is one of the mysteries which I have never been able to penetrate."

"It is a most beneficial, but a very strange institution," replied Madame de Rênal. "Women are not admitted; all that I know of it is that they all address one another as *tu*. For instance, this servant will find M. Valenod there, and that conceited fool will not be in the least annoyed at hearing himself called *tu* by Saint-Jean, and will answer him in the same tone. If you really want to know what they do there, I can ask M. de Maugiron and M. Valenod for details. We pay twenty francs for each servant so that if there should be another '93 they may not cut our throats."

The time flew. The memory of his mistress's charms distracted Julien from his black ambition. The necessity to refrain from speaking to her of serious, reasonable matters, since they were on opposite sides, added, without his suspecting it, to the happiness that he owed to her and to the power which she was acquiring over him.

At those moments when the presence of quick-eared children confined them to the language of cold reason, it was with a perfect docility that Julien, gazing at her with eyes that burned with love, listened to her explanations of the world as it really was. Often, in the middle

of an account of some clever piece of roguery, in connexion with the laying out of a road, or of some astounding
contract, Madame de Rênal's attention would suddenly go
completely astray; Julien was obliged to scold her, she
allowed herself to caress him in the same way as she
caressed her children. This was because there were days
on which she imagined that she loved him like a child of
her own. Had she not to reply incessantly to his artless
questions about a thousand simple matters of which a child
of good family is not ignorant at fifteen? A moment later,
she was admiring him as her master. His intelligence
positively frightened her; she thought she could perceive
more clearly every day the future great man in this young
cleric. She saw him as Pope, she saw him as First Minister,
like Richelieu.

"Shall I live long enough to see you in your glory?"
she said to Julien; "there is a place waiting for a great
man; the Monarchy, the Church need one; these gentlemen say so every day. If some Richelieu does not stem
the torrent of private judgment, all is lost."

CHAPTER EIGHTEEN

A KING AT VERRIÈRES

N'êtes-vous bons qu'à jeter là comme un cadavre de
peuple, sans âme, et dont les veines n'ont plus de sang?
*(From the Bishop's address, delivered in
the Chapel of Saint Clement.)*

ON the third of September, at ten o'clock in the
evening, a mounted constable aroused the whole
of Verrières by galloping up the main street; he
brought the news that His Majesty the King of ——
was coming the following Sunday, and it was now Tuesday. The Prefect authorized, that is to say ordered, the
formation of a Guard of Honour; he must be received
with all the pomp possible. A courier was sent to Vergy.
M. de Rênal arrived during the night and found the whole
town in a ferment. Everybody was claiming a right to
something; those who had no other duty were engaging
balconies to see the King enter the town.

Who was to command the Guard of Honour? M. de
Rênal saw at once how important it was, in the interest
of the houses that would have to be carried back, that M.
de Moirod should fill this post. It might be held to con-
stitute a claim to the place of Principal Deputy. There
was nothing to be said against M. de Moirod's devotion;
it went beyond all comparison, but he had never ridden
a horse in his life. He was a man of six and thirty, timid
in every way, and equally afraid of falls and of being
laughed at.

The Mayor sent for him at five o'clock in the morning.

"You see, Sir, that I am asking your advice, as though you already occupied the post in which all right-minded people would gladly see you. In this unfortunate town the manufacturers prosper, the Liberal Party are becoming millionaires, they aspire to power, they will forge themselves weapons out of everything. We must consider the King's interests, those of the Monarchy, and above all those of our holy religion. To whom do you think, Sir, that we ought to entrust the command of the Guard of Honour?"

In spite of the horrible fear that a horse inspired in him, M. de Moirod ended by accepting this honour like a martyr. "I shall manage to adopt the right manner," he told the Mayor. There was barely time to overhaul the uniforms which had been used seven years before on the passage of a Prince of the Blood.

At seven, Madame de Rênal arrived from Vergy with Julien and the children. She found her drawing-room full of Liberal ladies who were preaching the union of parties, and had come to implore her to make her husband find room in the Guard of Honour for theirs. One of them asserted that if her husband were not chosen he would go bankrupt from grief. Madame de Rênal sent them all packing at once. She seemed greatly occupied.

Julien was surprised and even more annoyed by her making a mystery to him of what was disturbing her. "I thought as much," he told himself bitterly, "her love is eclipsed by the joy of receiving a King in her house. All this excitement dazzles her. She will begin to love me again when her brain is no longer troubled by ideas of caste."

The surprising thing was that he loved her all the more for this.

The upholsterers began to invade the whole house, he long watched in vain for an opportunity of saying a word to her. At length he found her coming out of his own room, carrying one of his coats. They were alone. He tried to speak to her. She made off, declining to listen to him. "What a fool I am to be in love with a woman like that, ambition makes her just as stupid as her husband."

She was even more so: one of her great wishes, which she had never confessed to Julien, for fear of shocking him, was to see him discard, if only for a day, his gloomy black coat. With an ingenuity truly admirable in so natural a woman, she secured, first from M. de Moirod, and then from the Sub-Prefect M. de Maugiron, that Julien should be appointed to the Guard of Honour in preference to five or six young men, sons of manufacturers in easy circumstances, at least two of whom were of an exemplary piety. M. Valenod, who was reckoning on lending his carriage to the prettiest women of the town, in order to have his fine Norman horses admired, agreed to let Julien, the person he hated most, have one of them. But each of the members of the Guard of Honour possessed or had borrowed one of those sky-blue coats with a pair of colonel's epaulettes in silver, which had shone in public seven years before. Madame de Rênal wanted a new coat, and she had but four days in which to send to Besançon, and to procure from there the uniform, the weapons, the hat, and all the other requisites for a Guard of Honour. What is rather amusing is that she thought it imprudent to have Julien's coat made at Verrières. She wished to take him by surprise, him and the town.

The work of organizing the Guard of Honour and popular feeling finished, the Mayor had next to deal with a great religious ceremony; the King of —— refused to pass through Verrières without paying a visit to the famous relic of Saint Clement which is preserved at Bray-le-Haut, a short league from the town. The clergy must be present in full force, and this was the most difficult thing to arrange; M. Maslon, the new curé, was determined, at any price, to keep M. Chélan out. In vain did M. de Rênal point out to him the imprudence of this action. The Marquis de La Mole, whose ancestors for so long were Governors of the Province, had been chosen to accompany the King of ——. He had known the abbé Chélan for thirty years. He would be certain to inquire for him on arriving at Verrières, and, if he found that he was in disgrace, was quite capable of going in search of him, to the little house to which he had retired, accompanied by such of the procession as were under his orders. What a rebuff that would be!

"I am dishonoured here and at Besançon," replied the abbé Maslon, "if he appears among my clergy. A Jansenist, great heavens!"

"Whatever you may say, my dear abbé," M. de Rênal assured him, "I shall not expose the municipal government of Verrières to the risk of an insult from M. de La Mole. You don't know the man, he is sound enough at court; but here, in the country, he has a satirical, mocking spirit, and likes nothing so much as to embarrass people. He is capable, simply for his own amusement, of covering us with ridicule in the eyes of the Liberals."

It was not until the night between Saturday and Sunday, after three days of discussion, that the abbé Maslon's pride gave way before the Mayor's fear, which had turned to courage. The next thing was to write a honeyed note to the abbé Chélan, inviting him to be present at the veneration of the relic at Bray-le-Haut, his great age and infirmities permitting. M. Chélan asked for and obtained a letter of invitation for Julien, who was to accompany him in the capacity of sub-deacon.

Early on Sunday morning, thousands of peasants, arriving from the neighbouring mountains, flooded the streets of Verrières. It was a day of brilliant sunshine. At length, about three o'clock, a tremor ran through the crowd; they had caught sight of a beacon blazing on a rock two

leagues from Verrières. This signal announced that the
King had just entered the territory of the Department.
Immediately the sound of all the bells and the repeated
discharge of an old Spanish cannon belonging to the town
proclaimed its joy at this great event. Half the popula-
tion climbed up on the roofs. All the women were on
the balconies. The Guard of Honour began to move.
The brilliant uniforms were greatly admired, each of the
onlookers recognized a relative or friend. There was
general laughter at the alarm of M. de Moirod, whose
cautious hand lay ready at any moment to clutch hold of
his saddle. But one thing made them forget all the others:
the left hand man in the ninth section was a handsome lad,
very slender, who at first was not identified. Presently
a cry of indignation from some, the astonished silence of
others announced a general sensation. The onlookers recognized in this young man, riding one of M. Valenod's
Norman horses, young Sorel, the carpenter's son. There
was one unanimous outcry against the Mayor, especially
among the Liberals. What, because this young labourer
dressed up as a priest was tutor to his brats, he had the
audacity to appoint him to the Guard of Honour, to the
exclusion of M. This and M. That, wealthy manufacturers!
"Those gentlemen," said a banker's wife, "ought really
to offer an affront to the little upstart, born in the gutter."

"He has a wicked temper and he is wearing a sabre,"
replied her companion; "he would be quite treacherous
enough to slash them across the face."

The comments made by the aristocratic element were
more dangerous. The ladies asked themselves whether the
Mayor alone was responsible for this grave breach of
etiquette. On the whole justice was done to his contempt
for humble birth.

While he was giving rise to so much comment, Julien

was the happiest man alive. Bold by nature, he ⟨...⟩
better seat on a horse than most of the young m⟨..⟩ ⟨..⟩
this mountain town. He saw in the eyes of the women
that they were talking about him.

His epaulettes were more brilliant because they were
new. At every moment his horse threatened to rear; he
was in the seventh heaven of joy.

His happiness knew no bounds when, as they passed
near the old rampart, the sound of the small cannon made
his horse swerve out of the ranks. By the greatest accident, he did not fall off; from that moment he felt himself a hero. He was Napoleon's orderly officer and was
charging a battery.

There was one person happier than he. First of all
she had watched him pass from one of the windows of
the town hall; then, getting into her carriage, and rapidly
making a wide detour, she was in time to tremble when
his horse carried him out of the ranks. Finally, her carriage passing out at a gallop through another of the
gates of the town, she made her way back to the road
along which the King was to pass, and was able to follow
the Guard of Honour at a distance of twenty paces, in
a noble cloud of dust. Ten thousand peasants shouted:
"Long live the King" when the Mayor had the honour of
addressing His Majesty. An hour later, when, having
listened to all the speeches, the King was about to enter
the town, the small cannon began to fire again with frenzied
haste. But an accident occurred, not to the gunners who
had learned their trade at Leipsic and Montmirail, but
to the future Principal Deputy, M. de Moirod. His horse
dropped him gently into the one puddle to be found along
the whole road, which created a scandal, because he had
to be pulled out of the way to enable the King's carriage
to pass.

His Majesty alighted at the fine new church, which was
decked out for the occasion with all its crimson hangings.

*E 945

The King was to halt for dinner, immediately after which he would take the road again to go and venerate the famous relic of Saint Clement. No sooner was the King inside the church than Julien went off at a gallop to M. de Rênal's. There he discarded with a sigh his fine sky-blue coat, his sabre, his epaulettes, to resume the little threadbare black coat. He mounted his horse again, and in a few minutes was at Bray-le-Haut, which stands on the summit of an imposing hill. "Enthusiasm is multiplying these peasants," thought Julien. "One cannot move at Verrières, and here there are more than ten thousand of them round this old abbey." Half ruined by the vandalism of the Revolution, it had been magnificently restored since the Restoration, and there was already some talk of miracles. Julien joined the abbé Chélan, who scolded him severely, and gave him a cassock and surplice. He vested himself hurriedly in these and followed M. Chélan, who was going in search of the youthful Bishop of Agde. This was a nephew of M. de La Mole, recently appointed to the See, who had been selected to exhibit the relic to the King. But the Bishop was not to be found.
  The clergy were growing impatient. They awaited their leader in the sombre, gothic cloister of the ancient abbey. Four and twenty parish priests had been collected to represent the original chapter of Bray-le-Haut which prior to 1789 had consisted of four and twenty canons. Having spent three quarters of an hour in deploring the youthfulness of the Bishop, the priests decided that it would be a good thing if their Dean were to go and inform His Lordship that the King was on his way, and that it was time they were in the choir. M. Chélan's great age had made him Dean; despite the anger he shewed with Julien, he made a sign to him to follow him. Julien carried his surplice admirably. By some secret process of the ecclesiastical toilet-table, he had made his fine curly hair lie quite flat; but, by an oversight which intensified the anger

of M. Chélan, beneath the long folds of his cassock one could see the spurs of the Guard of Honour.

When they reached the Bishop's apartment, the tall lackeys smothered in gold lace barely condescended to inform the old curé that His Lordship could not be seen. They laughed at him when he tried to explain that in his capacity as Dean of the Noble Chapter of Bray-le-Haut, it was his privilege to be admitted at all times to the presence of the officiating Bishop.

Julien's proud spirit was offended by the insolence of the lackeys. He set off on a tour of the dormitories of the old abbey, trying every door that he came to. One quite small door yielded to his efforts and he found himself in a cell in the midst of His Lordship's body-servants, dressed in black with chains round their necks. Seeing his air of haste, these gentlemen supposed that the Bishop had sent for him and allowed him to pass. He went a little way and found himself in an immense gothic chamber, very dark and panelled throughout in black oak; with a single exception, its pointed windows had been walled up with bricks. There was nothing to conceal the coarse surface of this masonry, which formed a sorry contrast to the venerable splendour of the woodwork. Both sides of this room, famous among the antiquarians of Burgundy, which the Duke Charles the Bold built about the year 1470 in expiation of some offence, were lined with wooden stalls, richly carved. These displayed, inlaid in wood of different colours, all the mysteries of the Apocalypse.

This melancholy splendour, degraded by the intrusion of the bare bricks and white plaster, impressed Julien. He stood there in silence. At the other end of the room, near the only window through which any light came, he saw a portable mirror framed in mahogany. A young man, robed in violet with a lace surplice, but bare-headed, was standing three paces away from the mirror. This article appeared out of place in such a room, and had doubtless been brought there from the town. Julien thought that the young man seemed irritated; with his right hand he was gravely giving benedictions in the direction of the mirror.

"What can this mean?" he wondered. "Is it a preliminary ceremony that this young priest is performing? He is perhaps the Bishop's secretary . . . he will be rude like the lackeys . . . but what of that, let us try him."

He went forward and passed slowly down the length of the room, keeping his eyes fixed on that solitary window and watching the young man who continued to give benedictions, with a slow motion but in endless profusion, and without pausing for a moment.

As he drew nearer he was better able to see the other's look of annoyance. The costliness of his lace-bordered surplice brought Julien to a standstill some distance away from the magnificent mirror.

"It is my duty to speak," he reminded himself at length; but the beauty of the room had touched his feelings and he was chilled in anticipation by the harsh words that would be addressed to him.

The young man caught sight of him in the glass, turned round, and suddenly discarding his look of irritation said to him in the pleasantest tone:

"Well, Sir, is it ready yet?"

Julien remained speechless. As this young man turned towards him, Julien saw the pectoral cross on his breast: it was the Bishop of Agde. "So young," thought Julien; "at the most, only six or eight years older than myself!"

And he felt ashamed of his spurs.

"Monseigneur," he replied timidly. "I am sent by the Dean of the Chapter, M. Chélan."

"Ah! I have an excellent account of him," said the bishop in a courteous tone which left Julien more fascinated than ever. "But I beg your pardon, Sir, I took you for the person who is to bring me back my mitre. It was carelessly packed in Paris; the silver tissue has been dreadfully frayed at the top. It will create a shocking effect," the young Bishop went on with a sorrowful air, "and they are keeping me waiting too."

"Monseigneur, I shall go and find the mitre, with Your Lordship's permission."

Julien's fine eyes had their effect.

"Go, Sir," the Bishop answered with exquisite courtesy; "I must have it at once. I am sorry to keep the gentlemen of the Chapter waiting."

When Julien was halfway down the room, he turned to look at the Bishop and saw that he was once more engaged in giving benedictions. "What can that be?" Julien asked himself; "no doubt, it is a religious preparation necessary to the ceremony that is to follow." When he came to the cell in which the servants were waiting, he saw the mitre in their hands. These gentlemen, yielding in spite of themselves to Julien's imperious glance, surrendered it to him.

He felt proud to be carrying it: as he crossed the room, he walked slowly; he held it with respect. He found the Bishop seated before the glass; but, from time to time, his right hand, tired as it was, still gave the benediction. Julien helped him to put on the mitre. The Bishop shook his head.

"Ah! It will keep on," he said to Julien with a satisfied air. "Will you go a little way off?"

Whereupon the Bishop walked at a smart pace to the middle of the room, then returning towards the mirror with a slow step, he resumed his air of irritation and went on solemnly giving benedictions.

Julien was spellbound with astonishment; he was tempted to guess what this meant, but did not dare. The Bishop stopped, and looking at him with an air from which the solemnity rapidly vanished:

"What do you say to my mitre, Sir, does it look right?"

"Quite right, Monseigneur."

"It is not too far back? That would look rather silly; but it does not do, either, to wear them pulled down over one's eyes like an officer's shako."

"It seems to me to be quite right."

"The King of —— is accustomed to venerable clergy who are doubtless very solemn. I should not like, especially in view of my age, to appear too frivolous."

And the Bishop once more began to walk about the room scattering benedictions.

"It is quite clear," said Julien, at last venturing to understand, "he is practising the benediction."

A few moments later:

"I am ready," said the Bishop. "Go, Sir, and inform the Dean and the gentlemen of the Chapter."

Presently M. Chélan, followed by the two oldest of the curés, entered by an immense door, magnificently carved, which Julien had not noticed. But this time he remained in his place in the extreme rear, and could see the Bishop only over the shoulders of the ecclesiastics who crowded towards this door.

The Bishop crossed the room slowly; when he came to the threshold the curés formed in processional order. After a momentary confusion the procession began to move, intoning a psalm. The Bishop came last, between M. Chélan and another curé of great age. Julien found a place for himself quite close to His Lordship, as being attached to the abbé Chélan. They moved down the long corridors of the abbey of Bray-le-Haut; in spite of the brilliant sunshine, these were dark and damp. At length they arrived at the door of the cloister. Julien was speechless with admiration of so fine a ceremony. His heart was divided between the ambition aroused by the Bishop's youthfulness, and the sensibility and exquisite manners of this prelate. His courtesy was of a very different kind from M. de Rênal's, even on his good days. "The more one rises towards the highest rank of society," thought Julien, "the more one finds these charming manners."

They entered the church by a side door; suddenly an appalling crash made its ancient vaults resound; Julien thought that the walls were collapsing. It was again the small cannon; drawn by eight horses at a gallop, it had just arrived; and immediately on its arrival, brought into action by the gunners of Leipsic, it was firing five rounds a minute, as though the Prussians had been in front of it.

But this stirring sound no longer had any effect upon Julien, he dreamed no more of Napoleon and martial glory. "So young," he was thinking, "to be Bishop of Agde! But where is Agde? And how much is it worth? Two or three hundred thousand francs, perhaps."

His Lordship's servants appeared, carrying a magnificent dais; M. Chélan took one of the poles, but actually it was Julien that bore it. The Bishop took his place beneath it. He had really succeeded in giving himself the air of an old man; our hero's admiration knew no bounds. "What cannot one do if one is clever!" he thought.

The King made his entry. Julien was so fortunate as to see him at close range. The Bishop addressed him with unction, and did not forget to include a slight touch of confusion, extremely flattering to His Majesty. We shall not repeat the account of the ceremonies at Bray-le-Haut; for a fortnight they filled the columns of all the newspapers of the Department. Julien learned, from the Bishop's speech, that the King was descended from Charles the Bold.

Later on it was one of Julien's duties to check the accounts of what this ceremony had cost. M. de La Mole, who had secured a bishopric for his nephew, had chosen to pay him the compliment of bearing the whole of the expense himself. The ceremony at Bray-le-Haut alone cost three thousand eight hundred francs.

After the Bishop's address and the King's reply, His Majesty took his place beneath the dais; he then knelt down most devoutly upon a cushion close to the altar. The choir was enclosed with stalls, and these stalls were raised two steps above the pavement. It was on the second of these steps that Julien sat at the feet of M. Chélan, not unlike a train-bearer at the feet of his Cardinal, in the Sistine Chapel, in Rome. There were a Te Deum, clouds of incense, endless volleys of musketry and artillery; the peasants were frantic with joy and piety. Such a day undoes the work of a hundred numbers of the Jacobin papers.

Julien was within six paces of the King, who was praying with genuine fervour. He noticed for the first time a small man of intelligent appearance, whose coat was almost bare of embroidery. But he wore a sky-blue riband over this extremely simple coat. He was nearer to the King than many other gentlemen, whose coats were so covered with gold lace that, to use Julien's expression, one could not see the cloth. He learned a minute later that this was M. de La Mole. He decided that he wore a haughty, indeed an insolent air.

"This Marquis would not be polite like my dear Bishop," he thought. "Ah! The career of a churchman makes one gentle and wise. But the King has come to venerate the relic, and I see no relic. Where can Saint Clement be?"

A little clerk, who was next to him, informed him that the venerable relic was in the upper part of the building, in a *chapelle ardente*.

"What is a *chapelle ardente*?" Julien asked himself.

But he would not ask for an explanation of the words. He followed the proceedings with even closer attention.

On the occasion of a visit from a sovereign prince, etiquette requires that the canons shall not accompany the Bishop. But as he started for the *chapelle ardente* His Lordship of Agde summoned the abbé Chélan; Julien ventured to follow him.

After climbing a long stair, they came to a very small door, the frame of which was sumptuously gilded. This work had a look of having just been completed.

Outside the door were gathered on their knees four and twenty girls, belonging to the most distinguished families of Verrières. Before opening the door, the Bishop sank on his knees in the midst of these girls, who were all pretty. While he was praying aloud, it seemed as though they could not sufficiently admire his fine lace, his charm, his young and pleasant face. This spectacle made our hero lose all that remained of his reason. At that moment, he would have fought for the Inquisition, and in earnest. Suddenly the door flew open. The little chapel seemed to be ablaze with light. One saw upon the altar more than a thousand candles arranged in eight rows, separated from one another by clusters of flowers. The sweet odour of the purest incense rose in clouds from the gate of the sanctuary. The newly gilded chapel was quite small, but very lofty. Julien noticed that there were on the altar candles more than fifteen feet long. The girls could not restrain a cry of admiration. No one had been admitted to the tiny ante-chapel save the twenty-four girls, the two priests and Julien.

Presently the King arrived, followed only by M. de La Mole and his Great Chamberlain. The guards themselves remained outside, on their knees, presenting their arms.

His Majesty flung himself rather than knelt down on the faldstool. It was then only that Julien, pressed against the gilded door, caught sight, beneath a girl's bare arm, of the charming statue of Saint Clement. It was hidden beneath the altar, in the garb of a young Roman soldier. He had in his throat a large wound from which the blood seemed to be flowing. The artist had surpassed himself; the eyes, dying but full of grace, were half closed. A budding moustache adorned the charming mouth, which being slightly open had the effect of being still engaged in prayer. At the sight of this statue, the girl nearest to Julien wept hot tears; one of her tears fell upon Julien's hand.

After an interval of prayer in the most profound silence, disturbed only by the distant sound of the bells of all the villages within a radius of ten leagues, the Bishop of Agde asked the King's permission to speak. He concluded a brief but highly edifying discourse with these words, simple in themselves, but thereby all the better assured of their effect.

"Never forget, young Christian women, that you have seen one of the great Kings of the earth upon his knees before the servants of this all-powerful and terrible God. These servants, frail, persecuted, martyred upon earth, as you can see from the still bleeding wound of Saint Clement, are triumphant in heaven. All your lives, I think, young Christians, you will remember this day. You will detest impiety. Always you will remain faithful to this God who is so great, so terrible, but so good."

At these words, the Bishop rose with authority.

"You promise me?" he said, extending his arm with an air of inspiration.

"We promise," said the girls, bursting into tears.

"I receive your promise, in the name of our terrible God!" the Bishop concluded in a voice of thunder. And the ceremony was at an end.

The King himself was in tears. It was not until long afterwards that Julien was calm enough to inquire where were the bones of the Saint, sent from Rome to Philip the Bold, Duke of Burgundy. He was told that they were embodied in the charming wax figure.

His Majesty deigned to permit the girls who had accompanied him into the chapel to wear a red riband upon which were embroidered the words: "HATRED OF IMPIETY, PERPETUAL ADORATION."

M. de La Mole ordered ten thousand bottles of wine to be distributed among the peasants. That evening, at Verrières, the Liberals found an excuse for illuminating their houses a hundred times more brilliantly than the Royalists. Before leaving the town, the King paid a visit to M. de Moirod.

CHAPTER NINETEEN

TO THINK IS TO BE FULL OF SORROW

Le grotesque des évènements de tous les jours vous
cache le vrai malheur des passions.

BARNAVE.

WHILE he was replacing its ordinary furniture
in the room that M. de La Mole had occupied,
Julien found a piece of stout paper, folded
twice across. He read at the foot of the first page:

To H. E., M. le Marquis de La Mole, Peer of France,
Knight of the Royal Orders, etc., etc.

It was a petition in the rude handwriting of a cook.

"Monsieur le Marquis,

"All my life I have held religious principles. I was in
Lyons, exposed to the bombs, at the time of the siege,
in '93, of execrable memory. I am a communicant, I go
every Sunday to mass in my parish church. I have never
failed in my Easter duty, not even in '93, of execrable
memory. My cook, for before the revolution I kept servants, my cook observes Friday. I enjoy in Verrières
a general and I venture to say merited respect. I walk
beneath the dais in processions, beside the curé and the
mayor. I carry, on solemn occasions, a big candle bought
at my own cost. The certificates of all of which are in
Paris at the Ministry of Finance. I ask Monsieur le
Marquis for the Verrières lottery office, which cannot fail
to be vacant soon in one way or another, the present holder
being seriously ill, and besides voting the wrong way at
the elections; etc.   DE CHOLIN."

[144]

On the margin of this petition was an endorsement signed *de Moirod*, which began with the words:

"I had the honour *yesterday* to mention the respectable person who makes this request," and so forth.

"And so even that imbecile Cholin shews me the way that I must follow," Julien said to himself.

A week after the visit of the King of —— to Verrières, the chief thing to emerge from the innumerable falsehoods, foolish interpretations, absurd discussions, etc., etc., to which the King, the Bishop of Agde, the Marquis de La Mole, the ten thousand bottles of wine, the unseated Moirod (who, in the hope of a Cross, did not set foot outside his own door for a whole month after his fall) were in turn subjected, was the utter indelicacy of having jockeyed into the Guard of Honour, Julien Sorel, the son of a carpenter. You ought to have heard, on this topic, the wealthy calico printers, who, morning, noon and night, used to talk themselves hoarse in preaching equality. That proud woman, Madame de Rênal, was the author of this abomination. Her reason? The flashing eyes and pink cheeks of that young parson Sorel were reason enough and to spare.

Shortly after their return to Vergy, Stanislas Xavier, the youngest of the children, took fever; at once Madame de Rênal was seized by the most fearful remorse. For the first time she blamed herself for falling in love in a coherent fashion. She seemed to understand, as though by a miracle, the appalling sin into which she had let herself be drawn. Although deeply religious by nature, until this moment she had never thought of the magnitude of her crime in the eyes of God.

Long ago, at the convent of the Sacred Heart, she had loved God with a passionate love; she feared Him in the same way in this predicament. The struggles that rent her heart asunder were all the more terrible in that there was nothing reasonable in her fear. Julien discovered that any recourse to argument irritated instead of calming her; she saw in it the language of hell. However, as Julien himself was greatly attached to little Stanislas, he was more welcome to speak to her of the child's illness: presently it assumed a grave character. Then her incessant remorse deprived Madame de Rênal even of the power to sleep; she never emerged from a grim silence: had she opened her mouth, it would have been to confess her crime to God and before men.

"I beg of you," Julien said to her, as soon as they were alone, "say nothing to anyone; let me be the sole confidant of your griefs. If you still love me, do not speak! your words cannot cure our Stanislas of his fever."

But his attempts at consolation produced no effect; he did not know that Madame de Rênal had taken it into her head that, to appease the anger of a jealous God, she must either hate Julien or see her son die. It was because she felt that she could not hate her lover that she was so unhappy.

"Avoid my presence," she said to Julien one day; "in the name of God, leave this house: it is your presence here that is killing my son.

"God is punishing me," she added in a whisper; "He is just; I adore His equity; my crime is shocking, and I was living without remorse! It was the first sign of departure from God: I ought to be doubly punished."

Julien was deeply touched. He was unable to see in this attitude either hypocrisy or exaggeration. "She believes that she is killing her son by loving me, and yet the unhappy woman loves me more than her son. That, how can I doubt it, is the remorse that is killing her; there is true nobility of feeling. But how can I have inspired such love, I, so poor, so ill-bred, so ignorant, often so rude in my manners?"

One night the child's condition was critical. About two o'clock in the morning, M. de Rênal came to see him.

The boy, burning with fever, was extremely flushed and did not recognize his father. Suddenly Madame de Rênal threw herself at her husband's feet: Julien saw that she was going to reveal everything and to ruin herself for ever.

Fortunately, this strange exhibition annoyed M. de Rênal.

"Good night! Good night!" he said and prepared to leave the room.

"No, listen to me," cried his wife on her knees before him, seeking to hold him back. "Learn the whole truth. It is I that am killing my son. I gave him his life, and I am taking it from him. Heaven is punishing me; in the eyes of God, I am guilty of murder. I must destroy and humble myself; it may be that such a sacrifice will appease the Lord."

If M. de Rênal had been a man of imagination, he would have guessed everything.

"Romantic stuff," he exclaimed, thrusting away his wife who sought to embrace his knees. "Romantic stuff, all that! Julien, tell them to fetch the doctor at daybreak."

And he went back to bed. Madame de Rênal sank on her knees, half unconscious, with a convulsive movement thrusting away Julien, who was coming to her assistance.

Julien stood watching her with amazement.

"So this is adultery!" he said to himself. . . . "Can it be possible that those rascally priests are right after all? That they, who commit so many sins, have the privilege of knowing the true theory of sin? How very odd!"

For twenty minutes since M. de Rênal had left the room, Julien had seen the woman he loved, her head sunk on the child's little bed, motionless and almost unconscious. "Here we have a woman of superior intelligence reduced to the last extremes of misery, because she has known me," he said to himself.

The hours passed rapidly. "What can I do for her? I must make up my mind. I have ceased to count here. What do I care for men, and their silly affectations? What can I do for her? . . . Go from her? But I shall be leaving her alone, torn by the most frightful grief. That automaton of a husband does her more harm than good. He will say something offensive to her, in his natural coarseness; she may go mad, throw herself from the window.

"If I leave her, if I cease to watch over her, she will tell him everything. And then, for all one knows, in spite of the fortune he is to inherit through her, he will make a scandal. She may tell everything, great God, to that —— abbé Maslon, who makes the illness of a child of six an excuse for never stirring out of this house, and not without purpose. In her grief and her fear of God, she forgets all that she knows of the man; she sees only the priest."

"Leave me," came suddenly from Madame de Rênal as she opened her eyes.

"I would give my life a thousand times to know how I can be of most use to you," replied Julien; "never have I so loved you, my dear angel, or rather, from this instant only, I begin to adore you as you deserve to be adored. What is to become of me apart from you, and with the knowledge that you are wretched by my fault! But I must not speak of my own sufferings. I shall go, yes, my love. But, if I leave you, if I cease to watch over you, to be constantly interposing myself between you and your husband, you will tell him everything, you will be ruined. Think of the ignominy with which he will drive you from the house; all Verrières, all Besançon will ring with the scandal. All the blame will be cast on you; you will never be able to lift up your head again."

"That is all that I ask," she cried, rising to her feet. "I shall suffer, all the better."

"But, by this appalling scandal, you will be harming him as well!"

"But I humble myself, I throw myself down in the mud; and in that way perhaps I save my son. This humiliation, in the sight of all, is perhaps a public penance. So far as my frailty can judge, is it not the greatest sacrifice that I can make to God? Perhaps he will deign to accept my humiliation and to spare me my son! Shew me a harder sacrifice and I will hasten to perform it."

"Let me punish myself. I too am guilty. Would you have me retire to La Trappe? The austerity of the life there may appease your God . . . Oh, heaven! Why can I not take upon myself Stanislas's illness?"

"Ah! You love him," said Madame de Rênal, rising and flinging herself into his arms.

Immediately she thrust him from her with horror.

"I believe you! I believe you!" she went on, having fallen once more on her knees; "O my only friend, why are not you Stanislas's father? Then it would not be a horrible sin to love you more than your son."

"Will you permit me to stay, and henceforward only to love you as a brother? It is the only reasonable expiation; it may appease the wrath of the Most High."

"And I," she exclaimed, rising, and taking Julien's head in her hands, and holding it at arm's length before her eyes, "and I, shall I love you like a brother? Is it in my power to love you like a brother?"

Julien burst into tears.

"I will obey you," he said as he fell at her feet. "I will obey you, whatever you may bid me do; it is the one thing left for me. My brain is smitten with blindness; I can see no course to take. If I leave you, you tell your husband all; you ruin yourself, and him at the same time. After such a disgrace he will never be elected Deputy. If I stay, you regard me as the cause of your son's death, and you yourself die of grief. Would you

[149]

like to test the effect of my going? If you like, I will
punish myself for our sin by leaving you for a week. I
shall pass the time in retreat wherever you choose. At
the abbey of Bray-le-Haut, for instance; but swear to
me that during my absence you will reveal nothing to your
husband. Remember that I can never return if you speak."

She promised; he departed, but was recalled after two
days.

"It is impossible for me to keep my oath without you.
I must speak to my husband, if you are not constantly
there to order me with your eyes to be silent. Each hour
of this abominable life seems to me to last a day."

In the end, heaven took pity on this unhappy mother.
Gradually Stanislas passed out of danger. But the ice was
broken, her reason had learned the magnitude of her sin, she
could no more recover her equilibrium. Remorse still remained, and took the form that it was bound to take in so
sincere a heart. Her life was heaven and hell; hell when
she did not see Julien, heaven when she was at his feet.

"I am no longer under any illusion," she told him, even
at the moments when she ventured to give absolute rein
to her love: "I am damned, irremediably damned. You
are young, you have yielded to my seduction, heaven may
pardon you; but as for me, I am damned. I know it by
an infallible sign. I am afraid: who would not be afraid
at the sight of hell? But at heart, I am not in the least
repentant. I would commit my sin again, were it to be
committed. Let heaven only refrain from punishing me
in this world and in my children, and I shall have more
than I deserve. But you, at least, my Julien," she cried
at other moments, "are you happy? Do you feel that
I love you enough?"

Julien's distrust and suffering pride, which needed above
all a love that made sacrifices, could not stand out against
the sight of so great, so indubitable a sacrifice, and one

that was made afresh every moment. He adored Madame de Rênal. "She may well be noble, and I the son of a working man; she loves me . . . I am not to her a footman employed in the part of lover." Once rid of this fear, Julien fell into all the follies of love, into its mortal uncertainties.

"At least," she cried when she saw that he doubted her love, "let me make you happy during the few days we still have to spend together! Let us make haste; to-morrow perhaps I shall be no longer yours. If heaven strikes me through my children, in vain shall I seek to live only for love of you, not to see that it is my crime that is killing them. I shall not be able to survive that blow. Even if I would, I could not; I should go mad."

"Ah! If I could take your sin upon my conscience, as you so generously wished that you might take Stanislas's fever!"

This great moral crisis changed the nature of the sentiment that united Julien to his mistress. His love was no longer merely admiration of her beauty, pride in the possession of her.

Their joy was thenceforward of a far higher nature, the flame that devoured them was more intense. They underwent transports of utter madness. Their happiness would have seemed great in the eyes of other people. But they never recaptured the delicious serenity, the unclouded happiness, the spontaneous joy of the first days of their love, when Madame de Rênal's one fear was that of not being loved enough by Julien. Their happiness assumed at times the aspect of crime.

In what were their happiest, and apparently their calmest moments: "Oh! Great God! I see hell before me," Madame de Rênal would suddenly exclaim, gripping Julien's hand with a convulsive movement. "What fearful torments! I have well deserved them." She clutched him, clinging to him like the ivy to the wall.

Julien tried in vain to calm this agitated soul. She took his hand, which she covered with kisses. Then, relapsing into a sombre meditation; "Hell," she said, "hell would be a blessing to me; I should still have some days in this world to spend with him, but hell here on earth, the death of my children. . . . Yet, at that price, perhaps my crime would be forgiven me. . . . Oh! Great God! Grant me not my pardon at that price. These poor children have done nothing to offend thee; 'tis I, I, the guilt is mine alone! I love a man who is not my husband."

Julien next saw Madame de Rênal reach a state that was outwardly tranquil. She sought to take the burden upon herself, she wished not to poison the existence of him whom she loved.

In the midst of these alternations of love, remorse and pleasure, the days passed for them with lightning rapidity. Julien lost the habit of reflexion.

Miss Elisa went to conduct a little lawsuit which she had at Verrières. She found M. Valenod greatly annoyed with Julien. She hated the tutor and often spoke about him to M. Valenod.

"You would ruin me, Sir, if I told you the truth!" she said to him one day. "Employers all hang together in important things. They never forgive us poor servants for certain revelations. . . ."

After these conventional phrases, which the impatient curiosity of M. Valenod found a way of cutting short, he learned the most mortifying things in the world for his own self-esteem.

This woman, the most distinguished in the place, whom for six years he had surrounded with every attention, and, unluckily, before the eyes of all the world; this proudest of women, whose disdain had so often made him blush, had taken as her lover a little journeyman dressed up as a tutor. And that nothing might be wanting to the discomfiture of the governor of the poorhouse, Madame de Rênal adored this lover.

"And," the maid added with a sigh, "M. Julien went to no pains to make this conquest, he has never departed from his habitual coldness with Madame."

It was only in the country that Elisa had become certain of her facts, but she thought that this intrigue dated from far earlier.

"That, no doubt, is why," she continued bitterly, "he refused at the time to marry me. And I, like a fool, going to consult Madame de Rênal, begging her to speak to the tutor!"

That same evening M. de Rênal received from the town, with his newspaper, a long anonymous letter which informed him in the fullest detail of all that was going on under his roof. Julien saw him turn pale as he read this letter, which was written on blue paper, and cast angry glances at himself. For the rest of the evening the Mayor never recovered his peace of mind; it was in vain that Julien tried to flatter him by asking him to explain obscure points in the pedigrees of the best families of Burgundy.

CHAPTER TWENTY

THE ANONYMOUS LETTERS

> Do not give dalliance
> Too much the rein; the strongest oaths are straw
> To the fire i'the blood.
>
> *The Tempest.*

AS they left the drawing-room about midnight, Julien found time to say to his mistress:

"Do not let us meet to-night, your husband has suspicions; I would swear that that long letter he was reading with such displeasure is an anonymous one."

Fortunately, Julien locked himself into his room. Madame de Rênal conceived the mad idea that this warning was simply a pretext for not coming to see her. She lost her head absolutely, and at the usual hour came to his door. Julien, hearing a sound in the corridor, instantly blew out his lamp. Some one was attempting to open his door; was it Madame de Rênal, was it a jealous husband?

Early the next morning, the cook, who took an interest in Julien, brought him a book on the cover of which he read these words written in Italian: *Guardate alla pagina 130.*

Julien shuddered at the imprudence, turned to page one hundred and thirty and found fastened to it with a pin the following letter written in haste, bedewed with tears, and without the least attempt at spelling. Ordinarily Madame de Rênal spelt quite well; he was moved by this detail and began to forget the frightful imprudence.

"So you would not let me in to-night? There are moments when I feel that I have never seen into the depths of your heart. Your look frightens me. I am afraid of you. Great God! Can it be, you have never loved me? In that case, my husband can discover our love, and shut me up in lifelong imprisonment, in the country, apart from my children. Perhaps God wills it so. I shall soon die; but you will be a monster.

"Do you not love me? Are you tired of my follies, of my remorse, impious one? Do you wish to ruin me? I give you an easy method. Go, shew this letter to all Verrières, or rather shew it to M. Valenod alone. Tell him that I love you; but no, utter no such blasphemy; tell him that I adore you, that life only began for me on the day when I first saw you; that in the wildest moments of my girlhood, I had never even dreamed of the happiness that I owe to you; that I have sacrificed my life to you, that I am sacrificing my soul to you. You know that I am sacrificing far more.

"But what does he know of sacrifices, that man? Tell him, tell him, to make him angry, that I defy all evil-speakers, and that there is but one misfortune in the world for me, that of beholding a change in the one man who holds me to life. What a blessing for me to lose it, to offer it in sacrifice, and to fear no longer for my children!

"Doubt not, dear friend, if there be an anonymous letter, it comes from that odious being who, for the last six years, has pursued me with his loud voice, with a list of the jumps his horse has taken, with his fatuity and with the endless enumeration of all his advantages.

"Is there an anonymous letter? Wicked one, that is what I wished to discuss with you; but no, you were right. Clasping you in my arms, for the last time perhaps, I could never have discussed the matter calmly, as I do when I am alone. From this moment our happiness will not be so easily secured. Will that be an annoyance to you? Yes, on the days when you have not received some amusing book from M. Fouqué. The sacrifice is made; to-morrow, whether there be an anonymous letter or not, I shall tell my husband that I have received an anonymous letter, that he must instantly provide you with a golden ladder, find some decent pretext, and send you back without delay to your family.

"Alas, dear friend, we are going to be parted for a fortnight, perhaps a month! But there, I do you justice, you will suffer as much as I. Still, this is the only way to counteract the effect of this anonymous letter; it is not the first that my husband has received, and on my account too. Alas! How I have laughed at them!

"The whole purpose of my scheme is to make my husband think that the letter comes from M. Valenod; I have no doubt that he is its author. If you leave the house, do not fail to go and establish yourself at Verrières. I shall contrive that my husband conceives the idea of spending a fortnight there, to prove to the fools that there is no coolness between him and myself. Once you are at Verrières, make friends with everyone, even the Liberals. I know that all the ladies will run after you.

"Do not go and quarrel with M. Valenod, nor crop his ears, as you once threatened; on the contrary, shew him every politeness. The essential thing is that it should be known throughout Verrières that you are going to Valenod's, or to some other house, for the children's education.

"That is what my husband will never stand. Should he resign himself to it, well, at least you will be living in Verrières, and I shall see you sometimes. My children, who are so fond of you, will go to see you. Great God! I feel that I love my children more, because they love you. What remorse! How is all this going to end? I am wandering. . . . Well, you understand what you must do; be gentle, polite, never contemptuous with these vulgar personages, I implore you on my knees: they are to be the arbiters of our destiny. Doubt not for a moment that my husband in dealing with you will conform to whatever *public opinion* may prescribe.

"It is you that are going to provide me with this anonymous letter; arm yourself with patience and a pair of scissors. Cut out of a book the words you will see below; paste them together, with water-glue, on the sheet of blue paper that I send you; it came to me from M. Valenod. Be prepared for a search of your room; burn the pages of the book you mutilate. If you do not find the words ready made, have the patience to compose them letter by letter. To spare you trouble, I have cut the anonymous letter short. Alas! If you no longer love me, as I fear, how long mine must seem to you!

ANONYMOUS LETTER

" 'Madame,

All your little goings on are known; but the persons to whose interest it is to check them have been warned. From a lingering affection for yourself, I beg you to detach yourself entirely from the little peasant. If you have the wisdom to do this, your husband will believe that the warning he has received was misleading, and he will be left in his error. Bear in mind that I know your secret; tremble, unhappy woman; henceforward you must tread a straight path, driven by me.'

"As soon as you have finished pasting together the words that make up this letter (do you recognize the Governor's style in it?) come out of your room, I shall meet you about the house.

"I shall go to the village, and return with a troubled countenance; I shall indeed be greatly troubled. Great

God! What a risk I am running, and all because you *thought you detected* an anonymous letter. Finally, with a woebegone face, I shall give my husband this letter, which will have been handed to me by a stranger. As for you, go for a walk in the direction of the woods with the children, and do not return until dinner time.

"From the rocks above, you can see the tower of the pigeoncote. If all goes well, I shall place a white handkerchief there; if not, you will see nothing.

"Ungrateful wretch, will not your heart find out some way of telling me that you love me, before starting on this walk? Whatever may befall me, be certain of one thing: I should not survive for a day a final parting. Ah! bad mother! These are two idle words that I have written, dear Julien. I do not feel them; I can think only of you at this moment, I have written them only so as not to be blamed by you. Now that I find myself brought to the point of losing you, what use is there in pretence? Yes, let my heart seem black as night to you, but let me not lie to the man whom I adore! I have been all too deceitful already in my life. Go to, I forgive you if you love me no longer. I have not time to read my letter through. It is a small thing in my eyes to pay with my life for the happy days which I have spent in your arms. You know that they will cost me more than life."

CHAPTER TWENTY-ONE

CONVERSATION WITH A LORD AND MASTER

Alas! our frailty is the cause, not we!
For such as we are made of, such we be.
Twelfth Night.

IT was with a childish pleasure that Julien spent an
hour in pasting words together. As he left his room
he came upon his pupils and their mother; she took
the letter with a simplicity and courage, the calmness of
which terrified him.

"Is the gum quite dry?" she asked him.

"Can this be the woman who was being driven mad
by remorse?" he thought. "What are her plans at this
moment?" He was too proud to ask her; but never, perhaps, had she appealed to him more strongly.

"If things go amiss," she went on with the same coolness, "I shall be stripped of everything. Bury this store
somewhere in the mountains; it may some day be my last
resource."

She handed him a glass-topped case, in red morocco,
filled with gold and a few diamonds.

"Go now," she said to him.

She embraced her children, the youngest of them twice
over. Julien stood spellbound. She left him at a rapid
pace and without looking at him again.

From the moment of his opening the anonymous letter,
M. de Rênal's life had been a burden to him. He had

not been so agitated since a duel that he had nearly had
to fight in 1816, and, to do him justice, the prospect of
receiving a bullet in his person would now have distressed
him less. He examined the letter from every angle. "Is
not this a woman's hand?" he asked himself. "In that case,
what woman can have written it?" He considered in turn
all the women he knew at Verrières, without finding a
definite object for his suspicions. Could a man have
dictated the letter? If so, what man? Here again, a
similar uncertainty; he had earned the jealousy and no
doubt the hatred of the majority of the men he knew.
"I must consult my wife," he said to himself, from force
of habit, as he rose from the armchair in which he had
collapsed.

No sooner had he risen than "Good God!" he exclaimed,
clapping his hand to his head, "she is the one person whom
I cannot trust; from this moment she is my enemy." And
tears of anger welled into his eyes.

It was a fitting reward for that barrenness of heart in
which practical wisdom in the provinces is rooted, that the
two men whom, at that moment, M. de Rênal most dreaded
were his two most intimate friends.

"Apart from them, I have ten friends perhaps," and
he turned them over in his mind, calculating the exact
amount of comfort that he would be able to derive from
each. "To all of them, to all of them," he cried in his
rage, "my appalling misfortune will give the most intense
pleasure." Happily for him, he supposed himself to be
greatly envied, and not without reason. Apart from his
superb house in town on which the King of —— had just
conferred everlasting honour by sleeping beneath its roof,
he had made an admirable piece of work of his country
house at Vergy. The front was painted white, and the
windows adorned with handsome green shutters. He was
comforted for a moment by the thought of this magnificence. The fact of the matter was that this mansion was

visible from a distance of three or four leagues, to the great detriment of all the country houses or so-called *châteaux* of the neighbourhood, which had been allowed to retain the humble grey tones imparted to them by time.

M. de Rênal could reckon upon the tears and pity of one of his friends, the churchwarden of the parish; but he was an imbecile who shed tears at everything. This man was nevertheless his sole resource.

"What misfortune is comparable to mine?" he exclaimed angrily. "What isolation!

"Is it possible," this truly pitiable man asked himself, "is it possible that, in my distress, I have not a single friend of whom to ask advice? For my mind is becoming unhinged, I can feel it! Ah, Falcoz! Ah, Ducros!" he cried bitterly. These were the names of two of his boy-hood's friends whom he had alienated by his arrogance in 1814. They were not noble, and he had tried to alter the terms of equality on which they had been living all their lives.

One of them, Falcoz, a man of spirit and heart, a paper merchant at Verrières, had purchased a printing press in the chief town of the Department and had started a news-paper. The *Congregation* had determined to ruin him: his paper had been condemned, his printer's licence had been taken from him. In these unfortunate circumstances he ventured to write to M. de Rênal for the first time in ten years. The Mayor of Verrières felt it incumbent on him to reply in the Ancient Roman style: "If the King's Minister did me the honour to consult me, I should say to him: 'Ruin without compunction all provincial printers, and make printing a monopoly like the sale of tobacco.'" This letter to an intimate friend which had set the whole of Verrières marvelling at the time, M. de Rênal now recalled, word for word, with horror. "Who would have said that with my rank, my fortune, my Crosses, I should one day regret it?" It was in such transports of anger, now against himself, now against all around him, that he passed a night of anguish; but, fortunately, it did not occur to him to spy upon his wife.

"I am used to Louise," he said to himself, "she knows all my affairs; were I free to marry again to-morrow I could find no one fit to take her place." Next, he sought relief in the idea that his wife was innocent; this point of view made it unnecessary for him to shew his strength of character, and was far more convenient; how many slandered wives have we not all seen!

"But what!" he suddenly exclaimed, pacing the floor with a convulsive step, "am I to allow her, as though I were a man of straw, a mere ragamuffin, to make a mock of me with her lover? Is the whole of Verrières to be allowed to sneer at my complacency? What have they not said about Charmier?" (a notorious local cuckold) "When he is mentioned, is there not a smile on every face? He is a good pleader, who is there that ever mentions his talent for public speaking? 'Ah! Charmier!' is what they say; 'Bernard's Charmier.' They actually give him the name of the man that has disgraced him.

"Thank heaven," said M. de Rênal at other moments, "I have no daughter, and the manner in which I am going to punish their mother will not damage the careers of my children; I can surprise that young peasant with my wife, and kill the pair of them; in that event, the tragic outcome of my misfortune may perhaps make it less absurd." This idea appealed to him: he worked it out in the fullest detail. "The Penal Code is on my side, and, whatever happens, our *Congregation* and my friends on the jury will save me." He examined his hunting knife, which had a keen blade; but the thought of bloodshed frightened him.

"I might thrash this insolent tutor black and blue and turn him from the house; but what a stir in Verrières and, indeed, throughout the Department! After the suppression of Falcoz's paper, when his editor came out of prison, I was instrumental in making him lose a place worth six hundred francs. They say that the scribbler has dared to shew his face again in Besançon, he may easily attack me, and so cunningly that it will be impossible to bring him to justice! That insolent fellow will insinuate in a thousand ways that he has been speaking the truth. A man of family, who respects his rank as I do, is always hated by plebeians. I shall see myself in those frightful Paris papers; my God! what degradation! To see the ancient name of Rênal plunged in the mire of ridicule. . . . If I ever travel, I shall have to change my name; what! give up this name which is my pride and my strength. What a crowning infamy!

"If I do not kill my wife, if I drive her from the house with ignominy, she has her aunt at Besançon, who will hand over the whole of her fortune to her on the quiet. My wife will go and live in Paris with Julien; Verrières will hear of it, and I shall again be regarded as a dupe." This unhappy man then perceived, from the failing light of his lamp, that day was beginning to break. He went to seek a breath of air in the garden. At that moment, he had almost made up his mind to create no scene, chiefly because a scene of that sort would fill his good friends at Verrières with joy.

His stroll in the garden calmed him somewhat. "No," he cried, "I shall certainly not part with my wife, she is too useful to me." He pictured to himself with horror what his house would be like without his wife; his sole female relative was the Marquise de R——, who was old, idiotic and evil-minded.

An idea of the greatest good sense occurred to him, but to put it into practice required a strength of character far exceeding the little that the poor man possessed. "If I keep my wife," he said to himself; "I know my own nature; one day, when she taxes my patience, I shall reproach her with her offence. She is proud, we are bound to quarrel, and all this will happen before she has inherited her aunt's estate. And then, how they will all laugh at me! My wife loves her children, it will all come to them in the end. But I, I shall be the talk of Verrières. What, they will say, he couldn't even punish his wife! Would it not be better to stick to my suspicions and to verify nothing? Then I tie my own hands, I cannot afterwards reproach her with anything."

A moment later M. de Rênal, his wounded vanity once more gaining the mastery, was laboriously recalling all the stories told in the billiard-room of the Casino or Noble Club of Verrières, when some fluent talker interrupted the pool to make merry at the expense of some cuckolded husband. How cruel, at that moment, those pleasantries seemed.

"God! Why is not my wife dead! Then I should be immune from ridicule. Why am I not a widower! I should go and spend six months in Paris in the best society." After this momentary happiness caused by the idea of widowhood, his imagination returned to the methods of ascertaining the truth. Should he at midnight, after the whole household had gone to bed, sprinkle a few handfuls of bran outside the door of Julien's room? Next morning, at daybreak, he would see the footprints on it.

"But that would be no good," he broke out angrily, "that wretched Elisa would notice it, and it would be all over the house at once that I am jealous."

In another story that circulated at the Casino, a husband had made certain of his plight by fastening a hair with a little wax so as to seal up the doors of his wife's room and her lover's.

After so many hours of vacillation, this method of obtaining enlightenment seemed to him decidedly the best, and he was thinking of adopting it, when at a bend in the path he came upon that wife whom he would have liked to see dead.

She was returning from the village. She had gone to hear mass in the church of Vergy. A tradition of extremely doubtful value in the eyes of the cold philosopher, but one in which she believed, made out that the little church now in use had been the chapel of the castle of the Lord of Vergy. This thought obsessed Madame de Rênal throughout the time which she had meant to pass in prayer in this church. She kept on picturing to herself her husband killing Julien during the chase, as though by accident, and afterwards, that evening, making her eat his heart.

"My fate," she said to herself, "depends on what he will think when he hears me. After these terrible moments, perhaps I shall not find another opportunity to speak to him. He is not a wise creature, swayed by reason. I might, if he were, with the aid of my own feeble wits, forecast what he would do or say. But my fate lies in my cunning, in the art of directing the thoughts of this whimsical creature, who becomes blind with anger and incapable of seeing things. Great God! I require talent, coolness, where am I to find them?"

She recovered her calm as though by magic on entering the garden and seeing her husband in the distance. The disorder of his hair and clothes shewed that he had not slept.

She handed him a letter which, though the seal was broken, was still folded. He, without opening it, gazed at his wife with madness in his eyes.

"Here is an abomination," she said to him, "which an evil looking man who claims to know you and that you owe him a debt of gratitude, handed to me as I came past the back of the lawyer's garden. One thing I must ask of you, and that is that you send back to his own people, and without delay, that Monsieur Julien." Madame de Rênal made haste to utter this name, even beginning a little too soon perhaps, in order to rid herself of the fearful prospect of having to utter it.

She was filled with joy on beholding the joy that it gave her husband. From the fixed stare which he directed at her she realized that Julien had guessed aright. Instead of worrying about a very present trouble, "what intelligence," she thought to herself. "What perfect tact! And in a young man still quite devoid of experience! To what heights will he not rise in time? Alas! Then his success will make him forget me."

This little act of admiration of the man she adored completely restored her composure.

She congratulated herself on the step she had taken. "I have proved myself not unworthy of Julien," she said to herself, with a sweet and secret relish.

Without saying a word, for fear of committing himself, M. de Rênal examined this second anonymous letter composed, as the reader may remember, of printed words gummed upon a sheet of paper of a bluish tinge. "They are making a fool of me in every way," M. de Rênal said to himself, utterly worn out.

"Fresh insults to be looked into, and all owing to my wife!" He was on the point of deluging her with a stream of the coarsest invective; the thought of the fortune awaiting her at Besançon just stopped him. Overpowered by the necessity of venting his anger on something, he tore up the sheet on which this second anonymous letter was gummed, and strode rapidly away, feeling that he could not endure his wife's company. A minute later, he returned to her, already more calm.

"We must take action at once and dismiss Julien," she immediately began; "after all he is only the son of a working man. You can compensate him with a few crowns, besides, he is clever and can easily find another place, with M. Valenod, for instance, or the Sub-Prefect

Maugiron; they both have families. And so you will not
be doing him any harm. . . ."

"You speak like the fool that you are," cried M. de
Rênal in a voice of thunder. "How can one expect common sense of a woman? You never pay attention to what
is reasonable; how should you have any knowledge? Your
carelessness, your laziness leave you just enough activity
to chase butterflies, feeble creatures which we are so unfortunate as to have in our households. . . ."

Madame de Rênal let him speak, and he spoke at length;
he *passed his anger*, as they say in those parts.

"Sir," she answered him finally, "I speak as a woman
whose honour, that is to say her most priceless possession,
has been outraged."

Madame de Rênal preserved an unalterable calm throughout the whole of this trying conversation, upon which
depended the possibility of her continuing to live beneath
the same roof as Julien. She sought out the ideas that
seemed to her best fitted to guide her husband's blind
anger. She had remained unmoved by all the insulting
remarks that he had addressed to her, she did not hear
them, she was thinking all the time of Julien. "Will he
be pleased with me?"

"This little peasant upon whom we have lavished every
attention, including presents, may be innocent," she said
at length, "but he is none the less the occasion of the first
insult I have ever received. . . . Sir, when I read that
abominable document, I vowed that either he or I should
leave your roof."

"Do you wish to create a scandal that will dishonour
me and yourself as well? You'll be giving a fine treat
to many people in Verrières."

"That is true; they are all jealous of the state of prosperity to which your wise management has brought you,
your family and the town. . . . Very well, I shall go and
bid Julien ask you for leave to spend a month with that

timber merchant in the mountains, a fit companion for
that little workman."

"Take care what you do," put in M. de Rênal, calmly
enough. "The one thing I must insist on is that you do
not speak to him. You would shew temper and make him
cross with me; you know how touchy the little gentleman is."

"That young man has no tact," went on Madame de
Rênal; "he may be learned, you know about that, but
at bottom he is nothing but a peasant. For my own part,
I have never had any opinion of him since he refused to
marry Elisa, it was a fortune ready made; and all because
now and again she pays a secret visit to M. Valenod."

"Ah!" said M. de Rênal, raising his eyebrows as far
as they would go, "what, did Julien tell you that?"

"No, not exactly; he has always spoken to me of the
vocation that is calling him to the sacred ministry; but
believe me, the first vocation for the lower orders is to
find their daily bread. He made it fairly clear to me that
he was not unaware of these secret visits."

"And I, I, knew nothing about them!" cried M. de
Rênal, all his fury returning, emphasizing every word.
"There are things going on in my house of which I know
nothing. . . . What! There has been something between
Elisa and Valenod?"

"Oh, that's an old story, my dear friend," Madame de
Rênal said laughing, "and I daresay no harm was done.
It was in the days when your good friend Valenod would
not have been sorry to have it thought in Verrières that
there was a little love—of a purely platonic sort—ex-
changed between him and me."

"I had that idea at one time," cried M. de Rênal striking his head in his fury as he advanced from one discovery to another, "and you never said a word to me
about it?"

"Was I to make trouble between two friends all for a little outburst of vanity on the part of our dear Governor? What woman is there in society to whom he has not addressed one or more letters, extremely witty and even a trifle gallant?"

"Has he written to you?"

"He writes frequently."

"Shew me his letters this instant, I order you"; and M. de Rênal added six feet to his stature.

"I shall do nothing of the sort," the answer came in a tone so gentle as to be almost indifferent, "I shall let you see them some other day, when you are more yourself."

"This very instant, damn it!" cried M. de Rênal, blind with rage, and yet happier than he had been at any time in the last twelve hours.

"Will you swear to me," said Madame de Rênal solemnly, "never to quarrel with the Governor of the Poorhouse over these letters?"

"Quarrel or no quarrel, I can take the foundlings away from him; but," he continued, furiously, "I want those letters this instant; where are they?"

"In a drawer in my desk; but you may be certain, I shall not give you the key of it."

"I shall be able to force it," he cried as he made off in the direction of his wife's room.

He did indeed break open with an iron bar a valuable mahogany writing desk, imported from Paris, which he used often to polish with the tail of his coat when he thought he detected a spot on its surface.

Madame de Rênal meanwhile had run up the hundred and twenty steps of the dovecote; she knotted the corner of a white handkerchief to one of the iron bars of the little window. She was the happiest of women. With tears in her eyes she gazed out at the wooded slopes of the mountain. "Doubtless," she said to herself, "beneath one of those spreading beeches, Julien is watching for this glad signal." For long she strained her ears, then cursed the monotonous drone of the grasshoppers and the twitter of the birds. But for those tiresome sounds, a cry of joy, issuing from among the rocks, might have reached her in her tower. Her ravening gaze devoured that immense slope of dusky verdure, unbroken as the surface of a meadow, that was formed by the treetops. "How is it he has not the sense," she asked herself with deep emotion, "to think of some signal to tell me that his happiness is no less than mine?" She came down from the dovecote only when she began to be afraid that her husband might come up in search of her.

She found him foaming with rage. He was running through M. Valenod's anodyne sentences, that were little used to being read with such emotion.

Seizing a moment in which a lull in her husband's exclamations gave her a chance to make herself heard:

"I cannot get away from my original idea," said Madame de Rênal, "Julien ought to go for a holiday. Whatever talent he may have for Latin, he is nothing more, after all, than a peasant who is often coarse and wanting in tact; every day, thinking he is being polite, he plies me with extravagant compliments in the worst of taste, which he learns by heart from some novel. . . ."

"He never reads any," cried M. de Rênal; "I am positive as to that. Do you suppose that I am a blind master who knows nothing of what goes on under his roof?"

"Very well, if he doesn't read those absurd compliments anywhere, he invents them, which is even worse. He will have spoken of me in that tone in Verrières; and, without going so far," said Madame de Rênal, with the air of one making a discovery, "he will have spoken like that before Elisa, which is just as though he had spoken to M. Valenod."

"Ah!" cried M. de Rênal, making the table and the whole room shake with one of the stoutest blows that

human fist ever gave, "the anonymous letter in print and
Valenod's letters were all on the same paper."

"At last!" thought Madame de Rênal; she appeared
thunderstruck by this discovery, and without having the
courage to add a single word went and sat down on the
divan, at the farther end of the room.

The battle was now won; she had her work cut out
to prevent M. de Rênal from going and talking to the
supposed author of the anonymous letter.

"How is it you do not feel that to make a scene, without
sufficient proof, with M. Valenod would be the most
deplorable error? If you are envied, Sir, who is to blame?
Your own talents: your wise administration, the buildings
you have erected with such good taste, the dowry I
brought you, and above all the considerable fortune we
may expect to inherit from my worthy aunt, a fortune the
extent of which is vastly exaggerated, have made you the
principal person in Verrières."

"You forget my birth," said M. de Rênal, with a faint
smile.

"You are one of the most distinguished gentlemen in the
province," Madame de Rênal hastily added; "if the King
were free and could do justice to birth, you would doubtless be figuring in the House of Peers," and so forth.
"And in this magnificent position do you seek to provide
jealousy with food for comment?

"To speak to M. Valenod of his anonymous letter is to
proclaim throughout Verrières, or rather in Besançon,
throughout the Province, that this petty cit, admitted perhaps imprudently to the friendship of *a Rênal,* has found
out a way to insult him. Did these letters which you
have just discovered prove that I had responded to M.
Valenod's overtures, then it would be for you to kill me, I
should have deserved it a hundred times, but not to shew
anger with him. Think that all your neighbours only

await a pretext to be avenged for your superiority; think
that in 1816 you were instrumental in securing certain
arrests. That man who took refuge on your roof. . . ."

"What I think is that you have neither respect nor
affection for me," shouted M. de Rênal with all the bitter-
ness that such a memory aroused, "and I have not been
made a Peer!"

"I think, my friend," put in Madame de Rênal with a
smile, "that I shall one day be richer than you, that I
have been your companion for twelve years, and that
on all these counts I ought to have a voice in your councils,
especially in this business to-day. If you prefer Monsieur
Julien to me," she added with ill-concealed scorn, "I
am prepared to go and spend the winter with my aunt."

This threat was uttered *with gladness*. It contained
the firmness which seeks to cloak itself in courtesy; it
determined M. de Rênal. But, obeying the provincial
custom, he continued to speak for a long time, harked back
to every argument in turn; his wife allowed him to speak,
there was still anger in his tone. At length, two hours of
futile discourse wore out the strength of a man who had
been helpless with rage all night. He determined upon
the line of conduct which he was going to adopt towards
M. Valenod, Julien, and even Elisa.

Once or twice, during this great scene, Madame de
Rênal came within an ace of feeling a certain sympathy
for the very real distress of this man who for ten years
had been her friend. But our true passions are selfish.
Moreover she was expecting every moment an avowal of
the anonymous letter which he had received overnight,
and this avowal never came. To gain complete confidence,
Madame de Rênal required to know what ideas might have
been suggested to the man upon whom her fate depended.
For, in the country, husbands control public opinion. A
husband who denounces his wife covers himself with
ridicule, a thing that every day is becoming less dangerous

in France; but his wife, if he does not supply her with money, declines to the position of a working woman at fifteen sous daily, and even then the virtuous souls have scruples about employing her.

An odalisque in the seraglio may love the Sultan with all her heart; he is all powerful, she has no hope of evading his authority by a succession of clever little tricks. The master's vengeance is terrible, bloody, but martial and noble: a dagger blow ends everything. It is with blows dealt by public contempt that a husband kills his wife in the nineteenth century; it is by shutting the doors of all the drawing-rooms in her face.

The sense of danger was keenly aroused in Madame de Rênal on her return to her own room; she was horrified by the disorder in which she found it. The locks of all her pretty little boxes had been broken; several planks in the floor had been torn up. "He would have been without pity for me!" she told herself. "To spoil so this floor of coloured parquet, of which he is so proud; when one of his children comes in with muddy shoes, he flushes with rage. And now it is ruined for ever!" The sight of this violence rapidly silenced the last reproaches with which she had been blaming herself for her too rapid victory.

Shortly before the dinner bell sounded, Julien returned with the children. At dessert, when the servants had left the room, Madame de Rênal said to him very drily.

"You expressed the desire to me to go and spend a fortnight at Verrières; M. de Rênal is kind enough to grant you leave. You can go as soon as you please. But, so that the children shall not waste any time, their lessons will be sent to you every day, for you to correct."

"Certainly," M. de Rênal added in a most bitter tone, "I shall not allow you more than a week."

Julien read in his features the uneasiness of a man in cruel torment.

"He has not yet come to a decision," he said to his

mistress, during a moment of solitude in the drawing-room.

Madame de Rênal informed him rapidly of all that she had done since the morning.

"The details to-night," she added laughing.

"The perversity of woman!" thought Julien. "What pleasure, what instinct leads them to betray us?

"I find you at once enlightened and blinded by your love," he said to her with a certain coldness; "your behaviour to-day has been admirable; but is there any prudence in our attempting to see each other to-night? This house is paved with enemies; think of the passionate hatred that Elisa has for me."

"That hatred greatly resembles the passionate indifference that you must have for me."

"Indifferent or not, I am bound to save you from a peril into which I have plunged you. If chance decrees that M. de Rênal speaks to Elisa, by a single word she may disclose everything to him. What is to prevent him from hiding outside my room, well armed. . . ."

"What! Lacking in courage even!" said Madame de Rênal, with all the pride of a woman of noble birth.

"I shall never sink so low as to speak of my courage," said Julien coldly, "that is mean. Let the world judge by my actions. But," he went on, taking her hand, "you cannot conceive how attached I am to you, and what a joy it is to me to be able to take leave of you before this cruel parting."

CHAPTER TWENTY-TWO

MANNERS AND CUSTOMS IN 1830

Speech was given to man to enable him to conceal his thoughts.

MALAGRIDA, S. J.

THE first thing that Julien did on arriving in Verrières was to reproach himself for his unfairness to Madame de Rênal. "I should have despised her as a foolish woman if from weakness she had failed to bring off the scene with M. de Rênal! She carried it through like a diplomat, and my sympathies are with the loser, who is my enemy. There is a streak of middle-class pettiness in my nature; my vanity is hurt, because M. de Rênal is a man! That vast and illustrious corporation to which I have the honour to belong; I am a perfect fool."

M. Chélan had refused the offers of hospitality which the most respected Liberals of the place had vied with one another in making him, when his deprivation drove him from the presbytery. The pair of rooms which he had taken were littered with his books. Julien, wishing to shew Verrières what it meant to be a priest, went and fetched from his father's store a dozen planks of firewood, which he carried on his back the whole length of the main street. He borrowed some tools from an old friend and had soon constructed a sort of bookcase in which he arranged M. Chélan's library.

"I supposed you to have been corrupted by the vanity of the world," said the old man, shedding tears of joy; "this quite redeems the childishness of that dazzling guard of honour uniform which made you so many enemies."

M. de Rênal had told Julien to put up in his house. No one had any suspicion of what had happened. On the third day after his arrival, there came up to his room no less a personage than the Sub-Prefect, M. de Maugiron. It was only after two solid hours of insipid tittle-tattle, and long jeremiads on the wickedness of men, on the lack of honesty in the people entrusted with the administration of public funds, on the dangers besetting poor France, etc., etc., that Julien saw him come at length to the purpose of his visit. They were already on the landing, and the poor tutor, on the verge of disgrace, was ushering out with all due respect the future Prefect of some fortunate Department, when it pleased the latter gentleman to occupy himself with Julien's career, to praise his moderation where his own interests were concerned, etc., etc. Finally M. de Maugiron, taking him in his arms in the most fatherly manner, suggested to him that he should leave M. de Rênal and enter the household of an official who had children to educate, and who, like King Philip, would thank heaven, not so much for having given him them as for having caused them to be born in the neighbourhood of M. Julien. Their tutor would receive a salary of eight hundred francs, payable not month by month, "which is not noble," said M. de Maugiron, but quarterly, and in advance to boot.

It was now the turn of Julien who, for an hour and a half, had been waiting impatiently for an opportunity to speak. His reply was perfect, and as long as a pastoral charge; it let everything be understood, and at the same time said nothing definite. A listener would have found in it at once respect for M. de Rênal, veneration for the people of Verrières and gratitude towards the illustrious Sub-Prefect. The said Sub-Prefect, astonished at finding a bigger Jesuit than himself, tried in vain to obtain something positive. Julien, overjoyed, seized the opportunity to try his skill and began his answer over again in different terms. Never did the most eloquent Minister, seeking to monopolize the last hours of a sitting when the Chamber seems inclined to wake up, say less in more words. As soon as M. de Maugiron had left him, Julien broke out in helpless laughter. To make the most of his Jesuitical bent, he wrote a letter of nine pages to M. de Rênal, in which he informed him of everything that had been said to him, and humbly asked his advice. "Why, that rascal never even told me the name of the person who is making the offer! It will be M. Valenod, who sees in my banishment to Verrières the effect of his anonymous letter."

His missive dispatched, Julien, as happy as a hunter who at six in the morning on a fine autumn day emerges upon a plain teeming with game, went out to seek the advice of M. Chélan. But before he arrived at the good curé's house, heaven, which was anxious to shower its blessings on him, threw him into the arms of M. Valenod, from whom he did not conceal the fact that his heart was torn; a penniless youth like himself was bound to devote himself entirely to the vocation which heaven had placed in his heart, but a vocation was not everything in this vile world. To be a worthy labourer in the Lord's vineyard, and not to be altogether unworthy of all one's learned fellow-labourers, one required education; one required to spend in the seminary at Besançon two very expensive years; it became indispensable, therefore—and, one might, in a certain sense, say, a duty—to save money, which was considerably easier with a salary of eight hundred francs paid quarterly, than with six hundred francs which melted away month by month. On the other hand, did not heaven, by placing him with the Rênal boys, and above all by inspiring in him a particular attachment to them, seem to indicate to him that it would be a mistake to abandon this form of education for another? . . .

Julien arrived at such a pitch of perfection in this kind -

of eloquence, which has taken the place of the swiftness of action of the Empire, that he ended by growing tired of the sound of his own voice.

Returning to the house he found one of M. Valenod's servants in full livery, who had been looking for him all over the town, with a note inviting him to dinner that very day.

Never had Julien set foot in the man's house; only a few days earlier, his chief thought was how he might give him a thorough good thrashing without subsequent action by the police. Although dinner was not to be until one o'clock, Julien thought it more respectful to present himself at half past twelve in the study of the Governor of the Poorhouse. He found him displaying his importance amid a mass of papers. His huge black whiskers, his enormous quantity of hair, his night-cap poised askew on the top of his head, his immense pipe, his embroidered slippers, the heavy gold chains slung across his chest in every direction, and all the equipment of a provincial financier, who imagines himself to be a ladies' man, made not the slightest impression upon Julien; he only thought all the more of the thrashing that he owed him.

He craved the honour of being presented to Madame Valenod; she was making her toilet and could not see him. To make up for this, he had the privilege of witnessing that of the Governor of the Poorhouse. They then proceeded to join Madame Valenod, who presented her children to him with tears in her eyes. This woman, one of the most important people in Verrières, had a huge masculine face, which she had plastered with rouge for this great ceremony. She displayed all the pathos of maternal feelings.

Julien thought of Madame de Rênal. His distrustful nature made him scarcely susceptible to any memories save those that are evoked by contrast, but such memories moved him to tears. This tendency was increased by the sight

of the Governor's house. He was taken through it. Everything in it was sumptuous and new, and he was told the
price of each article. But Julien felt that there was
something mean about it, a taint of stolen money. Everyone, even the servants, wore a bold air that seemed to be
fortifying them against contempt.

The collector of taxes, the receiver of customs, the chief
constable and two or three other public officials arrived
with their wives. They were followed by several wealthy
Liberals. Dinner was announced. Julien, already in the
worst of humours, suddenly reflected that on the other
side of the dining-room wall there were wretched prisoners, whose rations of meat had perhaps been *squeezed* to
purchase all this tasteless splendour with which his hosts
sought to dazzle him.

"They are hungry perhaps at this moment," he said
to himself; his throat contracted, he found it impossible
to eat and almost to speak. It was much worse a quarter
of an hour later; they could hear in the distance a few
snatches of a popular and, it must be admitted, not too
refined song which one of the inmates was singing. M.
Valenod glanced at one of his men in full livery, who left
the room, and presently the sound of singing ceased. At
that moment, a footman offered Julien some Rhine wine
in a green glass, and Madame Valenod took care to inform
him that this wine cost nine francs the bottle, direct
from the grower. Julien, the green glass in his hand,
said to M. Valenod:

"I don't hear that horrid song any more."

"Gad! I should think not, indeed," replied the Governor triumphantly. "I've made the rascal shut up."

This was too much for Julien; he had acquired the manners but had not yet the heart appropriate to his station.
Despite all his hypocrisy, which he kept in such constant
practice, he felt a large tear trickle down his cheek.

He tried to hide it with the green glass, but it was

simply impossible for him to do honour to the Rhine wine.
"Stop the man singing!" he murmured to himself, "O my
God, and Thou permittest it!"

Fortunately for him, no one noticed his ill-bred emotion.
The collector of taxes had struck up a royalist ditty. During the clamour of the refrain, sung in chorus: "There,"
Julien's conscience warned him, "you have the sordid
fortune which you will achieve, and you will enjoy it only
in these conditions and in such company as this! You
will have a place worth perhaps twenty thousand francs,
but it must be that while you gorge to repletion you stop
the poor prisoner from singing; you will give dinner
parties with the money you have filched from his miserable
pittance, and during your dinner he will be more wretched
still! O Napoleon! How pleasant it was in thy time to
climb to fortune through the dangers of a battle; but
meanly to intensify the sufferings of the wretched!"

I admit that the weakness which Julien displays in this
monologue gives me a poor opinion of him. He would
be a worthy colleague for those conspirators in yellow
gloves, who profess to reform all the conditions of life in
a great country, and would be horrified at having to
undergo the slightest inconvenience themselves.

Julien was sharply recalled to his proper part. It was
not that he might dream and say nothing that he had been
invited to dine in such good company.

A retired calico printer, a corresponding member of the
Academy of Besançon and of that of Uzès, was speaking
to him, down the whole length of the table, inquiring
whether all that was commonly reported as to his astonishing prowess in the study of the New Testament was true.

A profound silence fell instantly; a New Testament
appeared as though by magic in the hands of the learned
member of the two academies. Julien having answered in
the affirmative, a few words in Latin were read out to him
at random. He began to recite: his memory did not

betray him, and this prodigy was admired with all the noisy energy of the end of a dinner. Julien studied the glowing faces of the women. Several of them were not ill looking. He had made out the wife of the collector who sang so well.

"Really, I am ashamed to go on speaking Latin so long before these ladies," he said, looking at her. "If M. Rubigneau" (this was the member of the two academies) "will be so good as to read out any sentence in Latin, instead of going on with the Latin text, I shall endeavour to improvize a translation."

This second test set the crown of glory on his achievement.

There were in the room a number of Liberals, men of means, but the happy fathers of children who were capable of winning bursaries, and in this capacity suddenly converted after the last Mission. Despite this brilliant stroke of policy, M. de Rênal had never consented to have them in his house. These worthy folk, who knew Julien only by reputation and from having seen him on horseback on the day of the King of ——'s visit, were his most vociferous admirers. "When will these fools tire of listening to this Biblical language, of which they understand nothing?" he thought. On the contrary, this language amused them by it unfamiliarity; they laughed at it. But Julien had grown tired.

He rose gravely as six o'clock struck and mentioned a chapter of the new theology of Liguori, which he had to learn by heart in order to repeat it next day to M. Chélan. "For my business," he added pleasantly, "is to make other people repeat lessons, and to repeat them myself."

His audience laughed heartily and applauded; this is the kind of wit that goes down at Verrières. Julien was by this time on his feet, everyone else rose, regardless of decorum; such is the power of genius. Madame Valenod kept him for a quarter of an hour longer; he really must hear the children repeat their catechism; they made the most absurd mistakes which he alone noticed. He made no attempt to correct them. "What ignorance of the first principles of religion," he thought. At length he said good-bye and thought that he might escape; but the children must next attempt one of La Fontaine's Fables.

"That author is most immoral," Julien said to Madame Valenod; "in one of his Fables on Messire Jean Chouart, he has ventured to heap ridicule on all that is most venerable. He is strongly reproved by the best commentators."

Before leaving the house Julien received four or five invitations to dinner. "This young man does honour to the Department," his fellow-guests, in great hilarity, were all exclaiming at once. They went so far as to speak of a pension voted out of the municipal funds, to enable him to continue his studies in Paris.

While this rash idea was making the dining-room ring, Julien had stolen away to the porch. "Oh, what scum! What scum!" he murmured three or four times, as he treated himself to the pleasure of drinking in the fresh air.

He felt himself a thorough aristocrat for the moment, he who for long had been so shocked by the disdainful smile and the haughty superiority which he found lurking behind all the compliments that were paid him at M. de Rênal's. He could not help feeling the extreme difference. "Even if we forget," he said to himself as he walked away, "that the money has been stolen from the poor prisoners, and that they are forbidden to sing as well, would it ever occur to M. de Rênal to tell his guests the price of each bottle of wine that he offers them? And this M. Valenod, in going over the list of his property, which he does incessantly, cannot refer to his house, his land and all the rest of it, if his wife is present, without saying *your* house, *your* land."

This lady, apparently so conscious of the joy of ownership, had just made an abominable scene, during dinner, with a servant who had broken a wineglass and *spoiled one of her sets;* and the servant had answered her with the most gross insolence.

"What a household!" thought Julien; "if they were to give me half of all the money they steal, I wouldn't live among them. One fine day I should give myself away; I should be unable to keep back the contempt they inspire in me."

He was obliged, nevertheless, obeying Madame de Rênal's orders, to attend several dinners of this sort; Julien was the fashion; people forgave him his uniform and the guard of honour, or rather that imprudent display was the true cause of his success. Soon, the only question discussed in Verrières was who would be successful in the struggle to secure the learned young man's services, M. de Rênal or the Governor of the Poorhouse. These two gentlemen formed with M. Maslon a triumvirate which for some years past had tyrannized over the town. People were jealous of the Mayor, the Liberals had grounds for complaint against him; but after all he was noble and created to fill a superior station, whereas M. Valenod's father had not left him an income of six hundred livres. He had been obliged to pass from the stage of being pitied for the shabby apple-green coat in which everybody remembered him in his younger days to that of being envied for his Norman horses, his gold chains, the clothes he ordered from Paris, in short, all his present prosperity.

In the welter of this world so new to Julien he thought he had discovered an honest man; this was a geometrician, was named Gros and was reckoned a Jacobin. Julien, having made a vow never to say anything except what he himself believed to be false, was obliged to make a show of being suspicious of M. Gros. He received from Vergy large packets of exercises. He was advised to see much of his father, and complied with this painful necessity. In a word, he was quite redeeming his reputation, when one morning he was greatly surprised to find himself awakened by a pair of hands which were clapped over his eyes.

It was Madame de Rênal who had come in to town and, running upstairs four steps at a time and leaving her children occupied with a favourite rabbit that they had brought with them, had reached Julien's room a minute in advance of them. The moment was delicious but all too brief: Madame de Rênal had vanished when the children arrived with the rabbit, which they wanted to shew to their friend. Julien welcomed them all, including the rabbit. He seemed to be once more one of a family party; he felt that he loved these children, that it amused him to join in their chatter. He was amazed by the sweetness of their voices, the simplicity and nobility of their manners; he required to wash his imagination clean of all the vulgar behaviour, all the unpleasant thoughts the atmosphere of which he had to breathe at Verrières. There was always the dread of bankruptcy, wealth and poverty were always fighting for the upper hand. The people with whom he dined, in speaking of the joint on their table, made confidences humiliating to themselves, and nauseating to their hearers.

"You aristocrats, you have every reason to be proud," he said to Madame de Rênal. And he told her of all the dinners he had endured.

"Why, so you are in the fashion!" And she laughed heartily at the thought of the rouge which Madame Valenod felt herself obliged to put on whenever she expected Julien. "I believe she has designs on your heart," she added.

Luncheon was a joy. The presence of the children, albeit apparently a nuisance, increased as a matter of fact the general enjoyment. These poor children did not know how to express their delight at seeing Julien again. The servants had not failed to inform them that he was being offered two hundred francs more to "bring up" the little Valenods.

In the middle of luncheon, Stanislas Xavier, still pale

after his serious illness, suddenly asked his mother what was the value of his silver spoon and fork and of the mug out of which he was drinking.

"Why do you want to know?"

"I want to sell them to give the money to M. Julien, so that he shan't be a *dupe* to stay with us."

Julien embraced him, the tears standing in his eyes. The mother wept outright, while Julien, who had taken Stanislas on his knees, explained to him that he must not use the word *dupe,* which, employed in that sense, was a servant's expression. Seeing the pleasure he was giving Madame de Rênal, he tried to explain, by picturesque examples, which amused the children, what was meant by a dupe.

"I understand," said Stanislas, "it's the crow who is silly and drops his cheese, which is picked up by the fox, who is a flatterer."

Madame de Rênal, wild with joy, smothered her children in kisses, which she could hardly do without leaning slightly upon Julien.

Suddenly the door opened; it was M. de Rênal. His stern, angry face formed a strange contrast with the innocent gaiety which his presence banished. Madame de Rênal turned pale; she felt herself incapable of denying anything. Julien seized the opportunity and, speaking very loud, began to tell the Mayor the incident of the silver mug which Stanislas wanted to sell. He was sure that this story would be ill received. At the first word M. de Rênal frowned, from force of habit at the mere name of silver. "The mention of that metal," he would say, "is always a preliminary to some call upon my purse."

But here there was more than money at stake; there was an increase of his suspicions. The air of happiness which animated his family in his absence was not calculated to improve matters with a man dominated by so sensitive a vanity. When his wife praised the graceful and witty manner in which Julien imparted fresh ideas to his pupils:

"Yes, yes, I know, he is making me odious to my children; it is very easy for him to be a hundred times pleasanter to them than I, who am, after all, the master. Everything tends in these days to bring *lawful* authority into contempt. Unhappy France!"

Madame de Rênal did not stop to examine the implications of her husband's manner. She had just seen the possibility of spending twelve hours in Julien's company. She had any number of purchases to make in the town, and declared that she absolutely must dine in a tavern; in spite of anything her husband might say or do, she clung to her idea. The children were in ecstasies at the mere word *tavern*, which modern prudery finds such pleasure in pronouncing.

M. de Rênal left his wife in the first linendraper's shop that she entered, to go and pay some calls. He returned more gloomy than in the morning; he was convinced that the whole town was thinking about nothing but himself and Julien. As a matter of fact, no one had as yet allowed him to form any suspicion of the offensive element in the popular comments. Those that had been repeated to the Mayor had dealt exclusively with the question whether Julien would remain with him at six hundred francs or would accept the eight hundred francs offered by the Governor of the Poorhouse.

The said Governor, when he met M. de Rênal in society, gave him the cold shoulder. His behaviour was not without a certain subtlety; there is not much thoughtless action in the provinces: sensations are so infrequent there that people suppress them.

M. Valenod was what is called, a hundred leagues from Paris, a *faraud;* this is a species marked by coarseness and natural effrontery. His triumphant existence, since 1815, had confirmed him in his habits. He reigned, so to speak, at Verrières, under the orders of M. de Rênal; but being far more active, blushing at nothing, interfering in everything, everlastingly going about, writing, speaking, forgetting humiliations, having no personal pretensions, he had succeeded in equalling the credit of his Mayor in the eyes of ecclesiastical authority. M. Valenod had as good as told the grocers of the place: "Give me the two biggest fools among you"; the lawyers: "Point me out the two most ignorant"; the officers of health: "Let me have your two biggest rascals." When he had collected the most shameless representatives of each profession, he had said to them: "Let us reign together."

The manners of these men annoyed M. de Rênal. Valenod's coarse nature was offended by nothing, not even when the young abbé Maslon gave him the lie direct in public.

But, in the midst of this prosperity, M. Valenod was obliged to fortify himself by little insolences in points of detail against the harsh truths which he was well aware that everyone was entitled to address to him. His activity had multiplied since the alarms which M. Appert's visit had left in its wake. He had made three journeys to Besançon; he wrote several letters for each mail; he sent others by unknown messengers who came to his house at nightfall. He had been wrong perhaps in securing the deprivation of the old curé Chélan; for this vindictive action had made him be regarded, by several pious ladies of good birth, as a profoundly wicked man. Moreover this service rendered had placed him in the absolute power of the Grand Vicar de Frilair, from whom he received strange orders. He had reached this stage in his career when he yielded to the pleasure of writing an anonymous letter. To add to his embarrassment, his wife informed him that she wished to have Julien in the house; the idea appealed to her vanity.

In this situation, M. Valenod foresaw a final rupture

with his former confederate M. de Rênal. The Mayor
would address him in harsh language, which mattered
little enough to him; but he might write to Besançon, or
even to Paris. A cousin of some Minister or other might
suddenly descend upon Verrières and take over the Gover-
norship of the Poorhouse. M. Valenod thought of making
friends with the Liberals; it was for this reason that several of them were invited to the dinner at which Julien
recited. He would find powerful support there against
the Mayor. But an election might come, and it went
without saying that the Poorhouse and a vote for the wrong
party were incompatible. The history of these tactics,
admirably divined by Madame de Rênal, had been imparted to Julien while he gave her his arm to escort her
from one shop to another, and little by little had carried
them to the Cours de la Fidélité, where they spent some
hours, almost as peaceful as the hours at Vergy.

At this period, M. Valenod was seeking to avoid a final
rupture with his former chief, by himself adopting a bold
air towards him. On the day of which we treat, this
system proved successful, but increased the Mayor's ill
humour.

Never can vanity, at grips with all the nastiest and
shabbiest elements of a petty love of money, have plunged
a man in a more wretched state than that in which M.
de Rênal found himself, at the moment of his entering
the tavern. Never, on the contrary, had his children been
gayer or more joyful. The contrast goaded him to fury.

"I am not wanted in my own family, so far as I can
see!" he said as he entered, in a tone which he sought to
make imposing.

By way of reply, his wife drew him aside and explained
to him the necessity of getting rid of Julien. The hours
of happiness she had just enjoyed had given her back
the ease and resolution necessary for carrying out the
plan of conduct which she had been meditating for the

last fortnight. What really and completely dismayed the poor Mayor of Verrières was that he knew that people joked publicly in the town at the expense of his attachment to *hard cash*: M. Valenod was as generous as a robber, whereas he had shewn himself in a prudent rather than a brilliant light in the last five or six subscription lists for the Confraternity of Saint Joseph, the Congregation of Our Lady, the Congregation of the Blessed Sacrament, and so forth.

Among the country gentlemen of Verrières and the neighbourhood, skilfully classified in the lists compiled by the collecting Brethren, according to the amount of their offerings, the name of M. de Rênal had more than once been seen figuring upon the lowest line. In vain might he protest that he *earned nothing*. The clergy allow no joking on that subject.

CHAPTER TWENTY-THREE

THE SORROWS OF AN OFFICIAL

Il piacere di alzar la testa tutto l'anno è ben pagato
da certi quarti d'ora che bisogna passar.

CASTI.

BUT let us leave this little man to his little fears;
why has he taken into his house a man of feeling,
when what he required was the soul of a flunkey?
Why does he not know how to select his servants? The
ordinary procedure of the nineteenth century is that when
a powerful and noble personage encounters a man of feeling, he kills, exiles, imprisons or so humiliates him that
the other, like a fool, dies of grief. In this instance it
so happens that it is not yet the man of feeling who suf-
fers. The great misfortune of the small towns of France
and of elected governments, like that of New York, is
an inability to forget that there exist in the world persons like M. de Rênal. In a town of twenty thousand
inhabitants, these men form public opinion, and public
opinion is a terrible force in a country that has the Char-
ter. A man endowed with a noble soul, of generous in-
stincts, who would have been your friend did he not live
a hundred leagues away, judges you by the public opinion
of your town, which is formed by the fools whom chance
has made noble, rich and moderate. Woe to him who
distinguishes himself!

Immediately after dinner, they set off again for Vergy;
but, two days later, Julien saw the whole family return
to Verrières.

An hour had not gone by before, greatly to his surprise, he discovered that Madame de Rênal was making a mystery of something. She broke off her conversations with her husband as soon as he appeared, and seemed almost to wish him to go away. Julien did not wait to be told twice. He became cold and reserved; Madame de Rênal noticed this, and did not seek an explanation. "Is she going to provide me with a successor?" thought Julien. "Only the day before yesterday, she was so intimate with me! But they say that this is how great ladies behave. They are like kings, no one receives so much attention as the minister who, on going home, finds the letter announcing his dismissal."

Julien remarked that in these conversations, which ceased abruptly on his approach, there was frequent mention of a big house belonging to the municipality of Verrières, old, but large and commodious, and situated opposite the church, in the most valuable quarter of the town. "What connexion can there be between that house and a new lover?" Julien asked himself. In his distress of mind, he repeated to himself those charming lines of Francis I, which seemed to him new, because it was not a month since Madame de Rênal had taught them to him. At that time, by how many vows, by how many caresses had not each line been proved false!

> Souvent femme varie
> Bien fol est qui s'y fie.

M. de Rênal set off by post for Besançon. This journey was decided upon at two hours' notice, he seemed greatly troubled. On his return, he flung a large bundle wrapped in grey paper on the table.

"So much for that stupid business," he said to his wife.

An hour later, Julien saw the bill-sticker carrying off this large bundle; he followed him hastily. "I shall learn the secret at the first street corner."

He waited impatiently behind the bill-sticker, who with his fat brush was slapping paste on the back of the bill. No sooner was it in its place than Julien's curiosity read on it the announcement in full detail of the sale by public auction of the lease of that large and old house which recurred so frequently in M. de Rênal's conversations with his wife. The assignation was announced for the following day at two o'clock, in the town hall, on the extinction of the third light. Julien was greatly disappointed; he considered the interval to be rather short: how could all the possible bidders come to know of the sale in time? But apart from this, the bill, which was dated a fortnight earlier and which he read from beginning to end in three different places, told him nothing.

He went to inspect the vacant house. The porter, who did not see him approach, was saying mysteriously to a friend:

"Bah! It's a waste of time. M. Maslon promised him he should have it for three hundred francs; and as the Mayor kicked, he was sent to the Bishop's Palace, by the Grand Vicar de Frilair."

Julien's appearance on the scene seemed greatly to embarrass the two cronies, who did not say another word.

Julien did not fail to attend the auction. There was a crowd of people in an ill-lighted room; but everyone eyed his neighbours in a singular fashion. Every eye was fixed on a table, where Julien saw, on a pewter plate, three lighted candle-ends. The crier was shouting: "Three hundred francs, gentlemen!"

"Three hundred francs! It is too bad!" one man murmured to another. Julien was standing between them. "It is worth more than eight hundred; I am going to cover the bid."

"It's cutting off your nose to spite your face. What are you going to gain by bringing M. Maslon, M. Valenod, the Bishop, his terrible Grand Vicar de Frilair and the whole of their gang down upon you?"

"Three hundred and twenty," the other shouted.

"Stupid idiot!" retorted his neighbour. "And here's one of the Mayor's spies," he added pointing at Julien.

Julien turned sharply to rebuke him for this speech; but the two Franc-Comtois paid no attention to him. Their coolness restored his own. At this moment the last candle-end went out, and the drawling voice of the crier assigned the house for a lease of nine years to M. de Saint-Giraud, chief secretary at the Prefecture of ——, and for three hundred and thirty francs.

As soon as the Mayor had left the room, the discussion began.

"That's thirty francs Grogeot's imprudence has earned for the town," said one.

"But M. de Saint-Giraud," came the answer, "will have his revenge on Grogeot, he will pass it on."

"What a scandal," said a stout man on Julien's left: "a house for which I'ld have given, myself, eight hundred francs as a factory, and then it would have been a bargain."

"Bah!" replied a young Liberal manufacturer, "isn't M. de Saint-Giraud one of the *Congregation?* Haven't his four children all got bursaries? Poor man! The town of Verrières is simply bound to increase his income with an allowance of five hundred francs; that is all."

"And to think that the Mayor hasn't been able to stop it!" remarked a third. "For he may be an ultra, if you like, but he's not a thief."

"He's not a thief?" put in another; "it's a regular thieves' kitchen. Everything goes into a common fund, and is divided up at the end of the year. But there's young Sorel; let us get away."

Julien went home in the worst of tempers; he found Madame de Rênal greatly depressed.

"Have you come from the sale?" she said to him.

"Yes, Ma'am, where I had the honour to be taken for the Mayor's spy."

"If he had taken my advice, he would have gone away somewhere."

At that moment, M. de Rênal appeared; he was very sombre. Dinner was eaten in silence. M. de Rênal told Julien to accompany the children to Vergy; they travelled in unbroken gloom. Madame de Rênal tried to comfort her husband.

"Surely you are accustomed to it, my dear."

That evening, they were seated in silence round the domestic hearth; the crackle of the blazing beech logs was their sole distraction. It was one of those moments of depression which are to be found in the most united families. One of the children uttered a joyful cry.

"There's the bell! The bell!"

"Egad, if it's M. de Saint-Giraud come to get hold of me, on the excuse of thanking me, I shall give him a piece of my mind; it's too bad. It's Valenod that he has to thank, and it is I who am compromised. What am I going to say if those pestilent Jacobin papers get hold of the story, and make me out a M. Nonante-Cinq?"[1]

A good-looking man, with bushy black whiskers, entered the room at this moment in the wake of the servant.

"M. le Maire, I am Signor Geronimo. Here is a letter which M. le Chevalier de Beauvaisis, attaché at the Embassy at Naples, gave me for you when I came away; it is only nine days ago," Signor Geronimo added, with a sprightly air, looking at Madame de Rênal. "Signor de Beauvaisis, your cousin, and my good friend, Madame, tells me that you know Italian."

[1] M. Marsan explains this allusion to a satire by Barthélemy at the expense of the Marseilles magistrate Mérindol, who in sentencing him to a fine had made use of the Common Southern expression "Nonante-cinq" for "Quatre-vingt-quinze."

C. K. S. M.

The good humour of the Neapolitan changed this dull evening into one that was extremely gay. Madame de Rênal insisted upon his taking supper. She turned the whole house upside down; she wished at all costs to distract Julien's thoughts from the description of him as a spy which twice in that day he had heard ringing in his ear. Signor Geronimo was a famous singer, a man used to good company, and at the same time the best of company himself, qualities which, in France, have almost ceased to be compatible. He sang after supper a little duet with Madame de Rênal. He told charming stories. At one o'clock in the morning the children protested when Julien proposed that they should go to bed.

"Just this story," said the eldest.

"It is my own, Signorino," replied Signor Geronimo. "Eight years ago I was, like you, a young scholar in the Conservatorio of Naples, by which I mean that I was your age; for I had not the honour to be the son of the eminent Mayor of the beautiful town of Verrières."

This allusion drew a sigh from M. de Rênal, who looked at his wife.

"Signor Zingarelli," went on the young singer, speaking with a slightly exaggerated accent which made the children burst out laughing, "Signor Zingarelli is an exceedingly severe master. He is not loved at the Conservatorio; but he makes them act always as though they loved him. I escaped whenever I could; I used to go to the little theatre of San Carlino, where I used to hear music fit for the gods: but, O heavens, how was I to scrape together the eight soldi which were the price of admission to the pit? An enormous sum," he said, looking at the children, and the children laughed again. "Signor Giovannone, the Director of San Carlino, heard me sing. I was sixteen years old. 'This boy is a treasure,' he said.

"'Would you like me to engage you, my friend?' he said to me one day.

" 'How much will you give me?'

" 'Forty ducats a month.' That, gentlemen, is one hundred and sixty francs. I seemed to see the heavens open.

" 'But how,' I said to Giovannone, 'am I to persuade the strict Zingarelli to let me go?'

" '*Lascia fare a me.*' "

"Leave it to me!" cried the eldest of the children.

"Precisely, young Sir. Signor Giovannone said to me: 'First of all, *caro,* a little agreement.' I signed the paper: he gave me three ducats. I had never seen so much money. Then he told me what I must do.

"Next day, I demanded an interview with the terrible Signor Zingarelli. His old servant shewed me into the room.

" 'What do you want with me, you scapegrace?' said Zingarelli.

" '*Maestro,*' I told him, 'I repent of my misdeeds; never again will I break out of the Conservatorio by climbing over the iron railings. I am going to study twice as hard.'

" 'If I were not afraid of spoiling the finest bass voice I have ever heard, I should lock you up on bread and water for a fortnight, you scoundrel.'

" '*Maestro,*' I went on, 'I am going to be a model to the whole school, *credete a me.* But I ask one favour of you, if anyone comes to ask for me to sing outside, refuse him. Please say that you cannot allow it.'

" 'And who do you suppose is going to ask for a good for nothing like you? Do you think I shall ever allow you to leave the Conservatorio? Do you wish to make a fool of me? Off with you, off with you!' he said, aiming a kick at my hindquarters, 'or it will be bread and water in a cell.'

"An hour later, Signor Giovannone came to call on the Director.

" 'I have come to ask you to make my fortune,' he began, 'let me have Geronimo. If he sings in my theatre this winter I marry my daughter.'

" 'What do you propose to do with the rascal?' Zingarelli asked him. 'I won't allow it. You shan't have him; besides, even if I consented, he would never be willing to leave the Conservatorio; he's just told me so himself.'

" 'If his willingness is all that matters,' said Giovannone gravely, producing my agreement from his pocket, *'carta canta!* Here is his signature.'

"Immediately Zingarelli, furious, flew to the bell-rope: 'Turn Geronimo out of the Conservatorio,' he shouted, seething with rage. So out they turned me, I splitting my sides with laughter. That same evening, I sang the *aria del Moltiplico.* Pulcinella intends to marry, and counts up on his fingers the different things he will need for the house, and loses count afresh at every moment."

"Oh, won't you, Sir, please sing us that air?" said Madame de Rênal.

Geronimo sang, and his audience all cried with laughter. Signor Geronimo did not go to bed until two in the morning, leaving the family enchanted with his good manners, his obliging nature and his gay spirits.

Next day M. and Madame de Rênal gave him the letters which he required for the French Court.

"And so, falsehood everywhere," said Julien. "There is Signor Geronimo on his way to London with a salary of sixty thousand francs. But for the cleverness of the Director of San Carlino, his divine voice might not have been known and admired for another ten years, perhaps. . . . Upon my soul, I would rather be a Geronimo than a Rênal. He is not so highly honoured in society, but he has not the humiliation of having to grant leases like that one to-day, and his is a merry life."

One thing astonished Julien: the weeks of solitude spent at Verrières, in M. de Rênal's house, had been for him a time of happiness. He had encountered disgust and

gloomy thoughts only at the dinners to which he had been
invited; in that empty house, was he not free to read,
write, meditate, undisturbed? He had not been aroused
at every moment from his radiant dreams by the cruel
necessity of studying the motions of a base soul, and that
in order to deceive it by hypocritical words or actions.

"Could happiness be thus within my reach? . . . The
cost of such a life is nothing; I can, as I choose, marry Miss
Elisa, or become Fouqué's partner. . . . But the traveller
who has just climbed a steep mountain, sits down on the
summit, and finds a perfect pleasure in resting. Would
he be happy if he were forced to rest always?"

Madame de Rênal's mind was a prey to carking thoughts.
In spite of her resolve to the contrary, she had revealed
to Julien the whole business of the lease. "So he will
make me forget all my vows!" she thought.

She would have given her life without hesitation to save
that of her husband, had she seen him in peril. Hers
was one of those noble and romantic natures, for which
to see the possibility of a generous action, and not to perform it gives rise to a remorse almost equal to that which
one feels for a past crime. Nevertheless, there were dread-
ful days on which she could not banish the thought of the
absolute happiness which she would enjoy, if, suddenly left
a widow, she were free to marry Julien.

He loved her children far more than their father; in
spite of his strict discipline, he was adored by them. She
was well aware that, if she married Julien, she would
have to leave this Vergy whose leafy shade was so dear
to her. She pictured herself living in Paris, continuing
to provide her sons with that education at which everyone
marvelled. Her children, she herself, Julien, all perfectly
happy.

A strange effect of marriage, such as the nineteenth
century has made it! The boredom of married life in-
evitably destroys love, when love has preceded marriage.

And yet, as a philosopher has observed, it speedily brings about, among people who are rich enough not to have to work, an intense boredom with all quiet forms of enjoyment. And it is only dried up hearts, among women, that it does not predispose to love.

The philosopher's observation makes me excuse Madame de Rênal, but there was no excuse for her at Verrières, and the whole town, without her suspecting it, was exclusively occupied with the scandal of her love. Thanks to this great scandal, people that autumn were less bored than usual.

The autumn, the first weeks of winter had soon come and gone. It was time to leave the woods of Vergy. The high society of Verrières began to grow indignant that its anathemas were making so little impression upon M. de Rênal. In less than a week, certain grave personages who made up for their habitual solemnity by giving themselves the pleasure of fulfilling missions of this sort, implanted in him the most cruel suspicions, but without going beyond the most measured terms.

M. Valenod, who was playing a close game, had placed Elisa with a noble and highly respected family, which included five women. Elisa fearing, she said, that she might not find a place during the winter, had asked this family for only about two thirds of what she was receiving at the Mayor's. Of her own accord, the girl had the excellent idea of going to confess to the retired curé Chélan as well as to the new curé, so as to be able to give them both a detailed account of Julien's amours.

On the morning after his return, at six o'clock, the abbé Chélan sent for Julien:

"I ask you nothing," he said to him; "I beg you, and if need be order you to tell me nothing, I insist that within three days you leave either for the Seminary at Besançon or for the house of your friend Fouqué, who is still willing to provide a splendid career for you. I have foreseen and settled everything, but you must go, and not return to Verrières for a year."

Julien made no answer; he was considering whether his honour ought to take offence at the arrangements which M. Chélan, who after all was not his father, had made for him.

"To-morrow at this hour I shall have the honour of seeing you again," he said at length to the curé.

M. Chélan, who reckoned upon overcoming the young man by main force, spoke volubly. His attitude, his features composed in the utmost humility, Julien did not open his mouth.

At length he made his escape, and hastened to inform Madame de Rênal, whom he found in despair. Her husband had just been speaking to her with a certain frankness. The natural weakness of his character, seeking encouragement in the prospect of the inheritance from Besançon, had made him decide to regard her as entirely innocent. He had just confessed to her the strange condition in which he found public opinion at Verrières. The public were wrong, had been led astray by envious ill-wishers, but what was to be done?

Madame de Rênal had the momentary illusion that Julien might be able to accept M. Valenod's offer, and remain at Verrières. But she was no longer the simple, timid woman of the previous year; her fatal passion, her spells of remorse had enlightened her. Soon she had to bear the misery of proving to herself, while she listened to her husband, that a separation, at any rate for the time being, was now inevitable. "Away from me, Julien will drift back into those ambitious projects that are so natural when one has nothing. And I, great God! I am so rich, and so powerless to secure my own happiness! He will forget me. Charming as he is, he will be loved, he will love. Ah, unhappy woman! Of what can I complain? Heaven is just, I have not acquired merit by putting a stop to my crime; it blinds my judgment. It rested with me alone to win over Elisa with a bribe, nothing would have been easier. I did not take the trouble to reflect for a moment, the wild imaginings of love absorbed all my time. And now I perish."

One thing struck Julien; as he conveyed to Madame de Rênal the terrible news of his departure, he was met with no selfish objection. Evidently she was making an effort not to cry.

"We require firmness, my friend."

She cut off a lock of his hair.

"I do not know what is to become of me," she said to him, "but if I die, promise me that you will never forget my children. Far or near, try to make them grow up honourable men. If there is another revolution, all the nobles will be murdered, their father may emigrate, perhaps, because of that peasant who was killed upon a roof. Watch over the family. . . . Give me your hand. Farewell, my friend! These are our last moments together. This great sacrifice made, I hope that in public I shall have the courage to think of my reputation."

Julien had been expecting despair. The simplicity of this farewell touched him.

"No, I do not accept your farewell thus. I shall go; they wish it; you wish it yourself. But, three days after my departure, I shall return to visit you by night."

Madame de Rênal's existence was changed. So Julien really did love her since he had had the idea, of his own accord, of seeing her again. Her bitter grief changed into one of the keenest bursts of joy that she had ever felt in her life. Everything became easy to her. The certainty of seeing her lover again took from these last moments all their lacerating force. From that instant the conduct, like the features of Madame de Rênal was noble, firm, and perfectly conventional.

M. de Rênal presently returned; he was beside himself.

For the first time he mentioned to his wife the anonymous letter which he had received two months earlier.

"I intend to take it to the Casino, to shew them all that it comes from that wretch Valenod, whom I picked up out of the gutter and made into one of the richest citizens of Verrières. I shall disgrace him publicly, and then fight him. It is going too far."

"I might be left a widow, great God!" thought Madame de Rênal. But almost at the same instant she said to herself: "If I do not prevent this duel, as I certainly can, I shall be my husband's murderess."

Never before had she handled his vanity with so much skill. In less than two hours she made him see, always by the use of arguments that had occurred first to him, that he must shew himself friendlier than ever towards M. Valenod, and even take Elisa into the house again. Madame de Rênal required courage to make up her mind to set eyes on this girl, the cause of all her troubles. But the idea had come to her from Julien.

Finally, after having been set three or four times in the right direction, M. de Rênal arrived of his own accord at the idea (highly distressing, from the financial point of view) that the most unpleasant thing that could happen for himself was that Julien, amid the seething excitement and gossip of the whole of Verrières, should remain there as tutor to M. Valenod's children. It was obviously in Julien's interest to accept the offer made him by the Governor of the Poorhouse. It was essential however to M. de Rênal's fair fame that Julien should leave Verrières to enter the seminary at Besançon or at Dijon. But how was he to be made to agree, and after that how was he to maintain himself there?

M. de Rênal, seeing the imminence of a pecuniary sacrifice, was in greater despair than his wife. For her part, after this conversation, she was in the position of a man of feeling who, weary of life, has taken a dose of *stramonium;* he ceases to act, save, so to speak, automatically, and no longer takes an interest in anything. Thus Louis XIV on his deathbed was led to say: "When I was king." An admirable speech!

On the morrow, at break of day, M. de Rênal received an anonymous letter. It was couched in the most insulting style. The coarsest words applicable to his position stared from every line. It was the work of some envious subordinate. This letter brought him back to the thought of fighting a duel with M. Valenod. Soon his courage had risen to the idea of an immediate execution of his design. He left the house unaccompanied, and went to the gunsmith's to procure a brace of pistols, which he told the man to load.

"After all," he said to himself, "should the drastic rule of the Emperor Napoleon be restored, I myself could not be charged with the misappropriation of a halfpenny. At the most I have shut my eyes; but I have plenty of letters in my desk authorizing me to do so."

Madame de Rênal was frightened by her husband's cold anger, it brought back to her mind the fatal thought of widowhood, which she found it so hard to banish. She shut herself up with him. For hours on end she pleaded with him in vain, the latest anonymous letter had determined him. At length she succeeded in transforming the courage required to strike M. Valenod into that required to offer Julien six hundred francs for his maintenance for one year in a Seminary. M. de Rênal, heaping a thousand curses on the day on which he had conceived the fatal idea of taking a tutor into his household, forgot the anonymous letter.

He found a grain of comfort in an idea which he did not communicate to his wife: by skilful handling, and by taking advantage of the young man's romantic ideas, he hoped to bind him, for a smaller sum, to refuse M. Valenod's offers.

Madame de Rênal found it far harder to prove to Julien that, if he sacrificed to her husband's convenience a post worth eight hundred francs, publicly offered him by the Governor of the Poorhouse, he might without blushing accept some compensation.

"But," Julien continued to object, "I have never had, even for a moment, the slightest thought of accepting that offer. You have made me too familiar with a life of refinement, the vulgarity of those people would kill me."

Cruel necessity, with its hand of iron, bent Julien's will. His pride offered him the self-deception of accepting only as a loan the sum offered by the Mayor of Verrières, and giving him a note of hand promising repayment with interest after five years.

Madame de Rênal had still some thousands of francs hidden in the little cave in the mountains.

She offered him these, trembling, and feeling only too sure that they would be rejected with fury.

"Do you wish," Julien asked her, "to make the memory of our love abominable?"

At length Julien left Verrières. M. de Rênal was overjoyed; at the decisive moment of accepting money from him, this sacrifice proved to be too great for Julien. He refused point-blank. M. de Rênal fell upon his neck, with tears in his eyes. Julien having asked him for a testimonial to his character, he could not in his enthusiasm find terms laudatory enough to extol the young man's conduct. Our hero had saved up five louis, and intended to ask Fouqué for a similar amount.

He was greatly moved. But when he had gone a league from Verrières, where he was leaving such a treasure of love behind him, he thought only of the pleasure of seeing a capital, a great military centre like Besançon.

During this short parting of three days, Madame de Rênal was duped by one of love's most cruel illusions. Her life was tolerable enough, there was between her and the last extremes of misery this final meeting that she was still to have with Julien. She counted the hours, the minutes that divided her from it. Finally, during the night that followed the third day, she heard in the distance the signal arranged between them. Having surmounted a thousand perils, Julien appeared before her.

From that moment, she had but a single thought: "I am looking at you now for the last time." Far from responding to her lover's eagerness, she was like a barely animated corpse. If she forced herself to tell him that she loved him, it was with an awkward air that was almost a proof to the contrary. Nothing could take her mind from the cruel thought of eternal separation. The suspicious Julien fancied for a moment that she had already forgotten him. His hints at such a possibility were received only with huge tears that flowed in silence, and with a convulsive pressure of his hand.

"But, Great God! How do you expect me to believe you?" was Julien's reply to his mistress's chill protestations. "You would shew a hundred times more of sincere affection to Madame Derville, to a mere acquaintance."

Madame de Rênal, petrified, did not know how to answer.

"It would be impossible for a woman to be more wretched. . . . I hope I am going to die. . . . I feel my heart freezing. . . ."

Such were the longest answers he was able to extract from her.

When the approach of day made his departure necessary, Madame de Rênal's tears ceased all at once. She saw him fasten a knotted cord to the window without saying a word, without returning his kisses. In vain might Julien say to her:

"At last we have reached the state for which you so longed. Henceforward you will live without remorse. At the slightest indisposition of one of your children, you will no longer see them already in the grave."

"I am sorry you could not say good-bye to Stanislas," she said to him coldly.

In the end, Julien was deeply impressed by the embraces, in which there was no warmth, of this living corpse; he could think of nothing else for some leagues. His spirit was crushed, and before crossing the pass, so long as he was able to see the steeple of Verrières church, he turned round often.

CHAPTER TWENTY-FOUR

A CAPITAL

Que de bruit, que de gens affairés! que d'idées pour
l'avenir dans une tête de vingt ans! quelle distraction
pour l'amour!

BARNAVE.

A T length he made out, on a distant mountain, a line
of dark walls; it was the citadel of Besançon.
"How different for me," he said with a sigh,
"if I were arriving in this noble fortress to be a sub-
lieutenant in one of the regiments entrusted with its defence!"

Besançon is not merely one of the most charming towns
in France, it abounds in men and women of feeling and
spirit. But Julien was only a young peasant and had no
way of approaching the distinguished people.

He had borrowed from Fouqué a layman's coat, and it
was in this attire that he crossed the drawbridges. His
mind full of the history of the siege of 1674, he was
determined to visit, before shutting himself up in the
Seminary, the ramparts and the citadel. More than once,
he was on the point of being arrested by the sentries for
making his way into places from which the engineers of
the garrison excluded the public, in order to make a profit
of twelve or fifteen francs every year by the sale of the
hay grown there.

The height of the walls, the depth of the moats, the
awe-inspiring appearance of the guns had occupied him
for some hours, when he happened to pass by the principal café, on the boulevard. He stood speechless
with admiration; albeit he could read the word

Café inscribed in huge letters over the two vast doors, he could not believe his eyes. He made an effort to master his timidity; he ventured to enter, and found himself in a hall thirty or forty feet long, the ceiling of which rose to a height of at least twenty feet. On this day of days everything wore an air of enchantment for him.

Two games of billiards were in progress. The waiters were calling out the scores; the players hurried round the tables through a crowd of onlookers. Streams of tobacco smoke, pouring from every mouth, enveloped them in a blue haze. The tall stature of these men, their rounded shoulders, their heavy gait, their bushy whiskers, the long frock coats that covered their bodies, all attracted Julien's attention. These noble sons of the ancient Bisontium conversed only in shouts; they gave themselves the air of tremendous warriors. Julien stood spellbound in admiration; he was thinking of the vastness and splendour of a great capital like Besançon. He felt that he could not possibly summon up courage to ask for a cup of coffee from one of those gentlemen with the proud gaze who were marking the score at billiards.

But the young lady behind the counter had remarked the charming appearance of this young country cousin, who, brought to a standstill three paces from the stove, hugging his little bundle under his arm, was studying the bust of the King, in gleaming white plaster. This young lady, a strapping Franc-Comtoise, extremely well made, and dressed in the style calculated to give tone to a café, had already said twice, in a low voice so modulated that only Julien should hear her: "Sir! Sir!" Julien's gaze met that of a pair of the most tender blue eyes, and saw that it was himself who was being addressed.

He stepped briskly up to the counter and the pretty girl, as he might have advanced in the face of the enemy. As he executed this great movement, his bundle fell to the ground.

What pity will not our provincial inspire in the young scholars of Paris, who at fifteen, have already learned how to enter a café with so distinguished an air! But these children, so stylish at fifteen, at eighteen begin to turn *common*. The passionate shyness which one meets in the provinces now and then overcomes itself, and then teaches its victim to desire. As he approached this beautiful girl who had deigned to speak to him, "I must tell her the truth," thought Julien, who was growing courageous by dint of his conquered shyness.

"Madame, I have come for the first time in my life to Besançon; I should like to have, and to pay for, a roll of bread and a cup of coffee."

The girl smiled a little and then blushed; she feared, for this good-looking young man, the satirical attention and witticisms of the billiard players. He would be frightened and would never shew his face there again.

"Sit down here, near me," she said, and pointed to a marble table, almost entirely hidden by the enormous mahogany counter which protruded into the room.

The young woman leaned over this counter, which gave her an opportunity to display a superb figure. Julien observed this; all his ideas altered. The pretty girl had just set before him a cup, some sugar and a roll of bread. She hesitated before calling to a waiter for coffee, realizing that on the arrival of the said waiter her private conversation with Julien would be at an end.

Julien, lost in thought, was comparing this fair and sprightly beauty with certain memories which often stirred him. The thought of the passion of which he had been the object took from him almost all his timidity. The pretty girl had only a moment; she read the expression in Julien's eyes.

"This pipe smoke makes you cough, come to breakfast to-morrow before eight o'clock; at that time, I am almost alone."

"What is your name?" said Julien, with the caressing smile of happy timidity.

"Amanda Binet."

"Will you permit me to send you, in an hour's time, a little parcel no bigger than this?"

The fair Amanda reflected for a while.

"I am watched: what you ask may compromise me; however, I am now going to write down my address upon a card, which you can attach to your parcel. Send it to me without fear."

"My name is Julien Sorel," said the young man. "I have neither family nor friends in Besançon."

"Ah! Now I understand," she exclaimed joyfully, "you have come for the law school?"

"Alas, no!" replied Julien; "they are sending me to the Seminary."

The most complete discouragement extinguished the light in Amanda's features; she called a waiter: she had the necessary courage now. The waiter poured out Julien's coffee, without looking at him.

Amanda was taking money at the counter; Julien prided himself on having ventured to speak to her: there was a dispute in progress at one of the billiard tables. The shouts and contradictions of the players, echoing through that vast hall, made a din which astonished Julien. Amanda was pensive and did not raise her eyes.

"If you like, Mademoiselle," he said to her suddenly with assurance, "I can say that I am your cousin."

This little air of authority delighted Amanda. "This is no good-for-nothing young fellow," she thought. She said to him very quickly, without looking at him, for her eye was occupied in watching whether anyone were approaching the counter:

"I come from Genlis, near Dijon; say that you are from Genlis too, and my mother's cousin."

"I shall not forget."

"On Thursdays, at five o'clock, in summer, the young gentlemen from the Seminary come past the café here."

"If you are thinking of me, when I pass, have a bunch of violets in your hand."

Amanda gazed at him with an air of astonishment; this gaze changed Julien's courage into temerity; he blushed deeply, however, as he said to her:

"I feel that I love you with the most violent love."

"Don't speak so loud, then," she warned him with an air of alarm.

Julien thought of trying to recollect the language of an odd volume of the *Nouvelle Héloïse*, which he had found at Vergy. His memory served him well; he had been for ten minutes reciting the *Nouvelle Héloïse* to Miss Amanda, who was in ecstasies; he was delighted with his own courage, when suddenly the fair Franc-Comtoise assumed a glacial air. One of her admirers stood in the doorway of the café.

He came up to the counter, whistling and swaying his shoulders; he stared at Julien. For the moment, the latter's imagination, always flying to extremes, was filled entirely with thoughts of a duel. He turned deadly pale, thrust away his cup, assumed an air of assurance and studied his rival most attentively. While this rival's head was lowered as he familiarly poured himself out a glass of brandy upon the counter, with a glance Amanda ordered Julien to lower his gaze. He obeyed, and for a minute or two sat motionless in his place, pale, determined, and thinking only of what was going to happen; he was really fine at that moment. The rival had been astonished by Julien's eyes; his glass of brandy drained at a gulp, he said a few words to Amanda, thrust his hands into the side pockets of his ample coat, and made his way to one of the billiard tables, breathing loudly and staring at Julien. The latter sprang to his feet in a transport of rage; but did not know what action to take to be insulting. He laid down his little bundle and, with the most swaggering gait that he could assume, strode towards the billiard table.

In vain did prudence warn him: "With a duel on the day of your arrival at Besançon, your career in the church is gone for ever."

"What does that matter, it shall never be said that I quailed before an insult."

Amanda observed his courage; it formed a charming contrast with the simplicity of his manners; in an instant, she preferred him to the big young man in the long coat. She rose, and, while appearing to be following with her eyes the movements of someone going by in the street, took her place swiftly between him and the billiard table.

"You are not to look askance at that gentleman; he is my brother-in-law."

"What do I care? He looked at me."

"Do you wish to get me into trouble? No doubt, he looked at you, perhaps he will even come up and speak to you. I have told him that you are one of my mother's family and that you have just come from Genlis. He is a Franc-Comtois and has never been farther than Dôle, on the road into Burgundy; so tell him whatever you like, don't be afraid."

Julien continued to hesitate; she added rapidly, her barmaid's imagination supplying her with falsehoods in abundance:

"I dare say he did look at you, but it was when he was asking me who you were; he is a man who is rude with everyone, he didn't mean to insult you."

Julien's eye followed the alleged brother-in-law; he saw him buy a number in the pool which was beginning at the farther of the two billiard tables. Julien heard his loud voice exclaim: "I volunteer!" He passed nimbly behind Miss Amanda's back and took a step towards the billiard table. Amanda seized him by the arm.

"Come and pay me first," she said to him.

"Quite right," thought Julien; "she is afraid I may leave without paying." Amanda was as greatly agitated as himself, and had turned very red; she counted out his change as slowly as she could, repeating to him in a whisper as she did so:

"Leave the café this instant, or I shan't like you any more; I do like you, though, very much."

Julien did indeed leave, but slowly. "Is it not incumbent upon me," he repeated to himself, "to go and stare at that rude person in my turn, and breathe in his face?" This uncertainty detained him for an hour on the boulevard, outside the café; he watched to see if his man came out. He did not however appear, and Julien withdrew.

He had been but a few hours in Besançon, and already he had something to regret. The old Surgeon-Major had long ago, notwithstanding his gout, taught him a few lessons in fencing; this was all the science that Julien could place at the service of his anger. But this embarrassment would have been nothing if he had known how to pick a quarrel otherwise than by striking a blow; and, if they had come to fisticuffs, his rival, a giant of a man, would have beaten him and left him discomfited.

"For a poor devil like me," thought Julien, "without protectors and without money, there will be no great difference between a Seminary and a prison; I must leave my lay clothes in some inn, where I can put on my black coat. If I ever succeed in escaping from the Seminary for an hour or two, I can easily, in my lay clothes, see Miss Amanda again." This was sound reasoning; but Julien, as he passed by all the inns in turn, had not the courage to enter any of them.

Finally, as he came again to the Hôtel des Ambassadeurs, his roving gaze met that of a stout woman, still reasonably young, with a high complexion, a happy and gay expression. He went up to her and told her his story.

"Certainly, my fine young priest," the landlady of the Ambassadeurs said to him, "I shall keep your lay clothes for you, indeed I will have them brushed regularly. In this weather, it is a mistake to leave a broadcloth coat lying." She took a key and led him herself to a bedroom, advising him to write down a list of what he was leaving behind.

"Lord, how nice you look like that, M. l'abbé Sorel," said the stout woman, when he came down to the kitchen. "I am going to order you a good dinner; and," she added in an undertone, "it will only cost you twenty sous, instead of the fifty people generally pay; for you must be careful with your little purse."

"I have ten louis," retorted Julien with a certain note of pride.

"Oh, good Lord!" replied the good landlady in alarm, "do not speak so loud; there are plenty of bad folk in Besançon. They will have that out of you in less than no time. Whatever you do, never go into the cafés, they are full of rogues."

"Indeed!" said Julien, to whom this last statement gave food for thought.

"Never go anywhere except to me, I will give you your coffee. Bear in mind that you will always find a friend here and a good dinner for twenty sous; that's good enough for you, I hope. Go and sit down at the table, I am going to serve you myself."

"I should not be able to eat," Julien told her. "I am too much excited, I am going to enter the Seminary as soon as I leave here."

The good woman would not allow him to leave until she had stuffed his pockets with provisions. Finally Julien set out for the dread spot, the landlady from her doorstep pointing out the way.

CHAPTER TWENTY-FIVE

THE SEMINARY

Three hundred and thirty-six dinners at 83 centimes, three hundred and thirty-six suppers at 38 centimes, chocolate to such as are entitled to it; how much is there to be made on the contract?

The VALENOD *of* BESANÇON.

HE saw from a distance the cross of gilded iron over the door; he went towards it slowly; his legs seemed to be giving way under him. "So there is that hell upon earth, from which I can never escape!" Finally he decided to ring. The sound of the bell echoed as though in a deserted place. After ten minutes, a pale man dressed in black came and opened the door to him. Julien looked at him and at once lowered his gaze. This porter had a singular physiognomy. The prominent green pupils of his eyes were convex as those of a cat's; the unwinking contours of his eyelids proclaimed the impossibility of any human feeling; his thin lips were stretched and curved over his protruding teeth. And yet this physiognomy did not suggest a criminal nature, so much as that entire insensibility which inspires far greater terror in the young. The sole feeling that Julien's rapid glance could discern in that long, smug face was a profound contempt for every subject that might be mentioned to him, which did not refer to another and a better world.

Julien raised his eyes with an effort, and in a voice which the palpitation of his heart made tremulous explained that he wished to speak to M. Pirard, the Director of the Seminary. Without a word, the man in black made a sign to him to follow. They climbed two flights of a wide staircase with a wooden baluster, the warped steps of which sloped at a downward angle from the wall, and seemed on the point of collapse. A small door, surmounted by a large graveyard cross of white wood painted black, yielded to pressure and the porter shewed him into a low and gloomy room, the whitewashed walls of which were adorned with two large pictures dark with age. There, Julien was left to himself; he was terrified, his heart throbbed violently; he would have liked to find the courage to weep. A deathly silence reigned throughout the building.

After a quarter of an hour, which seemed to him a day, the sinister porter reappeared on the threshold of a door at the other end of the room, and, without condescending to utter a word, beckoned to him to advance. He entered a room even larger than the first and very badly lighted. The walls of this room were whitewashed also; but they were bare of ornament. Only in a corner by the door, Julien noticed in passing a bed of white wood, two straw chairs and a little armchair made of planks of firwood without a cushion. At the other end of the room, near a small window with dingy panes, decked with neglected flowerpots, he saw a man seated at a table and dressed in a shabby cassock; he appeared to be in a rage, and was taking one after another from a pile of little sheets of paper which he spread out on his table after writing a few words on each. He did not observe Julien's presence. The latter remained motionless, standing in the middle of the room, where he had been left by the porter, who had gone out again shutting the door behind him.

Ten minutes passed in this fashion; the shabbily dressed man writing all the time. Julien's emotion and terror were such that he felt himself to be on the point of collapsing. A philosopher would have said, perhaps wrongly: "It is the violent impression made by ugliness on a soul created to love what is beautiful."

The man who was writing raised his head; Julien did not observe this for a moment, and indeed, after he had noticed it, still remained motionless, as though turned to stone by the terrible gaze that was fixed on him. Julien's swimming eyes could barely make out a long face covered all over with red spots, except on the forehead, which displayed a deathly pallor. Between the red cheeks and white forehead shone a pair of little black eyes calculated to inspire terror in the bravest heart. The vast expanse of his forehead was outlined by a mass of straight hair, as black as jet.

"Are you coming nearer, or not?" the man said at length impatiently.

Julien advanced with an uncertain step, and at length, ready to fall to the ground and paler than he had ever been in his life, came to a halt a few feet away from the little table of white wood covered with scraps of paper.

"Nearer," said the man.

Julien advanced farther, stretching out his hand as though in search of something to lean upon.

"Your name?"

"Julien Sorel."

"You are very late," said the other, once more fastening upon him a terrible eye.

Julien could not endure this gaze; putting out his hand as though to support himself, he fell full length upon the floor.

The man rang a bell. Julien had lost only his sense of vision and the strength to move; he could hear footsteps approaching.

He was picked up and placed in the little armchair of white wood. He heard the terrible man say to the porter:

"An epileptic, evidently; I might have known it."

When Julien was able to open his eyes, the man with the red face was again writing; the porter had vanished. "I must have courage," our hero told himself, "and above all hide my feelings." He felt a sharp pain at his heart. "If I am taken ill, heaven knows what they will think of me." At length the man stopped writing, and with a sidelong glance at Julien asked:

"Are you in a fit state to answer my questions?"

"Yes, Sir," said Julien in a feeble voice.

"Ah! That is fortunate."

The man in black had half risen and was impatiently seeking for a letter in the drawer of his table of firwood which opened with a creak. He found it, slowly resumed his seat, and once more gazing at Julien, with an air which seemed to wrest from him the little life that remained to him:

"You are recommended to me by M. Chélan, who was the best curé in the diocese, a good man if ever there was one, and my friend for the last thirty years."

"Ah! It is M. Pirard that I have the honour to address," said Julien in a feeble voice.

"So it seems," said the Director of the Seminary, looking sourly at him.

The gleam in his little eyes brightened, followed by an involuntary jerk of the muscles round his mouth. It was the physiognomy of a tiger relishing in anticipation the pleasure of devouring its prey.

"Chélan's letter is short," he said, as though speaking to himself. *"Intelligenti pauca;* in these days, one cannot write too little." He read aloud:

" 'I send you Julien Sorel, of this parish, whom I baptized nearly twenty years ago; his father is a wealthy carpenter but allows him nothing. Julien will be a noteworthy labourer in the Lord's vineyard. Memory, intelligence are not wanting, he has the power of reflexion. Will his vocation last? Is it sincere?' "

"*Sincere!*" repeated the abbé Pirard with an air of surprise, gazing at Julien; but this time the abbé's gaze was less devoid of all trace of humanity. "*Sincere!*" he repeated, lowering his voice and returning to the letter:

" 'I ask you for a bursary for Julien; he will qualify for it by undergoing the necessary examinations. I have taught him a little divinity, that old and sound divinity of Bossuet, Arnault, Fleury. If the young man is not to your liking, send him back to me; the Governor of our Poorhouse, whom you know well, offers him eight hundred francs to come as tutor to his children. Inwardly I am calm, thank God. I am growing accustomed to the terrible blow. *Vale et me ama.*' "

The abbé Pirard, relaxing the speed of his utterance as he came to the signature, breathed with a sigh the word "Chélan."

"He is calm," he said; "indeed, his virtue deserved that reward; God grant it to me, when my time comes!"

He looked upwards and made the sign of the Cross. At the sight of this holy symbol Julien felt a slackening of the profound horror which, from his entering the building, had frozen him.

"I have here three hundred and twenty-one aspirants for the holiest of callings," the abbé Pirard said at length, in a severe but not hostile tone; "only seven or eight have been recommended to me by men like the abbé Chélan; thus among the three hundred and twenty-one you will be the ninth. But my protection is neither favour nor weakness, it is an increase of precaution and severity against vice. Go and lock that door."

Julien made an effort to walk and managed not to fall. He noticed that a little window, near the door by which he had entered, commanded a view of the country. He looked at the trees; the sight of them did him good, as though he had caught sight of old friends.

"Loquerisne linguam latinam? (Do you speak Latin?)" the abbé Pirard asked him as he returned.

"Ita, pater optime (Yes, excellent Father)," replied Julien, who was beginning to come to himself. Certainly nobody in the world had appeared to him less excellent than M. Pirard, during the last half-hour.

The conversation continued in Latin. The expression in the abbé's eyes grew gentler; Julien recovered a certain coolness. "How weak I am," he thought, "to let myself be imposed upon by this show of virtue! This man will be simply a rascal like M. Maslon"; and Julien congratulated himself on having hidden almost all his money in his boots.

The abbé Pirard examined Julien in theology, and was surprised by the extent of his knowledge. His astonishment increased when he questioned him more particularly on the Holy Scriptures. But when he came to questions touching the doctrine of the Fathers, he discovered that Julien barely knew the names of Saint Jerome, Saint Augustine, Saint Bonaventure, Saint Basil, etc., etc.

"In fact," thought the abbé Pirard, "here is another instance of that fatal tendency towards Protestantism which I have always had to rebuke in Chélan. A thorough, a too thorough acquaintance with the Holy Scriptures."

(Julien had just spoken to him, without having been questioned on the subject, of the *true* date of authorship of Genesis, the Pentateuch, etc.)

"To what does all this endless discussion of the Holy Scriptures lead," thought the abbé Pirard, "if not to *private judgment,* that is to say to the most fearful Protestantism? And, in conjunction with this rash learning, nothing about the Fathers that can compensate for this tendency."

But the astonishment of the Director of the Seminary knew no bounds when, questioning Julien as to the authority of the Pope, and expecting the maxims of the ancient Gallican church, he heard the young man repeat the whole of M. de Maistre's book.

"A strange man, Chélan," thought the abbé Pirard; "has he given him this book to teach him to laugh at it?"

In vain did he question Julien, trying to discover whether he seriously believed the doctrine of M. de Maistre. The young man could answer him only by rote. From this moment, Julien was really admirable, he felt that he was master of himself. After a prolonged examination it seemed to him that M. Pirard's severity towards him was no more than an affectation. Indeed, but for the rule of austere gravity which, for the last fifteen years, he had imposed on himself in dealing with his pupils in theology, the Director of the Seminary would have embraced Julien in the name of logic, such clarity, precision, and point did he find in the young man's answers.

"This is a bold and healthy mind," he said to himself, "but *corpus debile* (a frail body)."

"Do you often fall like that?" he asked Julien in French, pointing with his finger to the floor.

"It was the first time in my life; the sight of the porter's face paralysed me," Julien explained, colouring like a child.

The abbé Pirard almost smiled.

"Such is the effect of the vain pomps of this world; you are evidently accustomed to smiling faces, positive theatres of falsehood. The truth is austere, Sir. But is not our task here below austere also? You will have to see that your conscience is on its guard against this weakness: *Undue sensibility to vain outward charms.*

"Had you not been recommended to me," said the abbé Pirard, returning with marked pleasure to the Latin tongue, "had you not been recommended to me by a man such as the abbé Chélan, I should address you in the vain language of this world to which it appears that you are too well accustomed. The entire bursary for which you apply is,

I may tell you, the hardest thing in the world to obtain. But the abbé Chélan has earned little, by fifty-six years of apostolic labours, if he cannot dispose of a bursary at the Seminary."

After saying these words, the abbé Pirard advised Julien not to join any secret society or congregation without his consent.

"I give you my word of honour," said Julien with the heartfelt warmth of an honest man.

The Director of the Seminary smiled for the first time.

"That expression is not in keeping here," he told him; "it is too suggestive of the vain honour of men of the world, which leads them into so many errors and often into crime. You owe me obedience in virtue of the seventeenth paragraph of the Bull *Unam Ecclesiam* of Saint Pius V. I am your ecclesiastical superior. In this house to hear, my dearly beloved son, is to obey. How much money have you?"

("Now we come to the point," thought Julien, "this is the reason of the 'dearly beloved son.'")

"Thirty-five francs, Father."

"Keep a careful note of how you spend your money; you will have to account for it to me."

This exhausting interview had lasted three hours. Julien was told to summon the porter.

"Put Julien Sorel in cell number 103," the abbé Pirard told the man.

As a special favour, he was giving Julien a room to himself.

"Take up his trunk," he added.

Julien lowered his eyes and saw his trunk staring him in the face; he had been looking at it for three hours and had never seen it.

On arriving at No. 103, which was a tiny room eight feet square on the highest floor of the building, Julien observed that it looked out towards the ramparts, beyond which one saw the smiling plain which the Doubs divides from the city.

"What a charming view!" exclaimed Julien; in speaking thus to himself he was not conscious of the feeling implied by his words. The violent sensations he had experienced in the short time that he had spent in Besançon had completely drained his strength. He sat down by the window on the solitary wooden chair that was in his cell, and at once fell into a profound slumber. He did not hear the supper bell, nor that for Benediction; he had been forgotten.

When the first rays of the sun awakened him next morning, he found himself lying upon the floor.

CHAPTER TWENTY-SIX

THE WORLD, OR WHAT THE RICH LACK

Je suis seul sur la terre, personne ne daigne penser
à moi. Tous ceux que je vois faire fortune ont une
effronterie et une dureté de cœur que je ne me sens
point. Ils me haïssent à cause de ma bonté facile. Ah!
bientôt je mourrai, soit de faim, soit du malheur de
voir les hommes si durs.

YOUNG.[1]

H E made haste to brush his coat and to go downstairs; he was late. An under-master rebuked him
severely; instead of seeking to excuse himself,
Julien crossed his arms on his breast:

"*Peccavi, pater optime,*" he said with a contrite air.

This was a most successful beginning. The sharp wits
among the seminarists saw that they had to deal with a
man who was not new to the game. The recreation hour
came, Julien saw himself the object of general curiosity.
But they found in him merely reserve and silence. Following the maxims that he had laid down for himself,
he regarded his three hundred and twenty-one comrades
as so many enemies; the most dangerous of all in his eyes
was the abbé Pirard.

A few days later, Julien had to choose a confessor, he
was furnished with a list.

"Eh; Great God, for what do they take me?" he said

[1] I leave this motto in French as quoted by Stendhal, having
failed to trace the original passage, which may be from one of
the works of Edward Young (1681-1765). C. K. S. M.

to himself. "Do they suppose I can't take a hint?" And he chose the abbé Pirard.

Though he did not suspect it, this step was decisive. A little seminarist, still quite a boy, and a native of Verrières, who, from the first day, had declared himself his friend, informed him that if he had chosen M. Castanède, the vice-principal of the Seminary, he would perhaps have shewn greater prudence.

"The abbé Castanède is the enemy of M. Pirard, who is suspected of Jansenism"; the little seminarist added, whispering this information in his ear.

All the first steps taken by our hero who fancied himself so prudent were, like his choice of a confessor, foolish in the extreme. Led astray by all the presumption of an imaginative man, he mistook his intentions for facts, and thought himself a consummate hypocrite. His folly went the length of his reproaching himself for his successes in this art of the weak.

"Alas! It is my sole weapon! In another epoch, it would have been by speaking actions in the face of the enemy that I should have *earned my bread.*"

Julien, satisfied with his own conduct, looked around him; he found everywhere an appearance of the purest virtue.

Nine or ten of the seminarists lived in the odour of sanctity, and had visions like Saint Teresa and Saint Francis, when he received the Stigmata upon Monte Verna, in the Apennines. But this was a great secret which their friends kept to themselves. These poor young visionaries were almost always in the infirmary. Some hundred others combined with a robust faith an unwearying application. They worked until they made themselves ill, but without learning much. Two or three distinguished themselves by real talent, and, among these, one named Chazel; but Julien felt himself repelled by them, and they by him.

The rest of the three hundred and twenty-one seminarists were composed entirely of coarse creatures who were by no means certain that they understood the Latin words which they repeated all day long. Almost all of them were the sons of peasants, and preferred to earn their bread by reciting a few Latin words rather than by tilling the soil. It was after making this discovery, in the first few days, that Julien promised himself a rapid success. "In every service, there is need of intelligent people, for after all there is work to be done," he told himself. "Under Napoleon, I should have been a serjeant; among these future curés, I shall be a Grand Vicar.

"All these poor devils," he added, "labourers from the cradle, have lived, until they came here, upon skim milk and black bread. In their cottages, they tasted meat only five or six times in a year. Like the Roman soldiers who found active service a holiday, these boorish peasants are enchanted by the luxuries of the Seminary."

Julien never read anything in their lack-lustre eyes beyond the satisfaction of a bodily need after dinner, and the expectation of a bodily pleasure before the meal. Such were the people among whom he must distingush himself; but what Julien did not know, what they refrained from telling him, was that to be at the top of the various classes of dogma, church history, etc., etc., which were studied in the Seminary, was nothing more in their eyes than a sin of *vainglory*. Since Voltaire, since Two Chamber government, which is at bottom only *distrust and private judgment,* and instils in the hearts of the people that fatal habit of *want of confidence,* the Church of France seems to have realized that books are its true enemies. It is heartfelt submission that is everything in its eyes. Success in studies, even in sacred studies, is suspect, and with good reason. What is to prevent the superior man from going over to the other side, like Sieyès or Grégoire? The trembling Church clings to the Pope as to her sole chance of salvation. The Pope alone can attempt to paralyse private judgment, and, by the pious pomps of the ceremonies of his court, make an impression upon the sick and listless minds of men and women of the world.

Having half mastered these several truths, which however all the words uttered in a Seminary tend to deny, Julien fell into a deep melancholy. He worked hard, and rapidly succeeded in learning things of great value to a priest, entirely false in his eyes, and in which he took no interest. He imagined that there was nothing else for him to do.

"Am I then forgotten by all the world?" he wondered. He little knew that M. Pirard had received and had flung in the fire several letters bearing the Dijon postmark, letters in which, despite the most conventional style and language, the most intense passion was apparent. Keen remorse seemed to be doing battle with this love. "So much the better," thought the abbé Pirard, "at least it is not an irreligious woman that this young man has loved."

One day, the abbé Pirard opened a letter which seemed to be half obliterated by tears, it was an eternal farewell. "At last," the writer informed Julien, "heaven has granted me the grace of hating not the author of my fault, he will always be dearer to me than anything in the world, but my fault itself. The sacrifice is made, my friend. It is not without tears, as you see. The salvation of the beings to whom I am bound, and whom you have loved so dearly, has prevailed. A just but terrible God can no longer wreak vengeance upon them for their mother's crimes. Farewell, Julien, be just towards men."

This ending to the letter was almost entirely illegible. The writer gave an address at Dijon, and at the same time hoped that Julien would never reply, or that at least he would confine himself to language which a woman restored to the ways of virtue could read without blushing.

Julien's melancholy, assisted by the indifferent food supplied to the Seminary by the contractor for dinners at

83 centimes a head, was beginning to have an effect on his health, when one morning Fouqué suddenly appeared in his room.

"At last I have found my way in. I have come five times to Besançon, honour bound, to see you. Always a barred door. I posted someone at the gate of the Seminary; why the devil do you never come out?"

"It is a test which I have set myself."

"I find you greatly altered. At last I see you again. Two good five franc pieces have just taught me that I was no better than a fool not to have offered them on my first visit."

The conversation between the friends was endless. Julien changed colour when Fouqué said to him:

"Have you heard, by the way? The mother of your pupils has become most devoutly religious."

And he spoke with that detached air which makes so singular an impression on the passionate soul whose dearest interests the speaker unconsciously destroys.

"Yes, my friend, the most exalted strain of piety. They say that she makes pilgrimages. But, to the eternal shame of the abbé Maslon, who has been spying so long upon that poor M. Chélan, Madame de Rênal will have nothing to do with him. She goes to confession at Dijon or Besançon."

"She comes to Besançon!" said Julien, his brow flushing.

"Quite often," replied Fouqué with a questioning air.

"Have you any *Constitutionnels* on you?"

"What's that you say?" replied Fouqué.

"I ask you if you have any *Constitutionnels*?" Julien repeated, in a calmer tone. "They are sold here for thirty sous a copy."

"What! Liberals even in the Seminary!" cried Fouqué. "Unhappy France!" he went on, copying the hypocritical tone and meek accents of the abbé Maslon.

This visit would have made a profound impression upon our hero, had not, the very next day, a remark addressed to him by that little seminarist from Verrières who seemed such a boy, led him to make an important discovery. Ever since he had been in the Seminary, Julien's conduct had been nothing but a succession of false steps. He laughed bitterly at himself.

As a matter of fact, the important actions of his life were wisely ordered; but he paid no attention to details, and the clever people in a Seminary look only at details. And so he passed already among his fellow students as a free thinker. He had been betrayed by any number of trifling actions.

In their eyes he was convicted of this appalling vice, *he thought, he judged for himself,* instead of blindly following *authority* and example. The abbé Pirard had been of no assistance to him; he had not once uttered a word to him apart from the tribunal of penitence, and even there he listened rather than spoke. It would have been very different had Julien chosen the abbé Castanède.

The moment that Julien became aware of his own folly, his interest revived. He wished to know the whole extent of the harm, and, with this object, emerged a little from that haughty and obstinate silence with which he repulsed his fellows. It was then that they took their revenge on him. His advances were received with a contempt which went the length of derision. He realized that since his entering the Seminary, not an hour had passed, especially during recreation, that had not borne some consequence for or against him, had not increased the number of his enemies, or won him the good will of some seminarist who was genuinely virtuous or a trifle less boorish than the rest. The damage to be repaired was immense, the task one of great difficulty. Thenceforward Julien's attention was constantly on the alert; it was a case of portraying himself in an entirely new character.

The control of his eyes, for instance, gave him a great deal of trouble. It is not without reason that in such places they are kept lowered. "What was not my presumption at Verrières!" Julien said to himself, "I imagined I was alive; I was only preparing myself for life; here I am at last in the world, as I shall find it until I have played out my part, surrounded by real enemies. What an immense difficulty," he went on, "is this incessant hypocrisy! It would put the labours of Hercules to shame. The Hercules of modern times is Sixtus V, who for fifteen years on end, by his modesty, deceived forty Cardinals, who had seen him proud and vigorous in his youth.

"So learning is really nothing here!" he told himself with scorn; "progress in dogma, in sacred history, and the rest of it, count only in appearance. All that is said on that topic is intended to make fools like myself fall into the trap. Alas, my sole merit consisted in my rapid progress, in my faculty for grasping all that nonsense. Can it be that in their hearts they esteem it at its true value; judge of it as I do? And I was fool enough to be proud of myself! Those first places in class which I always obtain have served only to give me bad marks for the real places which we obtain when we leave the Seminary and in which we earn our living. Chazel, who knows far more than I, always puts into his compositions some piece of stupidity which sends him down to the fiftieth place; if he obtains the first, it is when he is not thinking. Ah! one word, a single word from M. Pirard, how useful it would have been to me!"

From the moment in which Julien's eyes were opened, the long exercises of ascetic piety, such as the Rosary five times weekly, the hymns to the Sacred Heart, etc., etc., which had seemed to him of such deadly dulness, became the most interesting actions of his life. Sternly criticising his own conduct, and seeking above all not to exaggerate his methods, Julien did not aspire from the first, like the seminarists who served as models to the rest, to perform at every moment some *significant* action, that is to say one which gave proof of some form of Christian perfection. In Seminaries, there is a way of eating a boiled egg which reveals the progress one has made in the godly life.

The reader, who is perhaps smiling, will please to remember all the mistakes made, in eating an egg, by the abbé Delille when invited to luncheon by a great lady of the Court of Louis XVI.

Julien sought at first to arrive at the *non culpa,* to wit, the state of the young seminarist whose gait, his way of moving his arms, eyes, etc., do not, it is true, indicate anything worldly, but do not yet shew the creature absorbed by the idea of the next life and the *absolute nullity* of this.

Everywhere Julien found inscribed in charcoal, on the walls of the passages, sentences like the following: "What are sixty years of trial, set in the balance with an eternity of bliss or an eternity of boiling oil in hell!" He no longer despised them; he realized that he must have them always before his eyes. "What shall I be doing all my life?" he said to himself; "I shall be selling the faithful a place in heaven. How is that place to be made visible to them? By the difference between my exterior and that of a layman."

After several months of application kept up at every moment, Julien still had the air of a *thinker.* His way of moving his eyes and opening his lips did not reveal an implicit faith ready to believe everything and to uphold everything, even by martyrdom. It was with anger that Julien saw himself surpassed in this respect by the most boorish peasants. They had good reasons for not having the air of thinkers.

What pains did he not take to arrive at that smug and narrow face, that expression of blind and fervent faith, which is so frequently to be found in the convents of Italy, and such perfect examples of which Guercino has bequeathed to us laymen in his paintings in churches.[1]

On the greatest festivals the seminarists were given sausages with pickled cabbage. Julien's neighbours at table had observed that he remained unmoved by this good fortune; it was one of his first crimes. His comrades saw in it an odious mark of the most stupid hypocrisy; nothing made him so many enemies. "Look at that gentleman, look at that proud fellow," they would say, "pretending to despise our best ration, sausages with cabbage! The wretched conceit of the damned fellow!" He should have refrained as an act of penance from eating the whole of his portion, and should have made the sacrifice of saying to some friend, with reference to the pickled cabbage: "What is there that man can offer to an All Powerful Being, if it be not *voluntary suffering?*"

Julien lacked the experience which makes it so easy for us to see things of this sort.

"Alas! The ignorance of these young peasants, my comrades, is a great advantage to them," he would exclaim in moments of discouragement. "When they arrive in the Seminary, the teacher has not to rid them of the appalling number of worldly thoughts which I brought with me, and which they read or my face, do what I will."

Julien studied with an attention that bordered upon envy the more boorish of the young peasants who arrived at the Seminary. At the moment when they were stripped of their ratteen jackets to be garbed in the black cassock, their education was limited to an immense and unbounded respect for dry and liquid money, as the saying goes in the Franche-Comté.

[1] For instance, in the Louvre, no. 1130: "Francis Duke of Aquitaine laying aside the crown and putting on a monastic habit."

It is the sacramental and heroic fashion of expressing the sublime idea of ready cash.

Happiness, for these seminarists, as for the heroes of Voltaire's tales, consists first and foremost in dining well. Julien discovered in almost all of them an innate respect for the man who wears a coat of *fine cloth*. This sentiment estimates *distributive justice*, as it is dealt out to us by our courts, at its true worth, indeed below its true worth. "What is to be gained," they would often say among themselves, "by going to law with the big?"

"Big" is the word used in the valleys of the Jura to denote a rich man. One may imagine their respect for the richest party of all: the Government!

Not to smile respectfully at the mere name of the Prefect is reckoned, among the peasants of the Franche-Comté, an imprudence; and imprudence, among the poor, is promptly punished with want of bread.

After having been almost suffocated at first by his sense of scorn, Julien ended by feeling pity: it had often been the lot of the fathers of the majority of his comrades to come home on a winter evening to their cottages, and to find there no bread, no chestnuts, and no potatoes. "Is it surprising then," Julien asked himself, "if the happy man, in their eyes, is first of all the man who has just eaten a good dinner, and after that he who possesses a good coat! My comrades have a definite vocation; that is to say, they see in the ecclesiastical calling a long continuation of this happiness: dining well and having a warm coat in winter."

Julien happened to hear a young seminarist, endowed with imagination, say to his companion:

"Why should not I become Pope like Sixtus V, who was a swineherd?"

"They make none but Italians Popes," replied the friend; "but they'll draw lots among us, for sure, to fill places as Grand Vicars and Canons, and perhaps Bishops.

M. P—— the Bishop of Châlons, is the son of a cooper; that is my father's trade."

One day, in the middle of a lesson in dogma, the abbé Pirard sent for Julien. The poor young fellow was delighted to escape from the physical and moral atmosphere in which he was plunged.

Julien found himself greeted by the Director in the manner which had so frightened him on the day of his joining the Seminary.

"Explain to me what I see written upon this playing card," he said to him, looking at him in such a way as to make him wish that the earth would open and swallow him.

Julien read:

"Amanda Binet, at the Giraffe café, before eight o'clock. Say you are from Genlis, and a cousin of my mother."

Julien perceived the immensity of the danger; the abbé Castanède's police had stolen the address from him.

"The day on which I came here," he replied, gazing at the abbé Pirard's forehead, for he could not face his terrible eye, "I was trembling with fear: M. Chélan had told me that this was a place full of tale-bearing and spite of all sorts; spying and the accusation of one's comrades are encouraged here. Such is the will of heaven, to shew life as it is to young priests, and to inspire in them a disgust with the world and its pomps."

"And it is to me that you make these fine speeches"— the abbé Pirard was furious. "You young rascal!"

"At Verrières," Julien went on calmly, "my brothers used to beat me when they had any reason to be jealous of me. . . ."

"To the point! Get to the point!" cried M. Pirard, almost beside himself.

Without being the least bit in the world intimidated, Julien resumed his narrative.

"On the day of my coming to Besançon, about noon,

I felt hungry, I went into a café. My heart was filled with repugnance for so profane a spot; but I thought that my luncheon would cost me less there than at an inn. A lady, who seemed to be the mistress of the place, took pity on my raw looks. 'Besançon is full of wicked people,' she told me, 'I am afraid for you, Sir. If you find yourself in any trouble, come to me, send a message to me before eight o'clock. If the porters at the Seminary refuse to take your message, say that you are my cousin, and come from Genlis. . . .' "

"All this farrago will have to be investigated," exclaimed the abbé Pirard who, unable to remain in one place, was striding up and down the room.

"You will go back to your cell!"

The abbé accompanied Julien and locked him in. He himself at once proceeded to examine his trunk, in the bottom of which the fatal card had been carefully concealed. Nothing was missing from the trunk, but several things had been disarranged; and yet the key never left his possession. "How fortunate," Julien said to himself, "that during the time of my blindness I never made use of the permission to leave the building, which M. Castanède so frequently offered me with a generosity which I now understand. Perhaps I might have been so foolish as to change my clothes and pay the fair Amanda a visit, I should have been ruined. When they despaired of making any use of their information in that way, so as not to waste it they have used it to denounce me."

A couple of hours later, the Director sent for him.

"You have not lied," he said to him, looking at him less severely; "but to keep such an address is an imprudence the serious nature of which you cannot conceive. Unhappy boy! In ten years, perhaps, it will redound to your hurt."

CHAPTER TWENTY-SEVEN

FIRST EXPERIENCE OF LIFE

Le temps présent, grand Dieu! c'est l'arche du
Seigneur. Malheur a qui y touche.

DIDEROT.

THE reader will kindly excuse our giving but few
clear and precise details of this epoch in Julien's
life. Not that we lack them, far from it; but
perhaps the life he led in the Seminary is too black for
the modest colouring which we have sought to preserve in
these pages. People who have been made to suffer by
certain things cannot be reminded of them without a horror
which paralyses every other pleasure, even that to be
found in reading a story.

Julien met with little success in his attempts at hypocrisy
in action; he passed through moments of disgust and even
of complete discouragement. He was utterly unsuccessful,
and that moreover in a vile career. The slightest help
from without would have sufficed to sustain his resolution, the difficulty to be overcome was not great; but the
was alone, as lonely as a vessel abandoned in mid-ocean.
"And if I should succeed," he said to himself; "to have
to spend my whole life in such evil company! Gluttons
who think of nothing but the ham omelette they are going
to devour at dinner, or men like the abbé Castanède, to
whom no crime is too black! They will rise to power;
but at what a price, great God!

"Man's will is powerful, I see it written everywhere;
but is it sufficiently so to overcome such repulsion? The
task of great men has always been easy; however terrible

was their danger, it was beautiful in their eyes; and who but myself can realize the ugliness of all that surrounds me?"

This was the most trying moment in his life. It was so easy for him to enlist in one of the fine regiments that were stationed at Besançon! He might become a teacher of Latin; he wanted so little to keep himself alive! But then, no career, no future for his imagination: it was a living death. Here is a detailed account of one of his wretched days.

"My presumption has so often flattered itself upon my being different from the other young peasants! Well, I have lived long enough to see that difference breeds hatred," he said to himself one morning. This great truth had just been revealed to him by one of his most annoying failures. He had laboured for a week to make himself agreeable to a student who lived in the odour of sanctity. He was walking with him in the courtyard, listening submissively to idiocies that sent him to sleep as he walked. Suddenly a storm broke, the thunder growled, and the saintly student exclaimed, thrusting him rudely away:

"Listen, each for himself in this world, I have no wish to be struck by lightning: God may blast you as an infidel, another Voltaire."

His teeth clenched with rage and his eyes opened towards the sky furrowed by streaks of lightning: "I should deserve to be submerged, were I to let myself sleep during the storm!" cried Julien. "Let us attempt the conquest of some other drudge."

The bell rang for the abbé Castanède's class of sacred history.

These young peasants who lived in such fear of the hard toil and poverty of their fathers, were taught that day by the abbé Castanède that that being so terrible in their eyes, the Government, had no real or legitimate power save what was delegated to it by God's Vicar on Earth.

"Render yourselves worthy of the Pope's bounties by the sanctity of your lives, by your obedience, be *like a rod in his hands*," he went on, "and you will attain to a superb position where you will be in supreme command, under no man's control; a permanent position, of which the Government pays one third of the emoluments, and the faithful, roused by your preaching, the other two thirds."

On leaving his classroom, M. Castanède stopped in the courtyard among his students, who that day were most attentive.

"You may well say of a curé, each man gets what he deserves," he said to the students who gathered round him. "I myself have known mountain parishes where the fees came to more than those of many town curés. There was as much in money, not to speak of the fat capons, eggs, fresh butter, and endless little delicacies; and there the curé takes the first place without challenge: no good meal to which he is not invited, made much of," etc.

No sooner had M. Castanède gone up to his own room, than the students divided into groups. Julien belonged to none of these; they drew away from him as from a tainted wether. In each of the groups, he saw a student toss a copper in the air, and if he guessed head or tail aright, his companions concluded that he would soon have one of these livings with fat fees.

Stories followed. One young priest, barely a year in orders, having presented a gelt rabbit to an old curé's servant, had got the curé to ask for him as his assistant, and a few months afterwards, for the curé had died almost immediately, had succeeded him in a good living. Another had managed to have his name put forward for the eventual succession to the curacy of a prosperous country town, by attending all the meals of the paralytic old curé and carving his chickens for him gracefully.

The seminarists, like young men in every profession, exaggerated the effect of these little stratagems when they were out of the ordinary and struck the imagination.

"I must," thought Julien, "take part in these conversations." When they were not discussing sausages and rich livings, their talk ran on the worldly side of ecclesiastical teaching; the differences between Bishops and Prefects, mayors and curés. Julien saw lurking in their minds the idea of a second God, but of a God far more to be feared and far more powerful than the first; this second God was the Pope. It was said, but with lowered voice, and when the speaker was quite certain of not being overheard by M. Pirard, that if the Pope did not take the trouble to appoint all the Prefects and all the mayors in France, it was because he had delegated the King of France for that duty, by naming him the Eldest Son of the Church.

It was about this time that Julien thought he might derive some benefit from his admiration for M. de Maistre's book on the Pope. He did, as a matter of fact, astonish his fellow-students; but this was a fresh misfortune. He annoyed them by expressing their opinions better than they could themselves. M. Chélan had been a rash counsellor for Julien as he had been for himself. After training him to the habit of reasoning accurately and not letting himself be taken in by vain words, he had omitted to tell him that in a person of little repute this habit is a crime; for sound reasoning always gives offence.

Julien's fine speech was therefore only another crime against him. His companions, being compelled to think about him, succeeded in finding two words to express all the horror with which he filled them: they nicknamed him Martin Luther; "chiefly," they said, "because of that infernal logic of which he is so proud."

Several young seminarists had fresher complexions and might be reckoned better looking than Julien; but he had

white hands, and could not hide certain habits of personal
cleanliness. This distinction was none at all in the grim
dwelling into which destiny had cast him. The unclean
peasants among whom he lived declared that he had
extremely lax morals. We are afraid to tire the reader
by an account of our hero's endless mishaps. To take one
instance, the more vigorous among his companions tried
to make a practice of thrashing him; he was obliged to
arm himself with a metal compass and to inform them,
but only by signs, that he would use it. Signs cannot be
represented, in a spy's report, so damningly as words.

CHAPTER TWENTY-EIGHT

A PROCESSION

Tous les cœurs étaient émus. La présence de Dieu
semblait descendue dans ces rues étroites et gothiques,
tendues de toutes parts, et bien sablées par les soins
des fidèles.

YOUNG.[1]

IN vain might Julien make himself small and foolish,
he could not give satisfaction, he was too different.
"And yet," he said to himself, "all these Professors
are men of great discernment, and picked men, each of
them one in a thousand; how is it they do not like my
humility?" One alone seemed to him to be taking advantage of his readiness to believe anything and to appear
taken in by everything. This was the abbé Chas-Bernard,
Master of Ceremonies at the Cathedral, where, for the
last fifteen years, he had been kept in hopes of a Canonry;
in the meantime, he taught sacred eloquence at the
Seminary. In the period of his blindness, this class was
one of those in which Julien most regularly came out at
the top. The abbé Chas had been led by this to shew
a partiality for him, and, at the end of his class, would
gladly take his arm for a turn in the garden.

"What can his object be?" Julien asked himself. He
found with amazement that, for hours on end, the abbé
talked to him of the ornaments which the Cathedral
possessed. It had seventeen apparelled chasubles, apart
from the vestments worn at requiems. They had great

[1] As in Chapter XXVI I have left this motto in French. It
seems, however, to be taken from Arthur Young rather than
Edward. C. K. S. M.

hopes of President de Rubempré's widow; this lady, who was ninety years old, had preserved for at least seventy of those years her wedding garments of superb Lyons stuffs, figured in gold. "Just imagine, my friend," said the abbé Chas coming to a standstill and opening his eyes wide, "these stuffs stand by themselves, there is so much gold in them. It is the common opinion among the good people of Besançon that, under the Présidente's will, the treasury of the Cathedral will be enriched with more than ten chasubles, not to mention four or five copes for the greater feasts. I will go farther," the abbé Chas added, lowering his voice. "I have good reason to think that the Présidente will bequeath to us eight magnificent silver-gilt candlesticks, which are supposed to have been bought in Italy, by the Duke of Burgundy, Charles the Bold, whose favourite minister was an ancestor of hers."

"But what is this man really aiming at behind all this frippery?" Julien wondered. "This careful preparation has been going on for an age, and nothing comes of it. He must have singularly little faith in me! He is cleverer than any of the others, whose secret purposes one can see so plainly after a fortnight. I understand, this man's ambition has been in torment for fifteen years."

One evening, in the middle of the armed drill, Julien was sent for by the abbé Pirard, who said to him:

"To-morrow is the festival of Corpus Domini. M. l'abbé Chas-Bernard requires you to help him to decorate the Cathedral; go and obey."

The abbé Pirard called him back, and added, in a tone of compassion:

"It is for you to decide whether you wish to seize the opportunity of taking a stroll through the town."

"*Incedo per ignes,*" replied Julien: which is to say, I am treading on dangerous ground.

Next morning at daybreak, Julien made his way to the Cathedral, walking with lowered eyes. The sight of the streets and the activity which was beginning to pervade the town did him good. On every side people were draping the fronts of their houses for the procession. All the time that he had spent in the Seminary seemed to him no more than an instant. His thoughts were at Vergy, and with that charming Amanda Binet, whom he might meet, for her café was but little out of his way. He saw in the distance the abbé Chas-Bernard, standing by the door of his beloved Cathedral; he was a large man with a joyful countenance and an open air. This morning he was triumphant: "I have been waiting for you, my dear son," he called out, as soon as he caught sight of Julien, "you are welcome. Our labours this day will be long and hard, let us fortify ourselves with an early breakfast; the other we shall take at ten o'clock during high mass."

"I desire, Sir," Julien said to him with an air of gravity, "not to be left alone for a moment; kindly observe," he added, pointing to the clock above their heads, "that I have arrived at one minute before five."

"Ah! So you are afraid of those young rascals at the Seminary! It is too kind of you to give them a thought," said the abbé Chas; "is a road any the worse, because there are thorns in the hedges on either side of it? The traveller goes his way and leaves the wicked thorns to wither where they are. However, we must to work, my dear friend, to work."

The abbé Chas had been right in saying that their labours would be hard. There had been a great funeral service in the Cathedral the day before; it had been impossible to make any preparations; they were obliged, therefore, in the course of the morning, to drape each of the gothic pillars which separate the nave from the aisles in a sort of jacket of red damask which rose to a height of thirty feet. The Bishop had ordered four upholsterers from Paris by mail coach, but these gentlemen could not do everything themselves, and so far from encouraging the awkward efforts of their Bisontine colleagues they increased their awkwardness by laughing at it.

Julien saw that he would have to go up the ladders himself, his agility stood him in good stead. He undertook to direct the local upholsterers in person. The abbé Chas was in ecstasies as he watched him spring from one ladder to another. When all the pillars were hung with damask, the next thing was to go and place five enormous bunches of plumes on top of the great baldachino, over the high altar. A richly gilded wooden crown was supported on eight great twisted columns of Italian marble. But, in order to reach the centre of the baldachino, over the tabernacle, one had to step across an old wooden cornice, possibly worm-eaten, and forty feet from the ground.

The sight of this perilous ascent had extinguished the gaiety, so brilliant until then, of the Parisian upholsterers; they looked at it from beneath, discussed it volubly, and did not go up. Julien took possession of the bunches of plumes, and ran up the ladder. He arranged them admirably upon the ornament in the form of a crown in the centre of the baldachino. As he stepped down from the ladder, the abbé Chas-Bernard took him in his arms.

"Optime!" exclaimed the worthy priest, "I shall tell Monseigneur of this."

Their ten o'clock breakfast was a merry feast. Never had the abbé Chas seen his church looking so well.

"My dear disciple," he said to Julien, "my mother used to hire out chairs in this venerable fane, so that I was brought up in this great edifice. Robespierre's Terror ruined us; but, at eight years old, as I then was, I was already serving masses in private houses, and their owners gave me my dinner on mass days. No one could fold a chasuble better than I, the gold braid was never broken. Since the restoration of the Faith by Napoleon, it has been my happy lot to take charge of everything in this venerable mother church. On five days in the year, my eyes behold it decked out with these beautiful ornaments. But never has it been so resplendent, never have the damask strips been so well hung as they are to-day, have they clung so to the pillars."

"At last, he is going to tell me his secret," thought Julien, "here he is talking to me of himself; he is beginning to expand." But nothing imprudent was said by this man, evidently in an excited state. "And yet he has worked hard, he is happy," Julien said to himself, "the good wine has not been spared. What a man! What an example for me! He takes the prize." (This was a low expression which he had picked up from the old surgeon.)

When the Sanctus bell rang during high mass, Julien wished to put on a surplice so as to follow the Bishop in the superb procession.

"And the robbers, my friend, the robbers!" cried the abbé Chas, "you forget them. The procession is going out; the church will be left empty; we must keep watch, you and I. We shall be fortunate if we lose only a couple of ells of that fine braid which goes round the base of the pillars. That is another gift from Madame de Rubempré; it comes from the famous Count, her great-grandfather; it is pure gold, my friend," the abbé went on, whispering in his ear, and with an air of evident exaltation, "nothing false about it! I entrust to you the inspection of the north aisle, do not stir from it. I keep for myelf the south aisle and nave. Keep an eye on the confessionals; it is there that the robbers' women spies watch for the moment when our backs are turned."

As he finished speaking, the quarter before twelve struck, at once the big bell began to toll. It was being pulled with all the ringers' might; the rich and solemn sound stirred Julien deeply. His imagination rose from the ground.

The odour of the incense and of the rose leaves strewn

before the Blessed Sacrament by children dressed as little Saint Johns, intensified his excitement.

The sober note of the bell ought to have suggested to Julien only the thought of the work of a score of men earning fifty centimes, and assisted perhaps by fifteen or twenty of the faithful. He ought to have thought of the wear and tear of the ropes, of the timber, of the danger from the bell itself which fell every two hundred years, and to have planned some way of diminishing the wage of the ringers, or of paying them with some indulgence or other favour drawn from the spiritual treasury of the Church, with no strain upon her purse.

In place of these sage reflexions, Julien's soul, excited by these rich and virile sounds, was straying through imaginary space. Never will he make either a good priest or a great administrator. Souls that are moved thus are capable at most of producing an artist. Here Julien's presumption breaks out in the full light of day. Fifty, perhaps, of his fellow seminarists, made attentive to the realities of life by the public hatred and Jacobinism which, they are told, is lurking behind every hedge, on hearing the big bell of the Cathedral, would have thought only of the wages paid to the ringers. They would have applied the genius of a Barême to determine the question whether the degree of emotion aroused in the public was worth the money given to the ringers. Had Julien chosen to give his mind to the material interests of the Cathedral, his imagination flying beyond its goal would have thought of saving forty francs for the Chapter, and would have let slip the opportunity of avoiding an outlay of twenty-five centimes.

, While, in the most perfect weather ever seen, the procession wound its way slowly through Besançon, and halted at the glittering stations which all the local authorities had vied with one another in erecting, the church remained

wrapped in a profound silence. A suffused light, an agreeable coolness reigned in it; it was still balmy with the
fragrance of flowers and incense.

The silence, the profound solitude, the coolness of the
long aisles, made Julien's musings all the sweeter. He
had no fear of being disturbed by the abbé Chas, who
was occupied in another part of the building. His soul
had almost quitted its mortal envelope, which was strolling
at a slow pace along the north aisle committed to his
charge. He was all the more at rest, since he was certain
that there was nobody in the confessionals save a few
devout women; he saw without observing.

His distraction was nevertheless half conquered by the
sight of two women extremely well dressed who were kneeling, one of them in a confessional, the other, close beside
her, upon a chair. He saw without observing them; at
the same time, whether from a vague sense of his duty,
or from admiration of the plain but noble attire of these
ladies, he remarked that there was no priest in that confessional. "It is strange," he thought, "that these beautiful
ladies are not kneeling before some station, if they are
religious; or placed in good seats in the front of some
balcony, if they are fashionable. How well cut that gown
is! What grace!" He slackened his pace in order to see
their faces.

The one who was kneeling in the confessional turned her
head slightly on hearing the sound of Julien's step amid
the prevailing silence. All at once she gave a little cry,
and fainted.

As her strength left her, this kneeling lady fell back;
her friend, who was close at hand, hastened to the rescue.
At the same time Julien caught sight of the shoulders of
the lady who had fallen back. A rope of large seed pearls,
well known to him, caught his eye. What was his state
when he recognized the hair of Madame de Rênal! It
was she. The lady who was trying to hold up her head,

and to arrest her fall, was Madame Derville. Julien, beside himself with emotion, sprang forward; Madame de Rênal's fall would perhaps have brought down her friend if he had not supported them. He saw Madame de Rênal's head, pale, absolutely devoid of consciousness, drooping upon her shoulder. He helped Madame Derville to prop that charming head against the back of a straw chair; he was on his knees.

Madame Derville turned and recognized him.

"Fly, Sir, fly!" she said to him in accents of the most burning anger. "On no account must she see you again. The sight of you must indeed fill her with horror, she was so happy before you came! Your behaviour is atrocious. Fly; be off with you, if you have any shame left."

This speech was uttered with such authority, and Julien felt so weak at the moment, that he withdrew. "She always hated me," he said to himself, thinking of Madame Derville.

At that moment, the nasal chant of the leading priests in the procession rang through the church; the procession was returning. The abbé Chas-Bernard called repeatedly to Julien, who at first did not hear him: finally he came and led him by the arm from behind a pillar where Julien had taken refuge more dead than alive. He wished to present him to the Bishop.

"You are feeling unwell, my child," said the abbé, seeing him so pale and almost unable to walk; "you have been working too hard." The abbé gave him his arm. "Come, sit down here, on the sacristan's little stool, behind me; I shall screen you." They were now by the side of the main door. "Calm yourself, we have still a good twenty minutes before Monseigneur appears. Try to recover yourself; when he passes, I shall hold you up, for I am strong and vigorous, in spite of my age."

But when the Bishop passed, Julien was so tremulous that the abbé Chas abandoned the idea of presenting him.

"Do not worry yourself about it," he told him, "I shall find another opportunity."

That evening, he sent down to the chapel of the Seminary ten pounds of candles, saved, he said, by Julien's efforts and the rapidity with which he extinguished them. Nothing could have been farther from the truth. The poor boy was himself extinguished; he had not had a thought in his head after seeing Madame de Rênal.

CHAPTER TWENTY-NINE

THE FIRST STEP

Il a connu son siècle, il a connu son département, et
il est riche.

Le Précurseur.

JULIEN had not yet recovered from the profound
abstraction in which the incident in the Cathedral
had plunged him, when one morning the grim abbé
Pirard sent for him.

"Here is M. l'abbé Chas-Bernard writing to me to com-
mend you. I am quite satisfied with your conduct as a
whole. You are extremely imprudent and indeed stupid,
without shewing it; however, up to the present your heart
is sound and even generous; your intellect is above the
average. Taking you all in all, I see a spark in you which
must not be neglected.

"After fifteen years of labour, I am on the eve of leaving this establishment: my crime is that of having allowed
the seminarists to use their own judgment, and of having
neither protected nor unmasked that secret society of which
you have spoken to me at the stool of penitence. Before
I go, I wish to do something for you; I should have acted
two months ago, for you deserve it, but for the accusation
based upon the address of Amanda Binet, which was
found in your possession. I appoint you tutor in the
New and Old Testaments."

Julien, in a transport of gratitude, quite thought of falling on his knees and thanking God; but he yielded to a
more genuine impulse. He went up to the abbé Pirard
and took his hand, which he raised to his lips.

"What is this?" cried the Director in a tone of annoyance; but Julien's eyes were even more eloquent than his action.

The abbé Pirard gazed at him in astonishment, like a man who, in the course of long years, has fallen out of the way of meeting with delicate emotions. This attention pierced the Director's armour; his voice changed.

"Ah, well! Yes, my child, I am attached to you. Heaven knows that it is entirely against my will. I ought to be just, and to feel neither hatred nor love for anyone. Your career will be difficult. I see in you something that offends the common herd. Jealousy and calumny will pursue you. In whatever place Providence may set you, your companions will never set eyes on you without hating you; and if they pretend to love you, it will be in order to betray you the more surely. For this there is but one remedy: have recourse only to God, who has given you, to punish you for your presumption, this necessity of being hated; let your conduct be pure; that is the sole resource that I can see for you. If you hold fast to the truth with an invincible embrace, sooner or later your enemies will be put to confusion."

It was so long since Julien had heard a friendly voice, that we must forgive him a weakness: he burst into tears. The abbé Pirard opened his arms to embrace him; the moment was very precious to them both.

Julien was wild with joy; this promotion was the first that he had obtained; the advantages were immense. In order to realize them, one must have been condemned to pass whole months without a moment's solitude, and in immediate contact with companions at best tiresome, and mostly intolerable. Their shouts alone would have been enough to create disorder in a sensitive organism. The boisterous joy of these peasants well fed and well dressed, could find expression, thought itself complete only when they were shouting with the full force of their lungs.

Now Julien dined by himself, or almost so, an hour later than the rest of the seminarists. He had a key to the garden, and might walk there at the hours when it was empty.

Greatly to his surprise, Julien noticed that they hated him less; he. had been expecting, on the contrary, an intensification of their hatred. That secret desire that no one should speak to him, which was all too apparent and had made him so many enemies, was no longer a sign of absurd pride. In the eyes of the coarse beings among whom he lived, it was a proper sense of his own dignity. Their hatred diminished perceptibly, especially among the youngest of his companions, now become his pupils, whom he treated with great courtesy. In course of time he had even supporters; it became bad form to call him Martin Luther.

But why speak of his friends, his enemies? It is all so ugly, and all the more ugly, the more accurately it is drawn from life. These are however the only teachers of ethics that the people have, and without them where should we be? Will the newspaper ever manage to take the place of the parish priest?

Since Julien's promotion, the Director of the Seminary made a point of never speaking to him except in the presence of witnesses. This was only prudent, in the master's interest as well as the pupil's; but more than anything else it was a *test*. The stern Jansenist Pirard's invariable principle was: "Has a man any merit in your eyes? Place an obstacle in the way of everything that he desires, everything that he undertakes. If his merit be genuine, he will certainly be able to surmount or thrust aside your obstacles."

It was the hunting season. Fouqué took it into his head to send to the Seminary a stag and a boar in the name of Julien's family. The dead animals were left lying in the passage, between kitchen and refectory. There all the seminarists saw them on their way to dinner. They aroused much interest. The boar, although stone dead, frightened the younger boys; they fingered his tusks. Nothing else was spoken of for a week.

This present, which classified Julien's family in the section of society that one must respect, dealt a mortal blow to jealousy. It was a form of superiority consecrated by fortune. Chazel and the most distinguished of the seminarists made overtures to him, and almost complained to him that he had not warned them of his parents' wealth, and had thus betrayed them into shewing a want of respect for money.

There was a conscription from which Julien was exempt in his capacity as a seminarist. This incident moved him deeply. "And so there has passed now for ever the moment at which, twenty years ago, a heroic life would have begun for me!"

Walking by himself in the Seminary garden, he overheard a conversation between two masons who were at work upon the enclosing wall.

"Ah, well! One will have to go, here's another conscription."

"In the *other man's* days, well and good! A stone mason became an officer, and became a general, that has been known."

"Look what it's like now! Only the beggars go. A man with the *wherewithal* stays at home."

"The man who is born poor stays poor, and that's all there is to it."

"Tell me, now, is it true what people say, that the other is dead?" put in a third mason.

"It's the big ones who say that, don't you see? They were afraid of the other."

"What a difference, how well everything went in his time! And to think that he was betrayed by his Marshals! There must always be a traitor somewhere!"

This conversation comforted Julien a little. As he walked away he repeated to himself with a sigh:

"The only King whose memory the people cherish still!"

The examinations came round. Julien answered the questions in a brilliant manner; he saw that Chazel himself was seeking to display the whole extent of his knowledge.

On the first day, the examiners appointed by the famous Grand Vicar de Frilair greatly resented having always to place first, or at the very most second on their list this Julien Sorel who had been pointed out to them as the Benjamin of the abbé Pirard. Wagers were made in the Seminary that in the aggregate list of the examinations, Julien would occupy the first place, a distinction that carried with it the honour of dining with the Bishop. But at the end of one session, in which the subject had been the Fathers of the Church, a skilful examiner, after questioning Julien upon Saint Jerome, and his passion for Cicero, began to speak of Horace, Virgil and other profane authors. Unknown to his companions, Julien had learned by heart a great number of passages from these authors. Carried away by his earlier successes, he forgot where he was and, at the repeated request of the examiner, recited and paraphrased with enthusiasm several odes of Horace. Having let him sink deeper and deeper for twenty minutes, suddenly the examiner's face changed, and he delivered a stinging rebuke to Julien for having wasted his time in these profane studies, and stuffed his head with useless if not criminal thoughts.

"I am a fool, Sir, and you are right," said Julien with a modest air, as he saw the clever stratagem by which he had been taken in.

This ruse on the examiner's part was considered a dirty trick, even in the Seminary, though this did not prevent M. l'abbé de Frilair, that clever man, who had so ably organized the framework of the Bisontine *Congregation,* and whose reports to Paris made judges, prefect, and even the general officers of the garrison tremble, from setting, with his powerful hand, the number 198 against Julien's name. He was delighted thus to mortify his enemy, the Jansenist Pirard.

For the last ten years his great ambition had been to remove Pirard from control of the Seminary. That cleric, following in his own conduct the principles which he had outlined to Julien, was sincere, devout, innocent of intrigue, devoted to his duty. But heaven, in its wrath, had given him that splenetic temperament, bound to feel deeply insults and hatred. Not one of the affronts that were put upon him was lost upon his ardent spirit. He would have offered his resignation a hundred times, but he believed that he was of use in the post in which Providence had placed him. "I prevent the spread of Jesuitry and idolatry," he used to say to himself.

At the time of the examinations, it was perhaps two months since he had spoken to Julien, and yet he was ill for a week, when, on receiving the official letter announcing the result of the competition, he saw the number 198 set against the name of that pupil whom he regarded as the glory of his establishment. The only consolation for this stern character was to concentrate upon Julien all the vigilance at his command. He was delighted to find in him neither anger nor thoughts of revenge, nor discouragement.

Some weeks later, Julien shuddered on receiving a letter; it bore the Paris post-mark. "At last," he thought, "Madame de Rênal has remembered her promises." A gentleman who signed himself Paul Sorel, and professed to be related to him, sent him a bill of exchange for five hundred francs. The writer added that if Julien continued to study with success the best Latin authors, a similar sum would be sent to him every year.

' "It is she, it is her bounty!" Julien said to himself with emotion, "she wishes to comfort me; but why is there not one word of affection?"

He was mistaken with regard to the letter; Madame de Rênal, under the influence of her friend Madame Derville, was entirely absorbed in her own profound remorse. In spite of herself, she often thought of the strange creature whose coming into her life had so upset it, but she would never have dreamed of writing to him.

If we spoke the language of the Seminary, we might see a miracle in this windfall of five hundred francs, and say that it was M. de Frilair himself that heaven had employed to make this gift to Julien.

Twelve years earlier, M. l'abbé de Frilair had arrived at Besançon with the lightest of portmanteaux, which, the story went, contained his entire fortune. He now found himself one of the wealthiest landowners in the Department. In the course of his growing prosperity he had purchased one half of an estate of which the other half passed by inheritance to M. de La Mole. Hence a great lawsuit between these worthies.

Despite his brilliant existence in Paris, and the posts which he held at court, the Marquis de La Mole felt that it was dangerous to fight down at Besançon against a Grand Vicar who was reputed to make and unmake Prefects. Instead of asking for a gratuity of fifty thousand francs, disguised under some head or other that would pass in the budget, and allowing M. de Frilair to win this pettifogging action for fifty thousand francs, the Marquis took offence. He believed that he had a case: a fine reason!

For, if we may be so bold as to say it: what judge is there who has not a son, or at least a cousin to help on in the world?

To enlighten the less clear-sighted, a week after the first judgment that he obtained, M. l'abbé de Frilair took the Bishop's carriage, and went in person to convey the

Cross of the Legion of Honour to his counsel. M. de La Mole, somewhat dismayed by the bold front assumed by the other side, and feeling that his own counsel were weakening, asked the advice of the abbé Chélan, who put him in touch with M. Pirard.

At the date of our story they had been corresponding thus for some years. The abbé Pirard dashed into the business with all the force of his passionate nature. In constant communication with the Marquis's counsel, he studied his case, and finding him to be in the right, openly declared himself a partisan of the Marquis de La Mole against the all powerful Grand Vicar. The latter was furious at such insolence, and coming from a little Jansenist to boot!

"You see what these court nobles are worth who claim to have such power!" the abbé de Frilair would say to his intimates; "M. de La Mole has not sent so much as a wretched Cross to his agent at Besançon, and is going to allow him to be deprived of his post without a murmur. And yet, my friends write to me, this noble peer never allows a week to pass without going to shew off his blue riband in the drawing-room of the Keeper of the Seals, for what that is worth."

In spite of all M. Pirard's activity, and albeit M. de La Mole was always on the best of terms with the Minister of Justice and still more with his officials, all that he had been able to achieve, after six years of constant effort, was to avoid actually losing his case.

In ceaseless correspondence with the abbé Pirard, over an affair which they both pursued with passion, the Marquis came in time to appreciate the abbé's type of mind. Gradually, despite the immense gulf between their social positions, their correspondence took on a tone of friendship. The abbé Pirard told the Marquis that his enemies were seeking to oblige him, by their insults, to offer his resignation. In the anger which he felt at the infamous stratagem (according to him) employed against Julien, he related the latter's story to the Marquis.

Although extremely rich, this great nobleman was not in the least a miser. He had never once been able to make the abbé Pirard accept so much as the cost of postage occasioned by the lawsuit. He took the opportunity to send five hundred francs to the abbé's favourite pupil.

M. de La Mole took the trouble to write the covering letter with his own hand. This set him thinking of the abbé.

One day the latter received a short note in which he was requested to call at once, upon urgent business, at an inn on the outskirts of Besançon. There he found M. de La Mole's steward.

"M. le Marquis has instructed me to bring you his carriage," he was informed. "He hopes that after you have read this letter, you will find it convenient to start for Paris, in four or five days from now. I am going to employ the time which you will be so kind as to indicate to me in visiting the estates of M. le Marquis in the Franche-Comté. After which, on whatever day suits you, we shall start for Paris."

The letter was brief:

"Rid yourself, my dear Sir, of all these provincial bickerings, come and breathe a calmer air in Paris. I am sending you my carriage, which has orders to await your decision for four days. I shall wait for you myself, in Paris, until Tuesday. It requires only the word yes, from you, Sir, to make me accept in your name one of the best livings in the neighbourhood of Paris. The wealthiest of your future parishioners has never set eyes on you, but is devoted to you more warmly than you can suppose; he is the Marquis de La Mole."

Without knowing it, the stern abbé Pirard loved this Seminary, peopled with his enemies, to which, for fifteen years, he had devoted all his thoughts. M. de La Mole's letter was to him like the sudden appearance of a surgeon with the duty of performing a painful but necessary operation. His dismissal was certain. He gave the steward an appointment, in three days' time.

For the next forty-eight hours, he was in a fever of uncertainty. Finally, he wrote to M. de La Mole and composed, for the Bishop's benefit, a letter, a masterpiece of ecclesiastical diction, though a trifle long. It would have been difficult to find language more irreproachable, or breathing a more sincere respect. And yet this letter, intended to give M. de Frilair a trying hour with his patron, enumerated all the serious grounds for complaint and descended to the sordid little pinpricks which, after he had borne them, with resignation, for six years, were forcing the abbé Pirard to leave the diocese.

They stole the wood from his shed, they poisoned his dog, etc., etc.

This letter written, he sent to awaken Julien who, at eight o'clock in the evening, was already asleep, as were all the seminarists.

"You know where the Bishop's Palace is?" he said to him in the best Latin; "take this letter to Monseigneur. I shall not attempt to conceal from you that I am sending you amongst wolves. Be all eyes and ears. No prevarication in your answers; but remember that the man who is questioning you would perhaps take a real delight in trying to harm you. I am glad, my child, to give you this experience before I leave you, for I do not conceal from you that the letter which you are taking contains my resignation."

Julien did not move; he was fond of the abbé Pirard. In vain might prudence warn him:

"After this worthy man's departure, the Sacred Heart party will degrade and perhaps even expel me."

He could not think about himself. What embarrassed

him was a sentence which he wished to cast in a polite form, but really he was incapable of using his mind.

"Well, my friend, aren't you going?"

"You see, Sir, they say," Julien began timidly, "that during your long administration here, you have never put anything aside. I have six hundred francs."

Tears prevented him from continuing.

"That too will be noticed," said the ex-Director of the Seminary coldly. "Go to the Palace, it is getting late."

As luck would have it, that evening M. l'abbé de Frilair was in attendance in the Bishop's parlour; Monseigneur was dining at the Prefecture. So that it was to M. de Frilair himself that Julien gave the letter, but he did not know who he was.

Julien saw with astonishment that this priest boldly opened the letter addressed to the Bishop. The fine features of the Grand Vicar soon revealed a surprise mingled with keen pleasure, and his gravity increased. While he was reading, Julien, struck by his good looks, had time to examine him. It was a face that would have had more gravity but for the extreme subtlety that appeared in certain of its features, and would actually have suggested dishonesty, if the owner of that handsome face had ceased for a moment to control it. The nose, which was extremely prominent, formed an unbroken and perfectly straight line, and gave unfortunately to a profile that otherwise was most distinguished, an irremediable resemblance to the mask of a fox. In addition, this abbé who seemed so greatly interested in M. Pirard's resignation, was dressed with an elegance that greatly pleased Julien, who had never seen its like on any other priest.

It was only afterwards that Julien learned what was the abbé de Frilair's special talent. He knew how to amuse his Bishop, a pleasant old man, made to live in Paris, who regarded Besançon as a place of exile. This Bishop was extremely short-sighted, and passionately fond of fish.

The abbé de Frilair used to remove the bones from the fish that was set before Monseigneur.

Julien was silently watching the abbé as he read over again the letter of resignation, when suddenly the door burst open. A lackey, richly attired, passed rapidly through the room. Julien had barely time to turn towards the door; he saw a little old man, wearing a pectoral cross. He fell on his knees: the Bishop bestowed a kind smile upon him as he passed through the room. The handsome abbé followed him, and Julien was left alone in this parlour, the pious magnificence of which he could now admire at his leisure.

The Bishop of Besançon, a man of character, tried, but not crushed by the long hardships of the Emigration, was more than seventy-five, and cared infinitely little about what might happen in the next ten years.

"Who is that clever looking seminarist, whom I seemed to see as I passed?" said the Bishop. "Ought they not, by my orders, to be in their beds at this hour?"

"This one is quite wide awake, I assure you, Monseigneur, and he brings great news: the resignation of the only Jansenist left in your diocese. That terrible abbé Pirard understands at last the meaning of a hint."

"Well," said the Bishop with a roguish smile, "I defy you to fill his place with a man of his quality. And to shew you the value of the man, I invite him to dine with me to-morrow."

The Grand Vicar wished to insinuate a few words as to the choice of a successor. The prelate, little disposed to discuss business, said to him:

"Before we put in the next man, let us try to discover why this one is going. Fetch me in that seminarist, the truth is to be found in the mouths of babes."

Julien was summoned: "I shall find myself trapped between two inquisitors," he thought. Never had he felt more courageous.

At the moment of his entering the room, two tall valets, better dressed than M. Valenod himself, were disrobing Monseigneur. The prelate, before coming to the subject of M. Pirard, thought fit to question Julien about his studies. He touched upon dogma, and was amazed. Presently he turned to the Humanities, Virgil, Horace, Cicero. "Those names," thought Julien, "earned me my number 198. I have nothing more to lose, let us try to shine." He was successful; the prelate, an excellent humanist himself, was enchanted.

At dinner at the Prefecture, a girl, deservedly famous, had recited the poem of *La Madeleine*.[1] He was in the mood for literary conversation, and at once forgot the abbé Pirard and everything else, in discussing with the seminarist the important question, whether Horace had been rich or poor. The prelate quoted a number of odes, but at times his memory began to fail him, and immediately Julien would recite the entire ode, with a modest air; what struck the Bishop was that Julien never departed from the tone of the conversation; he said his twenty or thirty Latin verses as he would have spoken of what was going on in his Seminary. A long discussion followed of Virgil and Cicero. At length the prelate could not refrain from paying the young seminarist a compliment.

"It would be impossible to have studied to better advantage."

"Monseigneur," said Julien, "your Seminary can furnish you with one hundred and ninety-seven subjects far less unworthy of your esteemed approval."

"How so?" said the prelate, astonished at this figure.

"I can support with official proof what I have the honour to say before Monseigneur.

"At the annual examination of the Seminary, answering questions upon these very subjects which have earned me,

[1] A poem by Delphine Gay.

at this moment, Monseigneur's approval, I received the number 198."

"Ah! This is the abbé Pirard's Benjamin," exclaimed the Bishop, with a laugh, and with a glance at M. de Frilair; "we ought to have expected this; but it is all in fair play. Is it not the case, my friend," he went on, turning to Julien, "that they waked you from your sleep to send you here?"

"Yes, Monseigneur. I have never left the Seminary alone in my life but once, to go and help M. l'abbé Chas-Bernard to decorate the Cathedral, on the feast of Corpus Domini."

"Optime," said the Bishop; "what, it was you that shewed such great courage, by placing the bunches of plumes on the baldachino? They make me shudder every year; I am always afraid of their costing me a man's life. My friend, you will go far; but I do not wish to cut short your career, which will be brilliant, by letting you die of hunger."

And, on an order from the Bishop, the servants brought in biscuits and Malaga wine, to which Julien did honour, and even more so than abbé Frilair, who knew that his Bishop liked to see him eat cheerfully and with a good appetite.

The prelate, growing more and more pleased with the close of his evening, spoke for a moment of ecclesiastical history. He saw that Julien did not understand. He then passed to the moral conditions of the Roman Empire, under the Emperors of the Age of Constantine. The last days of paganism were accompanied by that state of uneasiness and doubt which, in the nineteenth century, is disturbing sad and weary minds. Monseigneur remarked that Julien seemed hardly to know even the name of Tacitus.

Julien replied with candour, to the astonishment of his

Bishop, that this author was not to be found in the library of the Seminary.

"I am really delighted to hear it," said the Bishop merrily. "You relieve me of a difficulty; for the last ten minutes, I have been trying to think of a way of thanking you for the pleasant evening which you have given me, and certainly in a most unexpected manner. Although the gift is scarcely canonical, I should like to give you a set of Tacitus."

The prelate sent for eight volumes handsomely bound, and insisted upon writing with his own hand, on the title-page of the first, a Latin inscription to Julien Sorel. The Bishop prided himself on his fine Latinity; he ended by saying to him, in a serious tone, completely at variance with his tone throughout the rest of the conversation:

"Young man, *if you are wise,* you shall one day have the best living in my diocese, and not a hundred leagues from my episcopal Palace; but you must be *wise.*"

Julien, burdened with his volumes, left the Palace, in great bewilderment, as midnight was striking.

Monseigneur had not said a word to him about the abbé Pirard. Julien was astonished most of all by the extreme politeness shewn him by the Bishop. He had never imagined such an urbanity of form, combined with so natural an air of dignity. He was greatly struck by the contrast when he set eyes once more on the sombre abbé Pirard, who awaited him with growing impatience.

"*Quid tibi dixerunt?* (What did they say to you?)" he shouted at the top of his voice, the moment Julien came within sight.

Then, as Julien found some difficulty in translating the Bishop's conversation into Latin:

"Speak French, and repeat to me Monseigneur's own words, without adding or omitting anything," said the ex-Director of the Seminary, in his harsh tone and profoundly inelegant manner.

"What a strange present for a Bishop to make to a young seminarist," he said as he turned the pages of the sumptuous Tacitus, the gilded edges of which seemed to fill him with horror.

Two o'clock was striking when, after a detailed report of everything, he allowed his favourite pupil to retire to his own room.

"Leave me the first volume of your Tacitus, which contains the Bishop's inscription," he said to him. "That line of Latin will be your lightning conductor in this place, when I have gone.

"Erit tibi, fili mi, successor meus tanquam leo quaerens quem devoret. (My successor will be to you, my son, as a lion seeking whom he may devour.)"

On the following morning, Julien detected something strange in the manner in which his companions addressed him. This made him all the more reserved. "Here," he thought, "we have the effect of M. Pirard's resignation. It is known throughout the place, and I am supposed to be his favourite. There must be an insult behind this attitude"; but he could not discover it. There was, on the contrary, an absence of hatred in the eyes of all whom he encountered in the dormitories. "What can this mean? It is doubtless a trap, we are playing a close game." At length the young seminarist from Verrières said to him with a laugh: *"Cornelii Taciti opera omnia."*

At this speech, which was overheard, all the rest seemed to vie with one another in congratulating Julien, not only upon the magnificent present which he had received from Monseigneur, but also upon the two hours of conversation with which he had been honoured. It was common knowledge, down to the most trifling details. From this moment, there was no more jealousy; everyone paid court to him most humbly; the abbé Castanède who, only yesterday, had treated him with the utmost insolence, came to take him by the arm and invited him to luncheon.

Owing to a weakness in Julien's character, the insolence of these coarse creatures had greatly distressed him; their servility caused him disgust and no pleasure.

Towards midday, the abbé Pirard took leave of his pupils, not without first delivering a severe allocution. "Do you seek the honours of this world," he said to them, "all social advantages, the pleasure of commanding men, that of defying the laws and of being insolent to all men with impunity? Or indeed do you seek your eternal salvation? The most ignorant among you have only to open their eyes to distinguish between the two paths."

No sooner had he left than the devotees of the Sacred Heart of Jesus went to chant a *Te Deum* in the chapel. Nobody in the Seminary took the late Director's allocution seriously. "He is very cross at being dismissed," was what might be heard on all sides. Not one seminarist was simple enough to believe in the voluntary resignation of a post which provided so many opportunities for dealing with the big contractors.

The abbé Pirard took up his abode in the best inn in Besançon; and on the pretext of some imaginary private affairs, proposed to spend a couple of days there.

The Bishop invited him to dinner, and, to tease his Grand Vicar de Frilair, endeavoured to make him shine. They had reached the dessert when there arrived from Paris the strange tidings that the abbé Pirard was appointed to the splendid living of N——, within four leagues of the capital. The worthy prelate congratulated him sincerely. He saw in the whole affair a well played game which put him in a good humour and gave him the highest opinion of the abbé's talents. He bestowed upon him a magnificent certificate in Latin, and silenced the abbé de Frilair, who ventured to make remonstrances.

That evening, Monseigneur carried his admiration to the drawing-room of the Marquise de Rubempré. It was a great piece of news for the select society of Besançon;

people were lost in conjectures as to the meaning of this extraordinary favour. They saw the abbé Pirard a Bishop already. The sharper wits supposed M. de La Mole to have become a Minister, and allowed themselves that evening to smile at the imperious airs which M. l'abbé de Frilair assumed in society.

Next morning, the abbé Pirard was almost followed through the streets, and the tradesmen came out to their shop-doors when he went to beg an audience of the Marquis's judges. For the first time, he was received by them with civility. The stern Jansenist, indignant at everything that he saw around him, spent a long time at work with the counsel whom he had chosen for the Marquis de La Mole, and then left for Paris. He was so foolish as to say to two or three lifelong friends who escorted him to the carriage and stood admiring its heraldic blason, that after governing the Seminary for fifteen years he was leaving Besançon with five hundred and twenty francs in savings. These friends embraced him with tears in their eyes, and then said to one another: "The good abbé might have spared himself that lie, it is really too absurd."

The common herd, blinded by love of money, were not fitted to understand that it was in his sincerity that the abbé Pirard had found the strength to fight single-handed for six years against Marie Alacoque, the Sacred Heart of Jesus, the Jesuits and his Bishop.

CHAPTER THIRTY

AMBITION

There is only one true nobility left; namely, the title
of Duke; Marquis is absurd, at the word Duke one turns
one's head.

The Edinburgh Review.[1]

THE abbé was astonished by the noble air and almost
gay tone of the Marquis. Nevertheless this future
Minister received him without any of those little
mannerisms of a great gentleman, outwardly so polite,
but so impertinent to him who understands them. It would
have been a waste of time, and the Marquis was so far
immersed in public business as to have no time to waste.

For six months he had been intriguing to make both
King and nation accept a certain Ministry, which, as a
mark of gratitude, would make him a Duke.

The Marquis had appealed in vain, year after year, to
his lawyer at Besançon for a clear and definite report
on his lawsuits in the Franche-Comté. How was the
eminent lawyer to explain them to him, if he did not understand them himself?

The little slip of paper which the abbé gave him explained everything.

"My dear abbé," said the Marquis, after polishing off
in less than five minutes all the polite formulas and personal inquiries, "my dear abbé, in the midst of my supposed prosperity, I lack the time to occupy myself seriously

[1] I have translated this motto, which is quoted in French by
Stendhal, but have not been able to find the original passage in
the *Edinburgh Review.* C. K. S. M.

with two little matters which nevertheless are of considerable importance: my family and my affairs. I take the
greatest interest in the fortunes of my house, I may carry
it far; I look after my pleasures, and that is what must
come before everything else, at least in my eyes," he went
on, noticing the astonishment in the eyes of the abbé
Pirard. Although a man of sense, the abbé was amazed
to see an old man talking so openly of his pleasures.

"Work does no doubt exist in Paris," the great nobleman continued, "but perched in the attics; and as soon as
I come in contact with a man, he takes an apartment on
the second floor, and his wife starts a *day;* consequently,
no more work, no effort except to be or to appear to be a
man of fashion. That is their sole interest once they are
provided with bread.

"For my lawsuits, to be strictly accurate, and also for
each lawsuit separately, I have lawyers who work themselves to death; one of them died of consumption, the day
before yesterday. But, for my affairs in general, would
you believe, Sir, that for the last three years I have given
up hope of finding a man who, while he is writing for me,
will deign to think a little seriously of what he is doing.
However, all this is only a preamble.

"I respect you, and, I would venture to add, although
we meet for the first time, I like you. Will you be my
secretary, with a salary of eight thousand francs, or indeed twice that sum? I shall gain even more, I assure
you; and I shall make it my business to keep your fine
living for you, for the day on which we cease to agree."

The abbé declined, but towards the end of the conversation, the sight of the Marquis's genuine embarrassment
suggested an idea to him.

"I have left down in my Seminary," he said to the Marquis, "a poor young man who, if I be not mistaken, is going
to be brutally persecuted. If he were only a simple religious he would be already *in pace.*

"At present this young man knows only Latin and the Holy Scriptures; but it is by no means impossible that one day he may display great talent, either for preaching or for the guidance of souls. I do not know what he will do; but he has the sacred fire, he may go far. I intended to give him to our Bishop, should one ever be sent to us who had something of your way of looking at men and affairs."

"What is your young man's origin?" said the Marquis.

"He is said to be the son of a carpenter in our mountains, but I am inclined to believe that he is the natural son of some rich man. I have seen him receive an anonymous or pseudonymous letter containing a bill of exchange for five hundred francs."

"Ah! It is Julien Sorel," said the Marquis.

"How do you know his name?" asked the astonished abbé; and, as he was blushing at his own question:

"That is what I am not going to tell you," replied the Marquis.

"Very well!" the abbé went on, "you might try making him your secretary, he has energy, and judgment; in short, it is an experiment worth trying."

"Why not?" said the Marquis; "but would he be the sort of man to let his palm be greased by the Prefect of Police or by anyone else, to play the spy on me? That is my only objection."

Receiving favourable assurances from the abbé Pirard, the Marquis produced a note for one thousand francs:

"Send this to Julien Sorel for his journey; tell him to come to me."

"Life in Paris must surely, M. le Marquis, have created this illusion in your mind; you are unaware, because you occupy an exalted social position, of the tyranny that weighs upon us poor provincials, and especially upon priests who are not on good terms with the Jesuits. They will never allow Julien Sorel to leave, they will manage to cover themselves with the cleverest excuses, they will reply that he is ill, letters will have gone astray in the post," etc., etc.

"One of these days I shall procure a letter from the Minister to the Bishop," said the Marquis.

"I was forgetting one thing," said the abbé: "this young man, although of quite humble birth, has a proud heart, he will be of no use to you in your business if his pride is offended; you will only make him stupid."

"I like that," said the Marquis, "I shall make him my son's companion, will that do?"

Some time after this, Julien received a letter in an unknown hand and bearing the postmark of Châlon, and found a draft upon a merchant in Besançon and instructions to proceed to Paris without delay. The letter was signed with an assumed name, but as he opened it Julien trembled: a great blot of ink had dropped full upon the thirteenth word.[1] It was the signal arranged between him and the abbé Pirard.

Within an hour, Julien was summoned to the Bishop's Palace, where he found himself greeted with a wholly fatherly welcome. Interspersed with quotations from Horace, Monseigneur paid him, with regard to the exalted destiny that awaited him in Paris, a number of very neat compliments, which required an explanation if he were to express his thanks. Julien could say nothing, chiefly because he knew nothing, and Monseigneur shewed a high regard for him. One of the minor clergy of the Palace wrote to the Mayor who made haste to appear in person bringing a passport already signed, but with a blank space for the name of the traveller.

Before midnight, Julien was with Fouqué, whose sober

---

[1] Originally this passage read: "A leaf from a tree had fallen out at his feet." In correcting a copy of the first edition, Stendhal added the marginal note: "The spy who opened the letter might fail to replace the leaf."

C. K. S. M.

mind was more astonished than delighted by the future
which seemed to be in store for his friend.

"The end of it will be," said this Liberal elector, "a post
under Government, which will oblige you to take some
action that will be pilloried in the newspapers. It will
be through your disgrace that I shall have news of you.
Remember that, even financially speaking, it is better to
earn one hundred louis in an honest trade in timber, where
you are your own master, than to receive four thousand
francs from a Government, were it that of King Solo-
mon himself."

Julien saw no more in this than the pettiness of a rustic
mind. He was at last going to appear on the stage of
great events. He preferred less certainty and greater
chances. In his heart there was no longer the slightest
fear of dying of hunger. The good fortune of going to
Paris, which he peopled in his imagination with men of
intelligence, great intriguers, great hypocrites, but as
courteous as the Bishop of Besançon and the Bishop of
Agde, eclipsed everything else in his eyes. He represented himself humbly to his friend as deprived of his free
will by the abbé Pirard's letter.

Towards noon on the following day he arrived in Verrières the happiest of men, he reckoned upon seeing Madame de Rênal again. He went first of all to his original
protector, the good abbé Chélan. He met with a stern
reception.

"Do you consider that you are under any obligation
to me?" said M. Chélan, without acknowledging his greeting. "You will take luncheon with me, meanwhile another
horse will be hired for you, and you will leave Verrières,
without seeing anyone."

"To hear is to obey," replied Julien, with the prim face
of a seminarist; and there was no further discussion save
of theology and Latin scholarship.

He mounted his horse, rode a league, after which, coming upon a wood, with no one to see him enter it, he hid himself there. At sunset he sent back the horse by a peasant to the nearest gate of the town. Later on, he entered the house of a vine-dresser who agreed to sell him a ladder, and to go with him, carrying the ladder, to the little wood that overhung the Cours de la Fidélité, in Verrières.

"We are a poor conscript deserting—or a smuggler," said the peasant, as he took leave of him, "but what do I care? My ladder is well paid for, and I myself have had to pass some awkward moments in my life."

The night was very dark. About one o'clock in the morning, Julien, carrying his ladder, made his way into Verrières. He climbed down as soon as he could into the bed of the torrent, which ran through M. de Rênal's magnificent gardens at a depth of ten feet, and confined between walls. Julien climbed up easily by his ladder. "What sort of greeting will the watch-dogs give me?" he wondered. "That is the whole question." The dogs barked, and rushed towards him; but he whistled softly, and they came and fawned upon him.

Then climbing from terrace to terrace, although all the gates were shut, he had no difficulty in arriving immediately beneath the window of Madame de Rênal's bedroom, which, on the garden side, was no more than nine or ten feet above the ground.

There was in the shutters a small opening in the shape of a heart, which Julien knew well. To his great dismay, this little opening was not lighted by the glimmer of a nightlight within.

"Great God!" he said to himself; "to-night, of all nights, this room is not occupied by Madame de Rênal! Where can she be sleeping? The family are at Verrières, since I found the dogs here; but I may in this room, without a light, come upon M. de Rênal himself or a stranger, and then what a scandal!"

The most prudent course was to retire; but the idea filled Julien with horror. "If it is a stranger, I shall make off as fast as my legs will carry me, leaving my ladder behind; but if it is she, what sort of welcome awaits me? She is steeped in repentance and the most extreme piety, I may be sure of that; but after all, she has still some memory of me, since she has just written to me." With this argument he made up his mind.

His heart trembling, but determined nevertheless to see her or to perish, he flung a handful of gravel against the shutter; no reply. He placed his ladder against the wall by the side of the window and tapped himself on the shutter, softly at first then more loudly. "Dark as it is, they may fire a gun at me," thought Julien. This thought reduced his mad undertaking to a question of physical courage.

"This room is unoccupied to-night," he thought, "or else whoever it is that is sleeping here is awake by this time. So there is no need for any further precaution here; all I need think of is not making myself heard by the people who are sleeping in the other rooms."

He stepped down, placed his ladder against one of the shutters, climbed up again and passing his hand through the heart-shaped opening, was fortunate in finding almost at once the wire fastened to the latch that closed the shutter. He pulled this wire; it was with an unspeakable joy that he felt that the shutter was no longer closed and was yielding to his efforts. "I must open it little by little and let her recognize my voice." He opened the shutter sufficiently to pass his head through the gap, repeating in a whisper: *It is a friend.*

He made certain, by applying his ear, that nothing broke the profound silence in the room. But decidedly, there was no nightlight, even half extinguished, on the hearth; this was indeed a bad sign.

"Beware of a gunshot!" He thought for a moment;

then, with one finger, ventured to tap the pane: no response; he tapped more loudly. "Even if I break the glass, I must settle this business." As he was knocking hard, he thought he could just make out, in the pitch darkness, something like a white phantom coming across the room. In a moment, there was no doubt about it, he did see a phantom which seemed to be advancing with extreme slowness. Suddenly he saw a cheek pressed to the pane to which his eye was applied.

He shuddered, and recoiled slightly. But the night was so dark that, even at this close range, he could not make out whether it was Madame de Rênal. He feared an instinctive cry of alarm; already he could hear the dogs prowling with muttered growls round the foot of his ladder. "It is I," he repeated, quite loudly, "a friend." No answer; the white phantom had vanished. "For pity's sake, open the window. I must speak to you, I am too wretched!" and he knocked until the window nearly broke.

A little sharp sound was heard; the catch of the window gave way; he pushed it open and sprang lightly into the room.

The white phantom moved away; he seized it by the arms; it was a woman. All his ideas of courage melted. "If it is she, what will she say to me?' What was his state when he realized from a faint cry that it was Madame de Rênal.

He gathered her in his arms; she trembled, and had barely the strength to repulse him.

"Wretch! What are you doing?"

Scarcely could her tremulous voice articulate the words. Julien saw that she was genuinely angry.

"I have come to see you after fourteen months of a cruel parting."

"Go, leave me this instant. Ah! M. Chélan, why did you forbid me to write to him? I should have prevented this horror." She thrust him from her with a force that was indeed extraordinary. "I repent of my crime; heaven has deigned to enlighten me," she repeated in a stifled voice. "Go! Fly!"

"After fourteen months of misery, I shall certainly not leave you until I have spoken to you. I wish to know all that you have been doing. Ah! I have loved you well enough to deserve this confidence. . . . I wish to know all."

In spite of herself Madame de Rênal felt this tone of authority exert its influence over her heart.

Julien, who was holding her in a passionate embrace, and resisting her efforts to liberate herself, ceased to press her in his arms. This relaxation helped to reassure Madame de Rênal.

"I am going to draw up the ladder," he said, "so that it may not compromise us if one of the servants, awakened by the noise, goes the rounds."

"Ah! Leave me, leave me rather," the answer came with unfeigned anger. "What do men matter to me? It is God that sees the terrible wrong you are doing me, and will punish me for it. You are taking a cowardly advantage of the regard that I once felt for you, but no longer feel. Do you hear, Master Julien?"

He drew up the ladder very slowly, so as not to make any noise.

"Is your husband in town?" he asked, not to defy her, but from force of habit.

"Do not speak to me so, for pity's sake, or I shall call my husband. I am all too guilty already of not having sent you away, at any cost. I pity you," she told him, seeking to wound his pride which she knew to be so irritable.

Her use of the plural pronoun, that abrupt method of breaking so tender a bond, and one upon which he still reckoned, roused Julien's amorous transport to a frenzy.

"What! Is it possible that you no longer love me!"

he said to her, in those accents of the heart to which it is so difficult to listen unmoved.

She made no reply; as for him, he was weeping bitter tears.

Really, he had no longer the strength to speak.

"And so I am completely forgotten by the one person who has ever loved me! What use to live any longer?" All his courage had left him as soon as he no longer had to fear the danger of encountering a man; everything had vanished from his heart, save love.

He wept for a long time in silence. She could hear the sound of his sobs. He took her hand, she tried to withdraw it; and yet, after a few almost convulsive movements, she let him keep it. The darkness was intense; they found themselves both seated upon Madame de Rênal's bed.

"What a difference from the state of things fourteen months ago!" thought Julien, and his flow of tears increased. "So absence unfailingly destroys all human feelings! The best thing will be for me to go!

"Be so kind as to tell me what has happened to you," Julien said at length, in a voice almost stifled by emotion.

"There can be no doubt," replied Madame de Rênal in a harsh voice, the tone of which offered a cutting reproach to Julien, "my misdeeds were known in the town, at the time of your departure. You were so imprudent in your behaviour. Some time later, when I was in despair, the respectable M. Chélan came to see me. It was in vain that, for a long time, he sought to obtain a confession. One day, the idea occurred to him to take me into that church at Dijon in which I made my first Communion. There, he ventured to broach the subject. . . ." Madame de Rênal's speech was interrupted by her tears. "What a shameful moment! I confessed all. That worthy man was kind enough not to heap on me the weight of his indignation: he shared my distress. At that time I was writing you day after day letters which I dared not send you; I concealed them carefully, and when I was too wretched used to shut myself up in my room and read over my own letters.

"At length, M. Chélan persuaded me to hand them over to him. . . . Some of them, written with a little more prudence than the rest, had been sent to you; never once did you answer me."

"Never, I swear to you, did I receive any letter from you at the Seminary."

"Great God! who can have intercepted them?"

"Imagine my grief; until the day when I saw you in the Cathedral, I did not know whether you were still alive."

"God in His mercy made me understand how greatly I was sinning against Him, against my children, against my husband," replied Madame de Rênal. "He has never loved me as I believed then that you loved me. . . ."

Julien flung himself into her arms, without any definite intention but with entire lack of self-control. But Madame de Rênal thrust him from her, and continued quite firmly:

"My respectable friend M. Chélan made me realize that, in marrying M. de Rênal, I had pledged all my affections to him, even those of which I was still ignorant, which I had never felt before a certain fatal intimacy. . . . Since the great sacrifice of those letters, which were so precious to me, my life has flowed on, if not happily, at any rate quietly enough. Do not disturb it any more; be a friend to me . . . the best of friends." Julien covered her hands with kisses; she could feel that he was still crying. "Do not cry, you distress me so. . . . Tell me, it is your turn now, all that you have been doing." Julien was unable to speak. "I wish to know what sort of life you led at the Seminary," she repeated, "then you shall go."

Without a thought of what he was telling her, Julien spoke of the endless intrigues and jealousies which he had encountered at first, then of his more peaceful life after he was appointed tutor.

"It was then," he added, "that after a long silence, which was doubtless intended to make me understand what I see only too clearly now, that you no longer love me, and that I had become as nothing to you. . . ."

Madame de Rênal gripped his hands. "It was then that you sent me a sum of five hundred francs."

"Never," said Madame de Rênal.

"It was a letter postmarked *Paris* and signed Paul Sorel, to avoid all suspicion."

A short discussion followed as to the possible source of this letter. The atmosphere began to change. Unconsciously, Madame de Rênal and Julien had departed from their solemn tone; they had returned to that of a tender intimacy. They could not see each other, so intense was the darkness, but the sound of their voices told all. Julien slipped his arm round the waist of his mistress; this movement was highly dangerous. She tried to remove Julien's arm, whereupon he, with a certain adroitness, distracted her attention by an interesting point in his narrative. The arm was then forgotten, and remained in the position that it had occupied.

After abundant conjectures as to the source of the letter with the five hundred francs, Julien had resumed his narrative; he became rather more his own master in speaking of his past life which, in comparison with what was happening to him at that moment, interested him so little. His attention was wholly concentrated on the manner in which his visit was to end. "You must leave me," she kept on telling him, in a curt tone.

"What a disgrace for me if I am shewn the door! The remorse will be enough to poison my whole life," he said to himself, "she will never write to me. God knows when I shall return to this place!" From that moment, all the element of heavenly bliss in Julien's situation vanished rapidly from his heart. Seated by the side of a woman whom he adored, clasping her almost in his arms, in this room in which he had been so happy, plunged in a black darkness, perfectly well aware that for the last minute she had been crying, feeling, from the movement of her bosom, that she was convulsed with sobs, he unfortunately became a frigid politician, almost as calculating and as frigid as when, in the courtyard of the Seminary, he saw himself made the butt of some malicious joke by one of his companions stronger than himself. Julien spun out his story, and spoke of the wretched life he had led since leaving Verrières. "And so," Madame de Rênal said to herself, "after a year's absence, almost without a single token of remembrance, while I was forgetting him, his mind was entirely taken up with the happy days he had enjoyed at Vergy." Her sobs increased in violence. Julien saw that his story had been successful. He realized that he must now try his last weapon: he came abruptly to the letter that he had just received from Paris.

"I have taken leave of Monseigneur, the Bishop."

"What! You are not returning to Besançon! You are leaving us for ever?"

"Yes," replied Julien, in a resolute tone; "yes, I am abandoning the place where I am forgotten even by her whom I have most dearly loved in all my life, and I am leaving it never to set eyes on it again. I am going to Paris. . . ."

"You are going to Paris!" Madame de Rênal exclaimed quite aloud.

Her voice was almost stifled by her tears, and shewed the intensity of her grief. Julien had need of this encouragement; he was going to attempt a course which might decide everything against him; and before this exclamation, seeing no light, he was absolutely ignorant of the effect that he was producing. He hesitated no longer; the fear of remorse gave him complete command of himself; he added coldly as he rose to his feet:

"Yes, Madame, I leave you for ever, may you be happy; farewell."

He took a few steps towards the window; he was already opening it. Madame de Rênal sprang after him. He felt her head droop on his shoulder, and that she was clasping him in her arms, pressing her cheek to his.

Thus, after three hours of conversation, Julien obtained what he had so passionately desired during the first two. Had they come a little earlier, this return to tender sentiments, the eclipse of remorse in Madame de Rênal would have been a divine happiness; obtained thus by artifice, they were no more than a formal triumph. Julien positively insisted, against the entreaties of his mistress, upon lighting the nightlight.

"Do you then wish me," he asked her, "to retain no memory of having seen you? The love that is doubtless glowing in those charming eyes, shall it then be lost to me? Shall the whiteness of that lovely hand be invisible to me? Think that I am leaving you for a very long time perhaps!"

"This is shocking," Madame de Rênal said to herself, but she could refuse nothing to this idea of lifelong separation, which made her dissolve in tears. Dawn was beginning to paint in clear hues the outline of the fir trees on the mountain to the east of Verrières. Instead of going away, Julien, drunken with pleasure, asked Madame de Rênal to let him spend the whole day hidden in her room, and not to leave until the following night.

"And why not?" was her answer. "This fatal relapse destroys all my self-esteem, and dooms me to lifelong misery," and she pressed him rapturously to her heart. "My husband is no longer the same, he has suspicions; he believes that I have been fooling him throughout this affair, and is in the worst of tempers with me. If he hears the least sound I am lost, he will drive me from the house like the wretch that I am."

"Ah! There I can hear the voice of M. Chélan," said Julien; "you would not have spoken to me like that before my cruel departure for the Seminary; you loved me then!"

Julien was rewarded for the coolness with which he had uttered this speech; he saw his mistress at once forget the danger in which the proximity of her husband involved her, to think of the far greater danger of seeing Julien doubtful of her love for him. The daylight was rapidly increasing and now flooded the room; Julien recovered all the exquisite sensations of pride when he was once more able to see in his arms and almost at his feet this charming woman, the only woman that he had ever loved, who, a few hours earlier, had been entirely wrapped up in the fear of a terrible God and in devotion to duty. Resolutions fortified by a year of constancy had not been able to hold out against his boldness.

Presently they heard a sound in the house; a consideration to which she had not given a thought now disturbed Madame de Rênal.

"That wicked Elisa will be coming into the room, what are we to do with that enormous ladder?" she said to her lover; "where are we to hide it? I am going to take it up to the loft," she suddenly exclaimed, with a sort of joviality.

"There, that is the face I remember," said the delighted Julien. "But you will have to go through the man's room."

"I shall leave the ladder in the corridor, call the man and send him on an errand."

"Remember to have some excuse ready in case the man notices the ladder when he passes it in the passage."

"Yes, my angel," said Madame de Rênal as she gave him a kiss. "And you, remember to hide yourself quickly under the bed if Elisa comes into the room while I am away."

Julien was amazed at this sudden gaiety. "And so," he thought, "the approach of physical danger, so far from disturbing her, restores her gaiety because she forgets her remorse! Indeed a superior woman! Ah! There is a heart in which it is glorious to reign!" Julien was in ecstasies.

Madame de Rênal took the ladder; plainly it was too heavy for her. Julien went to her assistance; he was admiring that elegant figure, which suggested anything rather than strength, when suddenly, without help, she grasped the ladder and picked it up as she might have picked up a chair. She carried it swiftly to the corridor on the third storey, where she laid it down by the wall. She called the manservant, and, to give him time to put on his clothes, went up to the dovecote. Five minutes later, when she returned to the corridor, the ladder was no more to be seen. What had become of it? Had Julien been out of the house, the danger would have been nothing. But, at that moment, if her husband saw the ladder! The consequences might be appalling. Madame de Rênal ran up and down the house. At last she discovered the ladder under the roof, where the man had taken and in fact hidden it himself. This in itself was strange, and at another time would have alarmed her.

"What does it matter to me," she thought, "what may happen in twenty-four hours from now, when Julien will have gone? Will not everything then be to me horror and remorse?"

She had a sort of vague idea that she ought to take her life, but what did that matter? After a parting which she had supposed to be for ever, he was restored to her, she saw him again, and what he had done in making his way to her gave proof of such a wealth of love!

In telling Julien of the incident of the ladder:

"What shall I say to my husband," she asked him, "if the man tells him how he found the ladder?" She meditated for a moment. "It will take them twenty-four hours to discover the peasant who sold it to you"; and flinging herself into Julien's arms and clasping him in a convulsive embrace: "Ah! to die, to die like this!" she cried as she covered him with kisses; "but I must not let you die of hunger," she added with a laugh.

"Come; first of all, I am going to hide you in Madame Derville's room, which is always kept locked." She kept watch at the end of the corridor and Julien slipped from door to door. "Remember not to answer, if anyone knocks," she reminded him as she turned the key outside; "anyhow, it would only be the children playing."

"Make them go into the garden, below the window," said Julien, "so that I may have the pleasure of seeing them, make them speak."

"Yes, yes," cried Madame de Rênal as she left him.

She returned presently with oranges, biscuits, a bottle of Malaga; she had found it impossible to purloin any bread.

"What is your husband doing?" said Julien.

"He is writing down notes of the deals he proposes to do with some peasants."

But eight o'clock had struck, the house was full of noise. If Madame de Rênal were not to be seen, people would begin searching everywhere for her; she was obliged to leave him. Presently she returned, in defiance of all the rules of prudence, to bring him a cup of coffee; she was afraid of his dying of hunger. After luncheon she managed to shepherd the children underneath the window of Madame Derville's room. He found that they had grown considerably, but they had acquired a common air, or else his ideas had changed. Madame de Rênal spoke to them of Julien. The eldest replied with affection and regret for his former tutor, but it appeared that the two younger had almost forgotten him.

M. de Rênal did not leave the house that morning; he was incessantly going up and downstairs, engaged in striking bargains with certain peasants, to whom he was selling his potato crop. Until dinner time, Madame de Rênal had not a moment to spare for her prisoner. When dinner was on the table, it occurred to her to steal a plateful of hot soup for him. As she silently approached the door of the room in which he was, carrying the plate carefully, she found herself face to face with the servant who had hidden the ladder that morning. At the moment, he too was coming silently along the corridor, as though listening. Probably Julien had forgotten to tread softly. The servant made off in some confusion. Madame de Rênal went boldly into Julien's room; her account of the incident made him shudder.

"You are afraid"; she said to him; "and I, I would brave all the dangers in the world without a tremor. I fear one thing only, that is the moment when I shall be left alone after you have gone," and she ran from the room.

"Ah!" thought Julien, greatly excited, "remorse is the only danger that sublime soul dreads!"

Night came at last. M. de Rênal went to the Casino.

His wife had announced a severe headache, she retired to her room, made haste to dismiss Elisa, and speedily rose from her bed to open the door to Julien.

It so happened that he really was faint with hunger. Madame de Rênal went to the pantry to look for bread. Julien heard a loud cry. She returned and told him that on entering the dark pantry, making her way to a cupboard in which the bread was kept, and stretching out her hand, she had touched a woman's arm. It was Elisa who had uttered the cry which Julien had heard.

"What was she doing there?"

"She was stealing sweets, or possibly spying on us," said Madame de Rênal with complete indifference. "But fortunately I have found a pie and a big loaf."

"And what have you got there?" said Julien, pointing to the pockets of her apron.

Madame de Rênal had forgotten that, ever since dinner, they had been filled with bread.

Julien clasped her in his arms with the keenest passion; never had she seemed to him so beautiful. "Even in Paris," he told himself vaguely, "I shall not be able to find a nobler character." She had all the awkwardness of a woman little accustomed to attentions of this sort, and at the same time the true courage of a person who fears only dangers of another kind and far more terrible.

While Julien was devouring his supper with a keen appetite, and his mistress was playfully apologizing for the simplicity of the repast, for she had a horror of serious speech, the door of the room was all at once shaken violently. It was M. de Rênal.

"Why have you locked yourself in?" he shouted to her.

Julien had just time to slip beneath the sofa.

"What! You are fully dressed," said M. de Rênal, as he entered; "you are having supper, and you have locked your door?"

On any ordinary day, this question, put with all the brutality of a husband, would have troubled Madame de Rênal, but she felt that her husband had only to lower his eyes a little to catch sight of Julien; for M. de Rênal had flung himself upon the chair on which Julien had been sitting a moment earlier, facing the sofa.

Her headache served as an excuse for everything. While in his turn her husband was giving her a long and detailed account of the pool he had won in the billiard room of the Casino, "a pool of nineteen francs, begad!" he added, she saw lying on a chair before their eyes, and within a few feet of them, Julien's hat. Cooler than ever, she began to undress, and, choosing her moment, passed swiftly behind her husband and flung a garment over the chair with the hat on it.

At length M. de Rênal left her. She begged Julien to begin over again the story of his life in the Seminary: "Yesterday I was not listening to you, I was thinking, while you were speaking, only of how I was to summon up courage to send you away."

She was the embodiment of imprudence. They spoke very loud; and it might have been two o'clock in the morning when they were interrupted by a violent blow on the door. It was M. de Rênal again:

"Let me in at once, there are burglars in the house!" he said, "Saint-Jean found their ladder this morning."

"This is the end of everything," cried Madame de Rênal, throwing herself into Julien's arms. "He is going to kill us both, he does not believe in the burglars; I am going to die in your arms, more fortunate in my death than I have been in my life." She made no answer to her husband, who was waiting angrily outside, she was holding Julien in a passionate embrace.

"Save Stanislas's mother," he said to her with an air of command. "I am going to jump down into the courtyard from the window of the closet, and escape through the garden, the dogs know me. Make a bundle of my clothes and throw it down into the garden as soon as you can. Meanwhile, let him break the door in. And whatever you do, no confession, I forbid it, suspicion is better than certainty."

"You will kill yourself, jumping down," was her sole reply and her sole anxiety.

She went with him to the window of the closet; she then took such time as she required to conceal his garments. Finally she opened the door to her husband, who was boiling with rage. He searched the bedroom, the closet, without uttering a word, and then vanished. Julien's clothes were thrown down to him, he caught them and ran quickly down the garden towards the Doubs.

As he ran, he heard a bullet whistle past him, and simultaneously the sound of a gun being fired.

"That is not M. de Rênal," he decided, "he is not a good enough shot." The dogs were running by his side in silence, a second shot apparently shattered the paw of one dog, for it began to emit lamentable howls. Julien jumped the wall of a terrace, proceeded fifty yards under cover, then continued his flight in a different direction. He heard voices calling to him, and could distinctly see the servant, his enemy, fire a gun; a farmer also came and shot at him from the other side of the garden, but by this time Julien had reached the bank of the Doubs, where he put on his clothes.

An hour later, he was a league from Verrières, on the road to Geneva. "If there is any suspicion," thought Julien, "it is on the Paris road that they will look for me."

(END OF VOLUME I)

EVERYMAN'S LIBRARY: A Selected List

BIOGRAPHY

ESSAYS AND CRITICISM

FICTION

4

HISTORY

LEGENDS AND SAGAS

POETRY AND DRAMA

REFERENCE

RELIGION AND PHILOSOPHY